The Reluctant Messenger of Science and Religion

The Reluctant Messenger of Science and Religion

Science and the World's Religions Are Pieces to a Puzzle That Need Each Other to Form a Complete Picture

Stephen W. Boston Ph.D.
Evelyn McKnight Boston Ph.D.

Writer's Showcase
New York Lincoln Shanghai

The Reluctant Messenger of Science and Religion
Science and the World's Religions Are Pieces to a Puzzle That Need Each Other to Form a Complete Picture

Writer's Showcase
an imprint of iUniverse, Inc.

For information address:
iUniverse, Inc.
2021 Pine Lake Road, Suite 100
Lincoln, NE 68512
www.iuniverse.com

The information contained within is a combination of fact and fiction. However, since names were changed and details were altered to preserve the privacy of certain individuals, the entire work is presented as fiction. Additional story elements have been added to help improve its overall flow and entertainment value.

ISBN: 0-595-26821-8 (pbk)
ISBN: 0-595-65628-5 (cloth)

Printed in the United States of America

Lovingly dedicated to our children:
Hunter Blake, Kathleen and Patricia Boston.

Facts before judgment and knowledge before wisdom.

—The Master

CONTENTS

Author's Foreword

The Reluctant Messenger began as a web project in 1997. Over the years, many people have requested a book version of the website. The website consists of about 500 pages. The theme of every page is science, religion, or both. What works well as a website doesn't translate easily into a novel. What makes for a good book doesn't work on the Internet. Few people want to read a novel sitting in front of a computer. The website is designed so readers can start anywhere and end anywhere without feeling they missed anything. The interesting side effect is that everybody experiences the pages in a different order, thus each person's expectation of the book will probably be different. This book is written with a logical, linear story flow but with much of the website missing. As a form of compensation, there is extra material that has never been on the website. The novel introduces several new characters and covers Lydia's perspective which the website doesn't reveal.

By late 2002, The Reluctant Messenger Website averaged over 100,000-page views a month. That works out to over a million hits a year. Reluctant-Messenger.com continues to have up-to-date information about upcoming books of spiritual fiction and nonfiction written by the authors as well as the wealth of research material.

Acknowledgements

For their help and support, our thanks and gratitude go to Lou Ann and Kenny Woliver, Leah Brothers-Grice, Tommy Grice, Carlos Kelly, Josiah Draper, Pranav Chavda, Urania, Simon, Diane, Jaci, and Gay

Prologue

The Master was free of thoughts as he slipped into his daily meditation. His mind was as calm as a lake on a windless night as the images took shape in his consciousness. The dreamlike quality of the vision suggested it was a glimpse of a future event instead of one in the past. The dark-haired man in his vision was the American he had seen in vision many times before. This time, however, the ruggedly handsome stranger was not alone. A picnic of sorts was taking place. The American was with a beautiful olive-skinned Indian woman. She looked alluring in her scanty outfit as she sat on his chest feeding him mushrooms she had dipped in honey. Dark and sinister shapes danced around them. The Master realized that at sometime in the future an important spiritual test would occur when this man least expected it. The vision ended before he found out whether the man passed or failed the test. That meant the outcome was still much in doubt.

When the images ebbed away, he unfolded slowly from the large pillow he had rested on and stretched. He walked into his parlor to do as he had done before. Lately, these visions of the man from America were happening more often. Each time he had recorded its essence with a painting. Once again, he prepared a canvas and got out his paintbrush.

San Francisco

Tina had no idea the next hour would change the lives of so many people. All she knew was that they were going to be late if Lydia didn't hurry up. She quietly tapped on the door connecting her hotel room with Lydia's. When there was no answer, she eased the door open just a bit and saw a reflection of Lydia in the mirror on the opposite wall. Lydia was kneeling quietly in the shadows with her hands folded, head bowed, and lips moving slightly. Tina smiled. Lydia always prayed just before a debate. Her friend's image looked so peaceful that she felt guilty disturbing her, but she had to do it. Tina was her assistant in this year's debate in San Francisco. The Hilton was hosting the finals and Lydia had qualified for them. On the debate circuit, she was a respected opponent in the Evolution vs. Creation category. Tina gave her a few more moments of privacy. Looking at the clock by her bed, she saw time was running out. She knocked louder. "Lydia, we *have* to go. If we're late, Chester will win by default."

Lydia quickly ended her prayer, took a deep breath, and looked up toward the narrowly open door linking her room to Tina's. "Okay, I'm coming." She grabbed her bag and her notes and rushed over to Tina's room. "How do I look?" She twirled around so Tina could see what she had chosen to wear. As usual, Lydia could rival Jackie O or Princess

Di in creating an air of understated elegance. The soft caramel of her suit enriched the golden highlights in her red hair and enhanced her fair skin. Her conservatively cut suit was slightly fitted at the waist with a slim skirt falling just below her knees. She wore little makeup—just a touch of mascara on her long lashes and tinted gloss on her full lips. Her only jewelry was a plain gold stud on each ear lobe and a thin gold chain with a small cross that nestled at the base of her long neck. Her nails were short, manicured, and buffed to a colorless sheen.

Tina grinned. "Chester doesn't have a chance. Now let's go."

Lydia didn't move for a moment and Tina saw that her friend was trembling. *What is that about? Lydia must be feeling more stress than normal before a debate.* When Lydia finally got her feet moving, she seemed distracted as they walked to the elevators. She looked at Tina and shook her head. "I don't know why I feel so nervous. I'm usually calm and confident."

This worried Tina. Normally, Lydia was well prepared and cool as ice. She almost always won her debates, especially when making it to the finals. This wasn't like her at all. "Calm down, this debate is just like all the others. Anyway, nobody can beat you in this subject now that you have the secret weapon. It's even better than your statistical argument; and when you combine the two, you can't lose."

The elevator dinged and both women got on. As the door closed, Tina had to reach around Lydia to hit the button for the third floor where the large meeting rooms were. Lydia was so distracted that she had stared at the row of buttons like she had never seen anything like that before. She shook her head and blushed, "Gosh, thanks, I don't know what I'm thinking."

*   *   *   *

Paul nudged Chester. "Come on buddy. You usually don't drink before a debate. Come on let's go; we can't be late."

Chester tipped the glass back and swallowed the rest of his scotch. "Hey, one drink to calm my nerves is *good* not bad." Chester glared at his friend.

Paul shook his head in concern. "This gal ain't any better than the others. Now that we know her whole argument is based on proving God exists, it can't be that solid. So she gets a few wins with novelty logic. Those never hold up in the finals. Why are you so nervous?"

Chester laid a five-dollar bill on the bar as he slid off the barstool. Gathering his stack of notes he said, "You and I know the best argument against evolution is the one based on the improbability of spontaneous life. I've got that one nailed. But rumor has it that she's not going to use it. Apparently she's come up with some weird statistical argument that hasn't been used before, but I couldn't find out what it is. The judges like innovative approaches regardless of how hairball they are. And you know judges go for the new ideas just to look unbiased so they can stay on the circuit." Chester and Paul headed out of the bar and into the main lobby.

"If you stay on the plan we came up with, you will win." Paul pushed through the crowd heading toward the escalators that led up to the conference rooms. He looked at his watch. It was a quarter to four. The gun control debate should be ending at four o'clock. He turned to tell Chester that they had time to go over the rebuttal points before he had to be onstage. His friend wasn't behind him. Peering over the crowd, he saw Chester heading back toward the bar.

* * * *

The judges were announcing the winner to the prior debate as Paul entered the auditorium. Several women overtly looked him over. His boyish good looks and sandy blond hair were enough to get any woman's attention. Add a tall chiseled body and the combination was irresistible. He looked for the area reserved for family and friends of those debating. The audience was clapping for the winner when the lights came up in the auditorium. As the judges and well-wishers cleared the stage, a rotund man wearing suspenders and carrying a huge camera motioned for the winner to get her pictures taken while standing at the podium holding her trophy. He flashed several shots off as the announcement came over the loud speaker there would be a ten-minute recess. Paul could see someone in the crowd waving at him. She cupped her hands around her mouth and called to get his attention. "Pau…l, Paul…"

He broke out in a big grin of recognition and headed down the aisle toward her. "Tina. Good to see you again." She reached up to shake his hand. He bowed and lifted the back of her hand to his lips. She shivered slightly as Paul's soft kiss brushed her skin. He smiled saying, "My lady, it is an honor to be in your fair presence."

She patted the seat next to her and cooed, "Aren't you a smooth one. I haven't seen you since we debated each other in Atlanta. What was that, summer of '92?"

Paul had a mischievous grin as he sat down. "Has it been two years already? Remember how hot it was in Atlanta that year?" Paul crossed his left leg so he could shift closer to Tina. Her complexion had a clear peach-colored translucence that spoke of health and good living. He noticed how her soft brown hair had blonde streaks in it like she'd been playing in the sun. Her dark brown eyes sparkled with interest as she smiled at him. A faint scent of flowers drifted to his nose as he leaned toward her. She had a wholesome girl-next-door beauty and a comfortable way about her that said *relationship material; take me home to meet mama*. Since his divorce five years earlier, Paul hadn't dated much; but Tina had a glow about her that shouted out loud that it was time to get back into the game or run for the hills. Paul whispered, "That was a great debate in Atlanta. I remember when we debated Roe vs. Wade in the quarterfinals. It was ironic that I as a man took the approach that women should have choices about what happens to their bodies. Your approach was so good that this baby killer didn't have a chance."

Tina frowned in disapproval and drew back. "I hate that term. It's bad enough abortions kill helpless unborn children." Tina's expression clouded over as she turned away and faced the stage, making it obvious that she wanted their conversation to be over.

Paul felt the sweat trickle down his back and sides. He tried desperately to fix his social misstep. "Look Tina, I was trying to give you a compliment. Remember, in your rebuttal you came up with the terms 'baby killer' and 'baby murderer' as a way to bring home the emotional impact of what abortion is all about. If it hadn't been for that emphasis, you might not have won. You affected my attitude about it with your argument."

Tina softened and turned back to Paul. "I'm sorry. I'm uptight tonight. You're right; I shouldn't be such a hypocrite. I've never been pregnant nor have I ever had to make such a difficult decision in my own life." Tina turned mournful eyes at Paul that pleaded, *forgive me?*

Paul jumped at the chance to reconnect. "No problem. Why are you so uptight? You love debate. This should be a good one."

The lights dimmed and the audience grew quiet. Tina leaned over and whispered to Paul. "See the redhead up onstage, on your right? I'm here with her. I helped her prepare for today."

Paul shook his head in the dark and wiped his hand over his face. *Man, do I have bad luck,* he thought. Shifting back toward Tina, he whispered back, "It's a small world. I'm here with Chester for the same reason. Good luck."

Tina reached her hand over and patted Paul on the knee. Paul relaxed. Tina was always that way. She never took a debate personally. He settled down in his padded chair, but his thoughts weren't on the debate. He was rehearsing ways to ask Tina out or at least get her phone number.

Paul could see that Lydia was focused yet calm. He noticed how collected she looked as the head judge approached the podium. Paul was hoping Chester hadn't consumed too much alcohol. Chester usually could hold his liquor just fine, but it wasn't like him to drink before such an important event. With scattered applause, a slender gray-haired judge shuffled to the microphone. He cleared his throat as he began. "Good afternoon, welcome to the 25th Annual West Coast Debate Society championship finals. Today's topic is Creation: Fiction not Fact. Dr. Chester Messenger is the proponent." The judge waited for the applause to die down. "Ms. Lydia Masters will argue the opposition." The applause was louder for Lydia, but Chester showed no emotion or concern. Paul watched his friend for signs of nervousness. He looked as solid as a rock. Tina leaned over to Paul. Whispering in his ear, she queried, "What would have happened if Lydia had won the semi-final defending science, what then? In Atlanta we never debated the same subject for the finals as in the semi-finals."

Paul admired her sharp mind. He murmured back, "This is a topic specific event. To win the semi-finals one has to win against someone of opposing views. If both semi-final winners won with the same viewpoint, they flip a coin to see who takes the opposition."

Tina started to say something, but the judge was explaining the rules. "Each participant has a maximum of fifteen minutes for opening statements. There is only one round of rebuttal and can last up to seven minutes. After both participants complete their rebuttals, they each have three minutes for closing statements. If the buzzer sounds, time is up; and the participant must close within ten seconds or will be disqualified. As the head judge, I will only vote if there is a tie. Otherwise, the other six judges will decide the winner, and their decision is final. Since Dr. Messenger has the affirmative viewpoint, he will go first. Now, please welcome Dr. Chester Messenger. Sir, you have the floor."

Chester got up from his table to strong applause. Paul couldn't help giving commentary. "Chester will counter the improbability argument to set up his affirmative position."

Tina turned and tried to speak as quietly as possible over the applause. "Lydia doesn't use the improbability argument anymore unless she gets into trouble and needs help during rebuttal."

Chester raised his hands to hush the crowd. He was elegant in his navy blue suit. His thick head of dark hair made it difficult to believe he was almost forty-seven years old. He looked more like a man in his middle thirties. His strong and vibrant voice went well with his rugged, intelligent looks. "Ladies and gentlemen, science has given us the keys to solving ancient puzzles including the origin of mankind. Until science gave us the ability to accurately date rocks, no one had a credible challenge to the Biblical account of how the universe and life on earth began. Genesis, the first book of the Bible, documents that God created the heavens, the earth, and the first man, Adam, in seven days. The Bible also lists the generations from Adam and his wife, Eve, to Christ. Just by using simple math, it's easy to calculate the universe and earth is roughly 6,000 years old according to the Bible.

Chester paused and looked over at the judges. He had their attention, which was a good sign. Without breaking the flow of his logic he continued in a strong and clear voice. "Science deals with facts. The facts are clear. The universe is at least 10 to 15 billion years old and the Earth is at least 4.5 billion years old. Genesis is a great story, but our planet has been here a lot longer than 6,000 years. The Big Bang Theory has years of solid astronomical and scientific data to support the premise the universe has been expanding for billions of years from its first expansion from a single point scientists call a *singularity*."

Chester paused and drank some water. He wanted that to sink into the minds of the judges before he brought up his next point. "Also, the fossil record shows that life began on this planet in a primitive state and, through the process called survival of the fittest, continued slowly to improve until life exists as we know it today. Carbon dating is fairly accurate and geological dating is very accurate. The fossil record does not support the premise that all the rocks, animals and plants suddenly came into existence just a few thousand years ago. Science has rock hard evidence to show that dinosaurs and other life lived on this planet millions and billions of years ago." Throughout the auditorium listeners chuckled or groaned at Chester's pun.

Chester smiled a little for he hoped the energy of the crowd would affect the judges who according to tradition remained without expression or reaction during a contestant's presentation. "Of course the question that science has yet to answer with certainty is how life began? It's obvious it started billions of years ago, and the fossil record makes it plain it started as one-celled plants and bacteria. What we don't know yet is how simple molecules came together to form complicated proteins. Laboratory experiments have shown that it isn't hard to form amino acids, the building blocks of proteins, from materials and conditions that would have existed on the planet three or four billion years ago. The key question that evolution must answer is, 'How did the amino acids combine to form DNA?'"

Chester sipped some more water then scanned the audience. He looked confident and sounded credible as he delivered the solution. Paul couldn't help himself. He gently nudged Tina and said, "I love this next part. It blows away the improbability argument."

Chester's voice rang out. "I'm sure you are familiar with the improbability argument that goes like this. It is possible for the molecules of amino acid randomly to combine to form DNA and simple life. However, the chance of it happening is so remote, so unlikely, that it would take a trillion universes a trillion years just to create a 50 percent chance of it occurring, statistically speaking. In other words, it would take billions of worlds, in a trillion universes, at least a trillion years for there to be even a fifty-fifty chance of a single molecule of DNA ever forming by chance. Some say the odds of an intact strand of DNA forming all at once by chance are the same as the odds of a tornado sweeping through a warehouse of jet parts and assembling a Boeing 747." Chester set up the argument and waited. The murmur that went throughout the crowd told him that they thought he was boxing himself into a logical corner. A couple of the judges had slightly raised eyebrows. Chester recognized the subtle positive clue in the otherwise stoic faces of the judges. Now he would tear up the straw man he had just built.

Chester cleared his throat a little and softened his voice. "Most know this as the improbability argument against the spontaneous evolution of life from simple molecules. However," Chester raised his index finger for emphasis. "Science once again comes to the rescue. The answer to this seemingly unsolvable problem comes from the greatest scientific achievement in modern physics, the Theory of Quantum Thermodynamics also known as Quantum Reality. Einstein's Theory of Relativity changed how we view the universe at large. Quantum Theory did the same for how we view the universe at the tiny, subatomic distances of reality."

Paul smiled. Chester always included entertainment in his presentations. He watched Tina as she listened carefully to the story Chester was weaving. She nudged him and leaned over. "I can understand why Lydia was nervous. Is Chester always this good?" She was so close her lips brushed his ear.

In the dark Tina could see Paul shake his head slightly. "No, he is in a different zone tonight. Must be the juice." Tina started to ask him what that meant, but Chester's debate was getting more interesting.

Chester's voice now took on a pace and flow that added extra substance to his logic. "When events are observed at the subatomic level, strange things happen. *Unobserved* subatomic events act like *probability waves*. They are called probability waves because, when unobserved, it is unknown where the subatomic building blocks of atoms are located or what they do. All anyone can do is mathematically predict where they *probably* can be found. This is a hazy area called a *wave* function. *Observed* subatomic events act like *separate particles* with a specific position or velocity and no ambiguity as to what they do or where they go." A ripple of whispering spread throughout the crowd.

Tina smiled and shared her pleasure with Paul. "If he gets too technical, he will lose the audience and possibly the judges."

Paul nodded his head. "You're right. This is the risky part."

Chester continued. "According to *John Horgan, Quantum Philosophy. Scientific American, July 1992: Photons, neutrons and even whole atoms act sometimes like waves, sometimes like particles, but they have no definite form until they are measured* or observed. According to Leonard Mandel, University of Rochester whose team pioneered the use of devices using photons to test quantum mechanics: *The mere 'threat' of obtaining information about which way the photon traveled forces it to travel only one route."* Chester paused to bring home the point. "The unbelievable conclusion is that observed subatomic events act differently than those that aren't."

As Chester took a drink Tina leaned over to Paul. "Did he explain that right?"

Paul put his fingers to his lips. "Shhhh...He will explain it."

As Chester paused, the crowd noise sounded like it was raining in the auditorium. Chester waited for the hubbub to die down. Speaking a little slower than before, he continued. "I want to give an example of what this means. Let's say I am a subatomic particle. This auditorium is the atom I'm in. If all of you were outside the auditorium with the doors closed, there is no way you could know for sure which seat I am sitting in. The seating capacity of this auditorium is 1,200. Quantum Reality would describe me as having a 1 in 1,200 chance of sitting in any one chair."

Chester paused and picked up his water glass. Paul looked up at the clock behind Chester and saw his time was running out. *He better wrap it up.*

Chester kept going. "However, if you looked into the auditorium, you would know exactly where I was sitting with 100% certainty. Quantum Reality isn't that simple. According to the data compiled by thousands of experiments, as a subatomic particle, the reason I have a 1 in 1,200 chance of sitting in a chair isn't because I'm in one specific chair. If that were the case, looking in to see where I'm sitting would be a simple act of discovery. Quantum Reality indicates that when no one is looking, I am in all the chairs and none of the chairs at the same time like wispy ghosts representing all of my *potential* locations. According to quantum physics, the act of someone looking into the auditorium would force me to materialize into just one chair. It's called the localization effect of observed phenomena."

Tina gloated and elbowed Paul. "He just lost it. That makes no sense at all."

Paul elbowed her back. "Just wait, here it comes."

Chester took a deep breath and looked confident. "This is called *quantum weirdness.* Neils Bohr who may be the greatest of the quantum theorists once said, 'Anyone who is not dizzy after his first acquaintance with the quantum of action has not understood a word.' And I agree. In 1957, Hugh Everett, while still a Ph.D. candidate under the famous John Wheeler, came up with a solution to the quantum observation problem that is both bold and insightful. I quote Nick Herbert's book *Quantum Reality: Beyond The New Physics.* On page 173, he says that Everett's solution *describes the world as a continually proliferating jungle of conflicting possibilities, each isolated inside its own universe.* Back to my example of me sitting in the auditorium; the most accurate theory of how quantum action happens is that instead of me being in one chair in one universe, I am in 1,200 universes and in each universe I am sitting in a different chair. The observer is also in 1,200 universes and in each one he sees me in a different chair." Heads were shaking all over the audience in disbelief.

Chester paused before explaining further. "Think about it. Our bodies are simply of a lot of subatomic particles bunched together. Don't *we* act a little different when we *know* someone is watching?" The audience snickered. Chester continued, "We take more risks when we are not being observed. Anybody not slow down when they see a cop with a radar gun?" Laughter rippled around the room. "But we always have a choice. And that choice is what creates a different result or consequence. Extensive experiments and calculations show us that this *quantum weirdness* is best explained by an infinite number of universes. In essence, every time there is a quantum event or action at the subatomic level, the universe splits into parallel universes or realities where there is a universe for every possible quantum result or outcome.

No other theory in quantum physics explains quantum action like the theory called the Many Worlds Solution. It is difficult to imagine an infinite number of universes in parallel with ours; however, the brightest minds of science support this explanation. This includes Stephen Hawking and Nobel Laureates Murray Gell-Mann and Richard Feynman. Let me quote further from Nick Herbert's book *Quantum Reality: Beyond The New Physics* so I can show you how Everett's solution to the observation problem solves the improbability enigma of life evolving on Earth. On pages 174 and 175, we find this logical gem. And I quote, *at a recent conference on the nature of quantum reality, Berkeley physicist Henry Stapp suggested an advantage that Everett's quantum reality confers on biological evolution and similar improbable but not impossible processes. Suppose, says Stapp, you could calculate the odds for life to begin on Earth and found them to be infinitesimally small but not actually zero. In the conventional single-universe model of things, something with a very small probability is effectively impossible: it will never happen. However, in the Everett picture everything that can happen does happen. If life on Earth is possible at all, then it is inevitable—in some corner of super reality."*

Leaning over the podium, Chester drove his point home. "Follow the logic with me. We can agree it is improbable but not impossible for amino acids randomly to combine to form DNA and the other proteins needed for simple life—even if the chance were only 1 in a trillion, trillion, trillion, trillion. In an infinite number of universes, the chance would be 100% that in one of the universes it would happen!" The crowd buzzed at the boldness of his statement. Throughout the auditorium Paul watched the silhouettes of heads leaning together as Chester's words sparked controversy. Most of the judges lowered their heads to take notes.

Chester waited until he had everybody's attention again. "For example; when you buy a lottery ticket, the chance of it winning may be 1 in 20 million. If a 100 million people play the lottery, there is a 100% chance that one or more will win. This is why the multi-state power ball lottery always has a winner when the money amount approaches 100 million dollars. So many people from all over the world play that a winner is certain." Paul could tell the audience was beginning to understand because heads were nodding all over.

"In an infinite number of universes, there would be at least one universe where the evolution of life would occur. By combining the evidence of the Big Bang with the evidence of Quantum Reality, we can trust the fossil record to mean what it shows us. Life *evolved* on this planet, as far-fetched as it may seem. The facts support this theory much better than the Genesis account of creation. Genesis describes a universe and an earth only 6,000 years old, but science has proven the earth is billions of years old in an even older universe."

As Chester took his seat the applause was thunderous. Even Tina was pounding her hands together as she acknowledged Chester's brilliant opening statement. The applause slowly subsided as Lydia got up and approached the podium. Paul nudged Tina, "Think your gal can match that?"

Tina put on a brave face. Over the applause she almost shouted, "I'm not worried."

Paul gloated back. "Well, you better worry. I bet your friend has never been against an opponent like Chester."

When the auditorium was quiet Lydia nodded toward the judges. She saw the head judge start the timer. As Lydia surveyed the crowd and the judges, she let the silence slip from a dramatic pause to an almost palpable tension. Paul admired Lydia's almost exotic features. She had a beauty that was both haunting and compelling. A heart-shaped face and a cascade of beautiful red hair framed her delicate features. Even though the auditorium was dark, it was as if her piercing green eyes looked right at him. "Science." Lydia paused and looked around. "Science comes to the rescue."

Paul smirked. "If she starts her rebuttal now, the judges will count off points."

Tina shushed him and watched her friend as she began her magic.

"For thousands of years Genesis has been a marvelous heritage of history and hope. Today in our modern world, it is easy to brush away this timeless message as the myths and legends of a desert people wanting to prove that they are special in the eyes of God. A beautiful message but not something the modern civilized world can count on as true and accurate. After all, science has taught us to remove such superstitions. But I say again. Science comes to the rescue." The crowd shifted throughout the auditorium. The excitement was contagious. Paul and Tina found themselves leaning forward in their chairs. Lydia stood straight and tall before the judges with a commanding presence and an air of defiance, looking like a regal princess defending her honor. "When I signed up to participate in this honorable debate, the committee accepted me as Lydia Masters because my signature is uniquely mine and recognized in a court of law as proof of my identify."

Paul smiled at the thought. *Lydia is rambling; she isn't going anywhere with this.*

"Just as you know who I am because of my signature, we can know who God is because of His signature. If Genesis is the poetic musing of men, then the story of Adam and Eve is just that, an interesting story to read to children and to learn in Sunday school. But if Genesis contains the revealed words of God, then we must not discard them as myth. We must recognize them as truth and the divine revelation of our true origin as the creation of Almighty God." Lydia paused and took a sip of water. She even used the same body language as Chester did when he paused for effect. Tina squeezed Paul's arm. By using Chester's words and mannerisms, she was slowly removing the spell he had woven by speaking first. Paul shook his head in admiration. Lydia was proving to be a formidable opponent.

"Science comes to the rescue. Imbedded in the words of Genesis is the signature of God. For centuries we have read in the book of Daniel these words. *'But thou, O Daniel, shut up the words, and seal the book, even to the time of the end: many shall run to and fro, and knowledge shall be increased,*' Daniel chapter twelve, verse four. The time for unsealing the book is here, and the unsealing proves God exists and that God is the author of Genesis."

Paul leaned over to Tina. "She is setting us up great. Now let's see if she can deliver the goods."

Tina quieted Paul with a dirty look.

"God revealed the Torah to Moses letter by letter. God gave strict commands on how scribes should copy his Holy Word. This was to insure that every letter would stay preserved in the original sequence and keep it uncorrupted. For centuries the people of Israel obeyed their God and took pride in the meticulous copying of the Holy Word. When scholars compared the scroll of Isaiah found among the Dead Sea Scrolls, they found a manuscript a thousand years older than any previously known manuscript, yet it was identical with the Hebrew scrolls used today."

The crowd was hooked. Lydia had them impressed yet wondering. "It wasn't until the computer's invention that we were able to discover why God commanded the Hebrews to use such rigorous methods to copy the Torah. Three Israeli mathematicians have unsealed the mystery for us. Imbedded in the Torah is a cryptographic code that proves that God wrote Genesis. God imbedded his digital signature, if you please."

Scattered shushes followed the noise of the crowd. The excitement was building. Tina wiggled in delight. Lydia had them now. All the judges stopped taking notes and looked up to watch her. She paused and stood up straighter. "Published in this year's August issue of the peer-review *Journal of Statistical Science* is a paper by three gentlemen that reveal a startling discovery. These mathematical statisticians, Doron Witztum, Eliyahu Rips and Yoav Rosenberg of the Jerusalem College of Technology and the Hebrew University discovered words encoded in the Genesis text that are humanly impossible to be there." Lydia paused and took a drink. She waited for the audience to settle down before continuing. "Taking the Hebrew text of Genesis, they ran statistical tests with mind-boggling results."

Paul was beginning to see where Lydia was going with her logic. Rumors had been circulating since 1992 that such a paper was being worked on, but he had discounted it as a hoax put forth by Jewish fanatics. He didn't realize it had passed peer review and had been published. If her logic held up, Chester might be in trouble after all.

"Torah Codes is the name of the discovery, and I would like to explain what these scientists found. First, let me give you a simple example of what they mean by 'Codes.' For years mankind has been imbedding secret codes in normal-looking messages. The term for this is 'cryptology.' It turns out God was the first cryptologist. I have made the example I am about to give you silly but simple by using words that are all four letters in length. By taking the beginning of each word, we can easily figure out the secret message. Here is the coded message, 'Hope Eggs Last Past Mom's Exit.'"

Lydia spoke each word slowly and clearly and then paused to give the audience time to figure out the secret message. "I'm sure most of you have figured it out by now. If we take the first letter of each word to form the new message, we get the secret message of HELP ME. If we made the words a long string without spaces, we would use the first letter and every fourth letter after that to insert the secret message. ELS or Equidistant Letter Sequences is the term used. 'Equidistant' because each letter in the secret message is the same distance apart every time. In this case, the equal distance between clues is four letters."

Tina whispered in glee. "Now comes the kicker."

Paul shook his head slowly in disbelief. *What could possibly be imbedded in the Torah that is so astounding?*

Lydia asked the same question. "What did the researchers find that was so remarkable? Using computers, they searched the Hebrew text. They discovered words comprised of letters at various equal skip distances or equidistant letter sequences, to use the technical term. Simply finding encoded words was nothing unusual, but they discovered something that was indeed unusual. They found related word-pairs or names and dates. To see if they had accidentally stumbled on a couple of related word-pairs, they selected at random 300 such related Hebrew word-pairs from names and events that occurred thousands of years after Genesis was written. And of these 300 related name-event pairs, all 300 were discovered to be in the Torah in close proximity. I say close proximity because the computer would print out the result of the equidistant letter sequences as a grid similar to a crossword puzzle or the word search puzzles you find in the paper. The related name pairs would be found close to each other in the two dimensional grid formed by whatever skip sequence they used."

This time the rumbling of the crowd was loud and long lasting until some in the crowd started to quiet those around them. A couple of the judges were furiously taking notes. To drive her point home, Lydia said in a clear loud voice. "The seemingly impossible related word-pairs they found are just as amazing as if they had found the first and last names of each one our judges who are on the stage with me right now. It's as if they had found each of their names embedded in the Torah as an ELS!"

Paul whispered to Tina, "What is an ELS again?"

"Equidistant letter sequences," she whispered back.

Lydia fed off the energy of the crowd. "They found the names of famous men of history in the Torah. Not just their first and last names but also their dates of birth. Looking for some coincidental explanation, they searched for the same word-pairs in simple randomized Hebrew texts but didn't find them. The word-pairs were only found in close proximity in the Torah, proving irrefutably the encoded word-pairs were not coincident or accidental but were put there by a superior intelligence. The scientists stated the statistical odds of this occurring by chance are fewer than one in 50 quadrillion. Most scientists consider one in a thousand as proof of non-coincidental phenomena."

Lydia paused and beamed. She knew she had made her point, but she wasn't through. "To test this awesome discovery with scientific precision, they took the Hebrew reference book *The Encyclopedia of Great Men in Israel* and found the 34 most prominent men in Israeli history from the ninth to the nineteenth centuries. They paired all the names with the dates of their birth or death. The reason they could do this is because Hebrew numbers are represented as letters much like roman numerals. If the Torah was just recorded stories as many people claim, there is no way those ancient people could foresee and record these men's names and birth dates 3,000 years in advance, but this is something God can do. Using computer analysis, the scientists searched the Torah for the 34 name-date pairs. Remember, they had to be equidistant and in close proximity to register a 'hit.' And how many did they find? They found every one of the 34 names and dates."

Lydia leaned over the podium and clearly and concisely made her most incredible claim yet. "Before the peer-review *Journal of Statistical Science* would publish their finding, they asked the scientists to do something they had never done before. They asked them to run the test again with new data. They told the scientists to use the next 34 most prominent men from the encyclopedia and rerun the test. Because the dates of the death for two of these men were not recorded, the second test only included 32 men. They found all 32 just like the 34 previous names and dates. The editors of the journal of *Statistical Science* were incredulous but published the paper anyway because it had passed the strictest controls they had ever required of a paper."

Lydia scanned the audience. She was almost out of time. Standing straight and proud once again she made her point emphatically. "This confirms without a doubt the information contained in Genesis is the revealed word of God, and we must not discard it as myth. We must recognize it as truth and the divine revelation of our true origin as the creation of Almighty God!"

As Lydia took her seat the applause was thunderous just as it had been for Chester. The crowd was restless as Chester stood up and approached the podium. As the sound of clapping died down, Paul remarked to Tina. "He doesn't even have notes. That's not a good sign for your gal."

Tina shrugged. He looked confident, almost cocky. His slight smile portrayed a man who was amused, not worried. She whispered to Paul. "I have to admire how well he handles himself onstage."

Chester grinned. "There are lies, damned lies, and then there are statistics!" Laughter rippled throughout the auditorium.

Chester waited for total silence. "How many here read Hebrew? No need to raise your hands. How many here understand the complexities of statistical analysis? I've read there are only three men in the entire field that understand the theory and how it works. The rest of us apply formulas and trust them. I know I do. How many here can program a computer? I for one can, and I can program a computer to prove just about anything I want and few could catch me doing it. Were these code words found horizontally, vertically, diagonally, backward or *just any which way* to force the data to reveal names and dates they wanted to find? I'm sure the writers of that remarkable paper were objective, and the fact they were invested in the result as it applied to their religious beliefs entered not into the equation. I'm sure that those Jewish men had Hebrew names spelled with Hebrew letters. Of course a computer search would turn up such names in skip letter sequences. As intriguing as the claims are, there is nobody here who can take the ancient Hebrew text and prove or disprove their claims. However, everybody here can go to museums and look for themselves at the fossils found and reassembled to show us our planet's past. Evolution's proof is in the rocks around us and anyone can view the evidence by going to the Museum of Natural History a few miles from here in this fine city of San Francisco. In fact, they have back-to-school specials for the entire month of September. If you want to go, I'll sell you my tickets." The crowd roared with laughter. Not only was he winning over the audience, he was winning.

Chester was grinning again as he looked at each judge. "That paper didn't explain how the earth is 4.5 billion years old and yet the Genesis account would have us believe our world has yet to have its six thousandth birthday. It didn't explain how the universe is anywhere from 10 billion to 15 billion years old yet Adam and Eve's appearance on Earth by some invisible hand happened just a few thousand years ago."

Paul leaned over to Tina. "That's my Chester; the king of rebuttal." Tina smiled back, her teeth flashing in the darkness of the auditorium.

Chester turned from gentle ridicule to good nature imploring. "Until other large-body texts are tested and analyzed just as the Torah was, we have no way of knowing how common this statistical anomaly is. Computer analysis of one text proves nothing. Folks, we love a good mystery; and I'm sure the mystery uncovered in that paper written by those three brilliant men will be solved one day. But meanwhile, leave the arcane analysis of the statistical anomalies claimed to be in an ancient text written by men, copied by men, and interpreted by men where it belongs." Chester grinned again. "I'm sorry, I guess I should mention where it belongs. There is a museum for oddities that boggle the mind. It's called 'Ripley's Believe It or Not'." As the audience roared with tension-releasing laughter, Chester shouted into the microphone, "I don't believe it, and I doubt Ripley would either."

Chester looked like a man conquering the world as he stately turned and strode back to his chair. Tina joined in the enthusiastic applause as he sat down with a flourish. He might be arrogant but right now it seemed fitting. Paul laughed out loud and poked Tina gently in her side. Tina elbowed him back only harder.

Loyal to her friend she put on her best haughty tone. "It ain't over 'till the fat lady sings and I don't see no fat lady."

Lydia was the picture of serenity and confidence as she took to the stage. The laughter and applause lingered but sympathetic shushes quieted everyone down. Lydia had the look of a librarian displeased at all the ruckus. She even put her hands on her hips for a second, and then she shook her finger at the naughty audience. Quickly her composure changed like the morning sun peeking behind a cloud trying to hide its warmth. Lydia smiled and held out her arms for the audience as if to embrace them all. Her voice rang with love and understanding as she put it in perspective for her audience craving entertainment but seeking truth. "If my opponent can't make it in debate, he would make a good clown. No, better yet, just a few blocks down is a comedy club I recommend. I know the manager. I can get him in as the opening act and get all of you discount tickets." Tina and Paul both laughed as did the audience. Many clapped as they admired her spunk and quick comeback.

Lydia waited for the focus to return to her like a conductor about to direct a concert. "Of course the earth is 4.5 billion years old and of course the universe is billions of years older than that. The Bible doesn't leave us without answers. Just because the questions are hard doesn't mean we lose faith. Seek and you shall find. Peter answered this question for us in his second epistle, chapter three verse eight, and I quote. '*But, beloved, be not ignorant of this one thing, that one day is with the Lord as a thousand years, and a thousand years as one day.*'"

Lydia drank some water and turned to the judges. "We know the Bible many times presents information in symbol and in metaphor. Jesus spoke in parables and the prophets recorded the future in a majestic language of vision and grandeur. Our great God did no less when he shared with us the work of his hands as recorded in Genesis. What seems like billions of years to mortal man is like a weekend project to the eternal all-powerful Creator."

Tina whispered in delight. "She must have expected Chester's rebuttal for she held back on this point." Paul shook his head in wonder; Lydia was resilient as well as brilliant.

"The fossil record is exactly that, a record. I am not asking you to ignore facts. I'm not asking you to ignore the findings of dedicated men and women who uncover the hidden history of our planet. Facts are facts but interpretation of those facts is just that, interpretation. Take the fossil record and recognize it for what it is; a record of the handiwork of our God over billions of years as he crafted our beautiful planet into the cradle and nursery for his dear children. It took millions of years for there to be enough oil to run our factories and to let us drive our cars and fly our planes. That was by design and was a gift from our Father, not some lottery we won in an infinite number of universes."

Murmurs of approval floated throughout the audience. "Those brilliant men did not write a paper that is a hoax or a con. They discovered something better than that. God wanted us to know we can believe his word and not just take it on faith. Only God could have put those men's names and the dates they began or ended their lives here among us. He did it to let us know we are not alone, to prove he is our Creator; and it isn't some incredibly lucky by-product of chance that put us here to wonder in vain why we are here. God placed us here as his children and to someday be with Him and Jesus forever and ever. Science has proven without a doubt that God wrote Genesis, and I want to remind you of what God wrote for us."

Lydia paused briefly to catch her breath and to quote her Bible correctly from memory. Her beautiful elegance and strong convictions radiated from the stage like a queen addressing her subjects. "*Then God said, 'Let us make man in our image, in our likeness.'*" Lydia paused and smiled and looked up as if to address the heavens. "*God saw all that he had made, and it was very good.*"

As the audience exploded into applause, she bowed her head and pressed a hand to her heart. Paul just blew out an incredulous, "Wow, I can't believe what I just witnessed. You would think Chester hadn't even spoken."

Tina stuck her tongue out at Paul. "The fat lady ain't sung. I told you."

The audience quieted down as the head judge took to the podium. "Ladies and Gentlemen, in a few moments Dr. Messenger and Ms. Masters will give their closing comments. After which, our panel of judges will cast their votes. After I read the decision, our sponsor from the International Society of Debate will present the trophy. Now to give his closing comments, Dr. Chester Messenger."

As he sat down, respectful applause for the judge gave Chester a space to approach the podium. He had the composure of a man with unshakable convictions and unwavering confidence. Spreading his hands in a gesture that asked for understanding from his listeners, Chester let his voice ring out. "We make choices every day. Not all decisions are easy. But we don't let ourselves be swayed by awe and wonder. David Copperfield can amaze and baffle us with his magic and illusion, but we still recognize it for what it is. It is entertaining, but we don't go home expecting ladies to float in midair or tigers to appear in a burst of flame. Why? Because we are logical creatures with logical minds, and we can think for ourselves. Statistical anomalies buried in a text written 3,000 years ago do not have more credibility than the fossil record that shows life evolved over millions, even billions of years. Let's examine the attempt to use the Bible to explain why Genesis doesn't match the scientific record. We'll assume that to God a thousand years is like a day. Then, God didn't create the heavens and the Earth in seven days. He did it in 7,000 years. Even *adding* the 6,000 years of genealogy from Adam to present, it is still not long enough. The fact is our Earth is over 4 billion years old. Science deals with facts and God is not a fact. God is a belief. Genesis doesn't speak of dinosaurs or flying reptiles. It speaks only of fish in the sea, birds of the air, and livestock that roam the earth. Be entertained by the amazing but believe the concrete and the reasonable. Science gives us a logical, irrefutable, documented explanation. It can be observed, measured, cataloged, and trusted. That explanation is the *Theory of Evolution*, and we can see its truth with our eyes and feel its truth with our hands."

The applause was respectable, but it lacked the enthusiasm generated after his previous presentations. Eyes were locked on Lydia as she approached the podium because they knew that Chester had left her a slight opening. She smiled and at that instant she was the most beautiful and compelling woman ever to take a stage. She wrapped the moment in magic and delivered her plea. "We all make choices, and we need to feel comfortable that we make the right ones. Science can give us facts that help us to understand, but facts alone are empty and not fulfilling. We are not machines that have no feelings. We are creatures of the mind, but we are also creatures of the heart. Before Witztum, Rips and Rosenberg unsealed the secrets of the Bible, we had only our hearts to go by. Now the precision of science and the power of the computer gives us the gift of seeing the hand of God in His Word. For any who need proof, it is here. For those who have faith, it need not be in vain. Genesis is a truth we can stand on like a rock. We can go confident into the future knowing we are not alone and that we have a Father who will guide us and love us for we are his creation. We are his children."

Several in the audience jumped to there feet clapping, including Tina, as Lydia walked back to her table and took her seat. Her stately elegance punctuated her compelling plea. Tina hooted like a kid at a matinee. "She did it! She did it!"

Paul clapped and hollered, too, but countered. "Don't count my guy out yet. He made the most sense. I would hate to be in those judges' shoes, but I have to root for my bud."

As the audience sat down, the judges flipped through their notes. Finally, each judge filled out a small form and handed it to the head judge. He quickly shuffled through the six squares of paper and put them down. Instead of getting up, he pressed his fingers into his eyes and then ran his hand through his thin gray hair. Tina rubbed her hands together and shivered. Whispering she pleaded, "Please, be Lydia."

With a sigh all could see, the elderly judge slowly rose and shuffled over to the podium. He looked down at the podium for a brief moment before looking up and addressing the audience. "We have all just witnessed a debate of conviction and of passion. I have seen hundreds and hundreds of debates, and this has to be the best one in many years. I was hoping the six panel judges would make it easy for me, but they didn't. The voting was three to three, and I must cast the deciding vote. If there were ever time for us to be able to let two deserving contestants each get a trophy, today would be that day." The room filled with the hum of the crowd's chatter. Tina and Paul could both hear snatches of conversation lobbying for either Chester or Lydia and even a few pleas for a tie. The judge tried to regain control. "Please, please." The room settled down reluctantly. "By the rules agreed on and accepted by the West Coast Debate Society, there can be no tie. Both contestants presented novel and new approaches to an old and honorable subject. We commend them for that. Although Ms. Master's approach was the more innovative, Dr. Messenger used quantum logic in a fresh new way. The one minor element that gave a slight edge to one over the other was the number of sources used. Dr. Messenger had more sources to back up his argument. It might sound technical and petty, but sometimes this is the only way such a close contest can be resolved. The 1994 West Coast Debate Society Champion for the topic of Creation: Fiction not Fact is Dr. Chester Messenger!"

As soon as he named Chester the winner, the room rumbled and buzzed with cheers, boos and unenthusiastic clapping. Many just sat in their chairs shaking their heads or looking around with puzzled looks. The judge leaned back into the microphone and almost shouted, "To present the trophy is Dr. Wayne Edge of the International Society of Debate." The scattered applause gained strength as Dr. Edge showed the trophy to the crowd as he crossed the stage. By the time he was shaking hands with Chester, the audience filled the auditorium with genuine applause of congratulations.

Cameras flashed as Chester shook the doctor's hand with one and took the beautiful golden trophy shaped like a podium with the other. As Chester held up the trophy, the doctor spoke into the microphone but no one could hear him over the applause and cheers of the crowd. As the crowd noise lessened the words were finally audible. "...worthy of this trophy and a debate to remember. Congratulations on a job well done."

The applause renewed as Chester stepped forward to make a few remarks. "I just want to…." The crowd respectfully quieted down. "I just want to thank the West Coast Debate Society and the city of San Francisco for their hospitality. And Ms. Masters…"

Chester turned to Lydia and held out his hand and motioned her forward. She blushed, got up and approached the podium. The applause rose again and no one seemed ready for it to stop. "And Ms. Masters, you sure gave me a run for the money. You are a formidable opponent and a brilliant debater. I admire your skill."

The applause dropped down and the crowd waited for her response. Chester was trying to be gracious and hadn't noticed how close Lydia was to tears. She managed a smile and leaned into the microphone. "Thanks, Dad, and congratulations."

Looking puzzled, Chester nodded and smiled. The crowd applauded politely. The lights went up for the whole auditorium. Folks wanting to congratulate him on his victory immediately went up onstage and surrounded Chester. Another group of people gathered near the podium to shake Lydia's hand. She held her composure until the last person, and then quickly headed for the stairs leading down from the stage. Even from where Paul and Tina stood they could see Lydia wasn't hiding her anguish. Tina left Paul in midsentence. She shouted over her shoulder, "Sorry, something is wrong with Lydia. I got to go see her."

Paul tried to follow Tina, but the crowd pushed him the wrong way. "Hey Tina, are you staying here at the hotel? Can I call you?" But Tina wasn't listening to him.

* * * *

Tina caught Lydia just as she reached the bottom of the stairs. "You were wonderful. You did great. I'm so proud of you!" The two women clung to each other for a moment. Lydia dabbed at her eyes. Tina took control. "Come on, if we go this way we can avoid the crowds." Tina hustled Lydia out a side entrance and around to the elevators. Most of the people were staying for the next debate so the outer lobby was almost empty. Once on the elevator, Lydia broke down crying. Tina supported her friend all the way to their floor and down the hall to their rooms. Once in her room, Lydia crumpled on her bed and sobbed. Tina couldn't understand Lydia's reaction. She had lost debates before and hadn't even shed a tear.

Lydia sobbed uncontrollably into her pillow. Tina could barely make out the words of Lydia's anguish. "Nobody believed me. Chester made it sound like I was lying. I was telling the truth, but I'm being punished anyway."

Tina sat next to her to console her. "You aren't being punished. It was just a debate."

Lydia turned away. "What do you know? Just leave me alone!" Not knowing what else to do, Tina retreated into her room.

* * * *

Paul gave up trying to fight the crowd to follow Tina. He watched as Lydia and Tina went out a side entrance. Maybe he could catch them in the hall outside the auditorium. Going with the flow of the crowd was easier, and he made good time. He couldn't find them in the crowd so he reversed course to see if he could locate Chester. He was gone, too. Inspired, Paul headed for the bar. There he was sitting on a stool by the bartender's station with his trophy in one hand and a drink in the other. From the downcast expression on his face, no one could have known he had just won the most thrilling debate Paul had ever witnessed. Clapping Chester on the back, Paul exclaimed, "I thought I would find you here. Great job, that was a superb piece of work up there. I told ya' you would win."

Chester mumbled something into his drink and tossed it back. Then barked toward the other end of the bar, "Hey Barkeep, how 'bout another one?"

Paul tried to lighten the mood. "If this is how you celebrate a victory, what do you do when you lose?"

Chester straightened up and swung around enough to face his friend. "I won on a technicality. I wasn't prepared. She caught me with my pants down and you know it. And the stuff with the number of sources quoted, it should never have come to that."

When the bartender returned with Chester's drink, Paul ordered a rum and coke. It didn't make sense for Chester to be so low, but Paul knew how to cheer up his friend. "You're just lucky you had a lousy opponent. It's not like she was actually a challenge or anything."

Chester chuckled. "Well, I guess I just proved I can't debate worth a damn." Chester and Paul were both laughing when the bartender sat their drinks in front of them.

Paul grabbed his drink and clinked his glass up against Chester's. "You're nuts not to be on top of the world. That was some debate we heard in there."

Chester slapped his friend on his back. "You're all right. I guess I should be celebrating, but it just amazes me that she did so well. I mean, come on, she didn't address a single creation issue. All she did was 'Torah Codes' this and 'Torah Codes' that and an appeal for feelings."

Paul mused, "But still, I wonder if there's anything to that encrypted stuff. What else could it be? Anything that will stand up for the long run has to be duplicable by other scholars. But, as you said, everyone's taking the word of just three men who are invested in the outcome."

Chester said, "I'll find out. You wait and see. If it's the last thing I do, I'll prove it's all smoke and mirrors. It's all just mumbo jumbo, funny numbers and hogwash."

Paul just shook his head and nursed his drink. Chester was a strange fellow sometimes, but he made a good friend. If anybody could get to the bottom of a mystery, Chester could. "Come on, you hungry? Let's go get one of those famous San Francisco steaks."

* * * *

After they got back from dinner, Paul called the front desk and asked for Tina's room. Surprisingly, he got her on the phone. "Hey Tina, it's Paul. How's Lydia. Is she okay?"

Tina was alone in her room finishing the dinner that she had ordered from room service. "Yeah, I guess. She's asleep. I'm kind of worried. I'm not sure why she's taking it so hard."

"You want go get some coffee or something."

Tina paused and finally said. "Sure, give me a couple of minutes, and I'll meet you at the café where they serve breakfast."

"Okay, great, I'll see ya there." Paul looked into the other room and saw Chester reading. I'm going to go downstairs, you okay?"

Chester didn't look up from his book. "Yeah, yeah. I just want to get some sleep and fly out of here tomorrow. Don't worry about me."

When Paul got to the café, Tina was already there. He beamed when she gave him a hug. "Sorry I ran off like that. Lydia needed me. Congratulations on your friend's win. I bet he is on top of the world."

The host seated them in a booth. When they were alone again, he answered her question. "No, he's acting more like someone who lost, not someone who just won. We had a few drinks and got some steaks. He's upstairs reading something, and all he wants to do is get out of here."

"Lydia and I plan to leave early tomorrow, also. We both need to get back to work. I hadn't planned this trip, but she was in a tight when her regular partner got sick. Lydia's a good friend and when she said the debate was in San Francisco, I quickly juggled my schedule to help out."

"How long have you known her?"

We were roommates in college; and we tried living together afterwards. Lydia is a neat freak and I have horizonalitis."

Paul laughed. "Horizonalitis?"

"Yeah, if it has a horizontal surface, I clutter it up. Drives Lydia crazy." Putting the menu down Tina said, "I guess I'll just have a glass of tea. How about you?"

The waitress showed up and Paul just said, "Two ice teas, please." She came right back carrying glasses of tea, both with a wedge of lemon on the side. After she left, Paul tried to see how much sugar he could get into the glass. Stirring the white mountain at the bottom of his glass, he tried to sound casual. "Where do you and Lydia live anyway?"

"Lydia and I are in Dallas not too far from the DFW airport. She owns a travel agency, and I work for Hertz. Where do you live?"

"Atlanta. It was our club that sponsored the debate a couple of years ago. That's why I was there."

"So how do you know Chester?"

"We met because he and I worked on a couple of projects together. He's a computer consultant and I'm a process consultant. But it was chess that got us started hanging out. We play in tournaments when we can. Last year we decided to share a condo. We both travel so much that half the time only one of us is there. Of course we discovered early on our mutual passion for debate. He and I were meant to be friends it seems."

"What's a process consultant?"

Paul rubbed the back of his neck. "Let me see. How can I explain it? In the old days they called us efficiency experts. Many times what a company needs isn't new technology or more people but a streamlined way of completing tasks with the people they already have. Often I work with strategic planning or new technologies, but those always involve processes sooner or later."

"Sounds like a lot more fun than running the counter of a rental car agency. At least Lydia gets to travel as part of her work. I just get to see people in a hurry all day."

Paul decided now was the time to go for broke. "Hey look, I go to Dallas a lot. Half of the time my work is in Dallas or Houston. Why don't I give you a call when I'm going to be in the area, and we can have dinner or something."

Tina didn't reply. She just looked in her purse and took out a business card and a pen. She wrote a phone number at the bottom of the card. As she handed the card to Paul, she said, "That's my home number and the card has my work number. Call me anytime. You don't have to wait until you're in Dallas, you know. Unless you don't think I'm worth a long-distance phone call." Tina cocked her head and winked.

Paul felt a flush in his chest and a shiver up his spine. He couldn't believe his luck; this beauty was interested in him. "I don't know, you might be worth a plane ride or three. Besides, I can make sure I get a lot more work in Dallas. I hear they're very inefficient around there." He winked back. "You know we have one more night here in San Francisco. Just because we have two friends that want to pout doesn't mean we have to. Want to do something; kick up our heels?"

"Do you dance?"

"I dance better than Chester debates."

"I've been wanting to go to the Backflip and dance. I hear it's *the* place to go, but I couldn't get Lydia to do anything besides go to Fisherman's Wharf and buy T-shirts and stuff. We did go to the aquarium, which was neat. Walking through the tunnel with all the fish swimming over our heads was so cool. But I couldn't even get Lydia to ride on one of the famous cable cars. I mean, that's what tourists *do* in San Francisco. So to heck with our party poopers. I want to go dancing, but I have to go change clothes. I can't go dancing in this!"

Paul went up to the cashier and paid for the tea before rejoining Tina by the elevators. "How much time do you need?"

"I'll meet you here in the lobby in fifteen minutes. I'll ask Lydia if she wants to go, but I know she will say no."

"I know Chester will say no, but I'll ask him anyway."

There was an embarrassed silence on the elevator. Both felt as excited as teenagers. Tina got off on her floor and blew Paul a kiss. Paul decided to he should change clothes, too. And to think, he almost didn't come to San Francisco with Chester."

Atlanta

Chester peeled the label off his beer and fretted. Paul shook his head and said, "You didn't even notice our waitress is a babe. What did we come to Hooters for if you ain't gonna look?"

Chester shook his head, "If I knew Hebrew, it would be easy to show that Rips was making the data prove out based on data bias. I don't think they did proper controls on the experiments."

"So you're back on that again? Can't you give it a rest? You won the damn debate for Christ's sake."

Chester leaned forward and with a glint and a firm jaw and said, "She shouldn't have gotten a single vote. After I prove the paper is hogwash no one will ever use it against me again."

Paul shook his head and with exasperation asked, "How are you going to do that?"

Chester grinned and said, "I'm going to India. There is a mathematician there who thinks he can prove that what was discovered in the Torah is nothing special at all. He needs a little help, and I'm going to help him."

Lydia and Mary's First Session

Lydia's hand shook as she reached for the door. The empty waiting room was different from others she'd been in before. It was smaller, quieter, and prettier. There were various green plants of different heights placed around the room. Two light blue comfortable-looking chairs were opposite a love seat. On the coffee table was a vase of fresh flowers. She smiled when she noticed the magazines on the table. They were current editions instead of the year-old stuff that was usually in reception areas. The aroma in this room was different, too. A vanilla scent was coming from a candle on a wall shelf. There were no overhead lights. A soft glow bathed the room from the table lamp and wall sconces. Taking a deep breath calming herself, she thought, *maybe this won't be so bad.*

At exactly 7:00 p.m., the door opened and a friendly face poked out. "Are you Lydia?" When Lydia nodded, the woman continued, "I'm Mary. Pleased to meet you." She held out her hand and gently motioned for Lydia to follow her. She was smiling so Lydia smiled back and tried to act confident. They walked toward the back of a suite of offices and entered one that had a warm look and feel, almost like a living room except there was a desk in one corner. On one end of the room was a soft floral sofa covered in a muted design with no particular pattern. Several pillows were on it near the armrests, and there were a couple of matching chairs across from it that looked comfortable. Lydia chose the sofa in case she was asked to lie down. Mary sat in a chair opposite and picked up a folder laying on the small table between the couch and chairs. She glanced over it and said to Lydia, "Can you tell me what reason you decided to come here today?"

"To be honest, I'm here because my doctor had the appointment set for me." Lydia dropped her gaze into her lap.

Mary nodded, "What did he say was the reason he was referring you?"

Lydia coughed nervously and replied, "I can't make myself do the work I need to do or go out with my friends or anything. It's like nothing matters anymore. I'm also having trouble sleeping. I'd probably be fine if I could just get a good night's sleep. I'm tired at night because I work long hours so I fall asleep quickly, but I wake up in a few hours and can't get back to sleep." After taking a deep breath she continued, "I've tried drinking warm milk, reading a boring book, listening to soft music; but I can't fall back to sleep until just about the time I have to get up for work. I thought I probably needed some vitamins or something. That's why I went to my doctor. After running me through the mill, he couldn't come up with anything physical so here I am."

"Are you currently taking any medication?" Lydia shook her head. "How about alcohol or other drugs?"

Again Lydia shook her head. "No, I don't even like to take aspirin and I don't drink alcohol at all. Well, maybe some champagne at weddings or on New Years, but that's all."

"You say nothing matters," Mary asked, "Do you ever get to the point of thinking about harming yourself?"

Lydia quickly responded, "Of course not! That's an unpardonable sin."

"Just checking," Mary casually accepted. "Would you mind telling me a little about yourself?"

Lydia leaned back and sighed. "I'm an only child and I grew up with my mom who loves me a lot. I visit with Mama about once a month. I'm single, never married. I live in a two-bedroom townhouse and own a small travel agency. I don't make much money, but I get to travel free or almost free."

Mary nodded and leaned back. "Your life sounds normal to me so far. Your father, where is he?"

Lydia picked up one of the pillows on the couch and hugged it to her stomach. "He lives in Alaska. I was in grade school the last time I saw him."

"How old were you? Is it a good memory?"

Lydia's gazed at the ceiling and lowered her voice. "It might have been for my eighth birthday. He bought me a backgammon set. I remember he taught me to play. It is the only legacy I have from him." She hugged the pillow tighter to her stomach. She shook her head and said, "But that is all in the past and has nothing to do with my life now." Looking back at Mary defiantly, she smiled and said. "What else do you want to know about me?"

Mary made a note on her pad, *father=pain,* to remind herself that this would be an area to explore later. Lydia's negative reaction told Mary she had better get to know more about her patient before pursuing that subject. She returned instead to something Lydia seemed more comfortable discussing. "The symptoms you mentioned earlier could be signs of depression. Can you remember how long you've been experiencing them?"

Lydia shifted on the couch and let the pillow fall to her lap. "I, uh, well, I know this will sound stupid, but I think they all started when I lost a debate a few months ago."

"Debate?" Mary prompted.

Lydia leaned forward and answered, "You see, I'm a member of a national organization that finds sponsors and organizes formal debates. I was on the debating team in college, and I still enjoy it. I'm good at it, too, so I usually win. I've debated on many subjects, but now I just enter the ones where the focus is 'God vs. Science' or 'Evolution vs. Creation.'"

Mary added to the pad, *religion,* as she asked, "Have you experienced similar symptoms other times you didn't win a contest?"

Lydia shook her head. "Not usually. I'm disappointed but not bummed out. This time it was different." Lydia spread her hands and shrugged.

"I see. What was different about this one?" Mary leaned back into her chair to listen.

Lydia perked up and sat up straight. Her face lit up in a smile and a slight flush came to her cheeks. "Well, not too long ago I was in San Francisco; and I debated this older man named Chester Messenger." Lydia held up her right hand. "I swear that is his real name. He's got a Ph.D. in something so I guess it's *Dr.* Chester. Anyway, he argued for evolution and I countered with creation. I was sure I had the winning points nailed, but he still won. I used a paper written by Jewish scientists that proves God exists and the book of Genesis is literal. Some of the judges saw the logic, but I guess not enough did." Lydia hung her head and her eyes filled up. It was clear she was fighting to keep control.

Mary wasn't sure if this was the direction she needed to take the session but decided it was best to follow along with whatever Lydia wanted to tell her. "Go on."

Lydia sniffed and composed herself as she started to explain what her argument was. "Have you heard of the Torah Codes or the Bible Codes?"

Mary shook her head and looked puzzled. "No, can you explain them to me."

Lydia took a deep breath. "These guys named Witztum, Rips and Rosenberg wrote a research paper in which they proved the first five books of the Bible, called the Torah, have hidden messages buried in them. It's so cool because the messages are encrypted codes like what spies use."

Confused, Mary asked. "I don't understand."

Lydia tried again, "They call it equidistant letters meaning 'equal-distant' letters. Related words and phrases can be found in the Bible. The words could start anywhere, but the letters making up the word are scattered in the text the same distance apart, say every 50 letters or every 125 letters. The scientists in Israel used a computer to find these secret codes. They are mathematical statisticians, and they discovered words and phrases encoded in the Genesis text that would be humanly impossible to put there. They found names, events, and dates from the nineteenth and twentieth century. Only God could have put that information there." Excited, Lydia continued. "This proves beyond a doubt that God wrote Genesis and the other four books of the Torah. So you see, obviously God created the heavens and the earth like it says in Genesis which means evolution *can't* be true."

"So this was your argument in the debate and the judges didn't buy it?" Mary queried.

Lydia sighed and slumped back. "Some of the judges believed me. Chester argued that people could make statistics prove anything. He made fun of everything I said. He talked about the fossil record that goes back 3.6 billion years and how we can't believe the Bible since it only documents the past 6,000 years. I thought I countered with solid rebuttals, but it wasn't enough. Four of the seven judges decided that Chester's fossil records were worth more points than the research done by those wonderful men."

Mary tried to get back to Lydia's symptoms of depression. "So you almost won but you've felt bad ever since then?

Lydia nodded her head. "Yes, I made it to my hotel room after the debate ended and cried for hours. I still can't stop thinking about it. I don't know what I did wrong. I know the debate is past and all, but I want to know..." Tears reddened Lydia's eyes but didn't fall. She looked up and pressed her lips together. Taking a deep breath, she looked back at Mary and said. "See what I mean?"

Mary pursed her lips for a second and shifted thoughtfully. "I can see you're distressed. Is there anything else that could be contributing to your unhappiness? You said you don't make much money. How about financial, social, romantic or sexual problems? Are you having difficulty with co-workers or friends? I once had a client who discovered her depression started when one of her friends didn't invite her to a small party. Her mind had instantaneously jumped back to high school when no boy asked her to the senior prom. Even minor incidents can remind us of similar events or people in our past when we were hurt and vulnerable."

Lydia laughed through her tears. "I wish it were that simple. I pay my bills on time and have good credit. My best friend, Tina, and I get together once a month. The only parties I go to are the ones around Christmas for the travel industry. As to a boyfriend, I don't think I have the energy for one right now. When I get my act together, I might want more of a social life." Lydia picked up a pillow off the couch again, pressed it to her abdomen and started rocking back and forth. "I'm sure there's nothing else."

Mary smiled on the inside. She knew she was getting close to something because of Lydia's reaction. There was something too painful there, but Lydia couldn't see it or didn't want to. Mary also knew it would probably take some time for Lydia to reveal whatever it was. She used the rest of the session to just learn more about her.

Before their time was up, Mary decided the best course was to start Lydia off with tried and proven stress management techniques. She asked her to get some type exercise, like taking a walk at least three times a week. She also told her to take a short morning and afternoon break from work each day and get away from the office for lunch a whole hour each day even if she just ate a sandwich in the park. She also asked her to limit her caffeine and sugar intake explaining how those chemicals contribute to mood shifts. She asked Lydia to write down her thoughts and feelings at the end of each day. It could be like a diary or just a list of thoughts and feelings she remembered experiencing at specific times during the day.

Before Lydia left she set an appointment for the same time the next week.

French India

Chester pushed himself from the keyboard and rubbed his tired eyes. His legs were cramping and he was sick of the cluttered papers, coffee cups, and computer printouts that littered his tiny cubicle. It was late at night, and he was glad to finally finish. He glanced at the clock perched on his monitor. The red digital glow displayed 12:34. Chester felt that all too frequent, strange and eerie feeling of someone watching him. He flicked his wrist up and around to look at his watch. It rhythmically displayed 12:34:54, 12:34:55 then 12:34:56. He shivered slightly as a strong and disturbing déjà vu passed through him. Since he had arrived in Mahe, located in French India, his personal coincidence quirk of seeing 12:34 had started up again. He shook the feeling off and continued to shut down the computer. He felt frustrated. The project hadn't been going well, at least by his standards. The software he had written was working flawlessly but the results were not what he had hoped they would be. He couldn't duplicate with nonbiblical text the results that Witzum, Rips and Rosenburg had with the Torah. He had come to India to prove the Bible Codes were simple statistical quirks common to all large texts regardless of their language or subject matter. The Swami had hired him to find hidden messages from God in the ancient Sanskrit texts, but he hadn't been able to do it so far. He wished he had never heard of the blasted Bible Codes. *What made him take on this hairball project, anyway?* His frustration and exhaustion made him crave the relief of a round of strong drinks. He was leaving for the U.S. tomorrow afternoon, and he could sleep late. Besides, he deserved a drink after slaving nonstop for six weeks. The strange culture and incessant heat didn't help either. He patted his jacket pocket to make sure he had his billfold, tickets, and passport. He was nervous about leaving them at the hotel room so he always carried them with him. After a relaxing visit home in the U.S. of A., he would come back and help out again; but he had to have a break in more familiar surroundings. He muttered after he signed out at the guard's desk, "It ain't my fault it ain't working. I did my part."

Mahe is a busy city in the lower southwest of India that has a section catering to tourists. It didn't take him long to find a place that served drinks. Chester didn't drink often, but when he did he liked to "tear a big one" as he liked to call it. In India the custom is to drink fast and that suited Chester just fine. After a couple of hours of downing stiff drinks and boring the patrons of the bar with his stories and arrogant attitude, he stumbled out to find a bus to his hotel.

He found a bus stop that was on a route back to his hotel. He didn't realize the bus that pulled up to let out some laughing tourists wasn't the right one. To make matters worse, he was so drunk he passed out after sitting down. He woke up lying across a bus bench seat with his head on the crook of his arm. He was alone on a silent bus parked on the side of a narrow road surrounded by tall trees. He sat up and looked around.

Chester wondered if he was in the forest of Thusharagiri. From what he remembered from the guidebook, this fit the description. He had read about its hiking trails. It was about 100 km from Mahe and famous for its dense evergreen trees populated with exotic birds and wild animals. Chester knew the forest was at least a day's walk from Mahe. He wasn't sure in which direction. All he knew for sure was that he was far away from the comfort of his hotel room.

Confused as to why he was the only one on the bus, he investigated. He stumbled off the bus and walked around to see if he could find anything wrong with blame thing. All the tires looked okay. He got back on the bus and tried to hot-wire it since the keys were missing. He got it to turn over a few times. It had plenty of battery, but the gas gauged showed it was empty. He slapped the steering wheel so hard it made his hand sting. He looked up into the mirror and realized the bus driver couldn't have seen him lying down because the seats blocked the view. He shouted at the mirror, "He could have at least checked to see if anybody was on the damn bus!" Satisfied his predicament wasn't his fault, he started looking around. He got off the bus and tried to get his bearings.

It was dark and noisy with the sound of insects and other nightlife. Down the road behind the bus and over the trees was the slight glow of light pollution reflected off the clouds. Chester began to worry and his sense of panic woke him up and made him sweat. He cussed out loud at the nameless people responsible for leaving him in this dark place. "You sons of bitches better get back with some gas or there'll be hell to pay." His outburst caused the insects to pause their serenades for a second or two only to begin their symphony again in earnest. To Chester it sounded like they were mocking him. He sat down and put his aching head in his hands.

A half hour dragged along and no one drove or walked by. He had to get back to town or he would miss his flight. Another one wouldn't be available for at least two days, but he had no idea where he was. All he knew for sure was his head was pounding and his mouth tasted like sour milk. He decided to walk down the road in the direction the bus had come from hoping it led to Mahe and his hotel room. He mumbled out loud, "I know I've said this before, but I'm always amazed where I find myself after I've been drinking." Chester continued to chew himself out as he trudged wearily down the dark road.

The Master's Sanctuary

He was deep into the relaxed state of his evening meditation when the silent vivid images played across the screen of his awareness.

When they faded, he got up and sketched what he had witnessed. It was like a movie had played within his mind's eye. He could remember clearly the details of the scene that unfolded before him. It was a man whose dress resembled that of an American rather than a European. He used some charcoal to shade in the night around the donkey that carried him. He paid special attention to the features of the man's face.

After an hour, a beautiful drawing in distinct tones of black and grays showed a tired unshaven man sitting on the back of a donkey. The man in the sketch was holding a candle. The flame lit up his face in the dark. After the sketch was as close to his vision as he could manage, he drew a smaller one of just the man's face. It was time to prepare for a long-awaited visitor.

The Master called for his servant. Soon Sanjiv shuffled into the parlor rubbing the sleep from his eyes. Anybody else would have questioned the wisdom of going out into the forest late at night with a charcoal sketch and a donkey to look for a stranger. But Sanjiv had never known of his Master to be wrong so he always obeyed the man who had rescued him from the orphanage many years ago. If Master said a man that looked liked his drawing would be on the old forest road needing help, then that's where he would be and that's where Sanjiv would go.

* * * *

Chester trudged slowly down the dark road still feeling the affects of the drinks he had consumed. As he rounded a corner, he saw someone approaching him with a flashlight. The light bobbed in a way that made it look like someone was on foot. Soon, a young Indian man appeared out of the darkness. In his right hand he held a tether clipped to a halter on a donkey's head. A large flashlight and a piece of paper were in his other hand.

When the young man saw Chester, he handed him the flashlight and the piece of paper. He spoke halted but understandable English and seemed delighted he had found Chester. "Me Sanjiv, me look for you, me find you."

Chester blinked not knowing what to make of this excited young man. "I'm Chester, what do you mean you're looking for me." In his inebriated state it came out more like "I'm Shesher, washa mean ur looking fer me." Sanjiv nodded vigorously and pointed repeatedly at the piece of paper now in Chester's hand. Chester unfolded the piece of paper. It was a sketch of him from the neck up. Chester's vision blurred slightly so he shook his head and refocused on the drawing the young man had handed him. He shook his head and looked again. There was Chester's face drawn on a sheet of paper. It looked a lot like the sketches he had seen done at circuses and fairs. "Do you work for the bus company? Who gave you that drawing of me? Who made the drawing?" Even confused and foggy-headed he could still recognize the obvious impossibility of a likeness of his face showing up on a deserted road in the middle of a forest in India. However, the young man did act as if he was looking for him.

All Sanjiv would do was point to the donkey and say, "Ride for mister, yes? Me help, yes?"

Chester was in no condition to walk much further but somehow it didn't feel ridiculous. In a strange way, he felt a subtle tremor of recognition. He felt like he should trust this man with a donkey, but he couldn't figure out why. It calmed his fears that the young stranger seemed relieved to have found him. Chester felt weak and shaky so he accepted the offer of a ride. Fatigue made his eyelids heavy and his stomach was in knots. He leaned forward until the bristles of the donkey's short mane pricked his cheek. A dozen jostles later, he was asleep.

* * * *

The Master heard the sound of an animal plodding along nearer and nearer, so he went out onto the porch of his cottage. His dim porch light cast his shadow onto the grass and the path beyond. Through some bushes the Master could see the silhouette of a man on a donkey. Just past the bushes came Sanjiv leading his donkey. Sitting on his donkey was an rumpled-looking American man holding a flashlight. The man looked exhausted and barely awake. In fact, the sight before the Master was identical with his vision, except in his vision the man on the donkey had been holding a candle. Sanjiv helped the American slide off the donkey and made sure he could stand on his own.

The Master told Sanjiv to put up the donkey and to leave him and their visitor alone. Chester was a little confused and protested that he had to catch a plane. The Master smiled and said, "No, first you need sleep. Later we will learn much from each other." Stepping back and holding the door open, he motioned, "Come in. Come in. Please, come in. I have been expecting you for a long time. But enough talk. You need sleep, my friend."

Chester realized that he had to sober up before going anywhere so he might as well sleep it off here. He stumbled up the steps of this gentleman's porch and walked into a parlor. It was a comfortable room cluttered with the accouterments used for painting and other arts. Chester's eyes did a double-take and he walked over to an easel holding a charcoal drawing of a man on a donkey that looked just like him. Shivers went up and down his spine just as they had back at the forest road with Sanjiv. Chester pointed at the canvas, "Wh…what, whee… where?"

The Master smiled as he watched Chester's reaction to his drawing. "You will see and learn many more wonders soon. But first you need sleep."

"Like I'll be able to sleep now," grumped Chester.

Sanjiv walked into the parlor. The Master nodded at Sanjiv. Sanjiv moved over to Chester and said, "Please mister, I show you bed."

Chester took one last look at the drawing. He shivered and felt goose bumps cascade from his head to his toes before following Sanjiv. He walked down a short hall into a small room with a bed, a table, and a few pillows. He fell with a groan onto the bed and quickly fell asleep.

Mary Finds a Pattern

Mary shuffled through the folders on her desk. She was going through her daily ritual of reviewing the files of the clients she would see that day. She came to Lydia's file and smiled. This case was interesting and challenging. Her notes reminded her that when Lydia wasn't comfortable discussing something, she would grab a pillow and hug it to her stomach like a shield. There were two topics that needed more investigation: religion and her father. Mary decided to explore these areas in today's session. She would watch Lydia's reactions closely and back off if she started getting too agitated. Setting that file aside, she went on to review the notes of other clients.

* * * *

Lydia felt antsy sitting in Mary's office waiting for her to return with their drinks. She thought, *only crazy people go to therapists. Maybe I'm crazy.* Mary seemed friendly and concerned, but she was scared to trust a worldly woman to help her instead of the Lord or her pastor. She moved from the chair to the couch to put more distance between them. Besides, it had those fluffy soft pillows. Mary returned carrying a Diet Coke for herself and ice water for Lydia. She gave Lydia her glass and sat in the chair opposite the couch. Each set their glass on the coffee table between them using coasters to protect the oak finish. Lydia shifted nervously not knowing what to say.

Mary smiled and started telling Lydia about a movie she had seen recently. Surprised, Lydia perked up as she responded, "I've heard it's great. I wish I could see it."

"What's stopping you," Mary inquired.

Lydia skirted the question, "Oh, the usual, work, work, work and more work."

"That's a bummer," Mary commiserated. "Owning your own business is a responsibility and accomplishment. How did you swing that?"

Lydia was eager to talk about work. She told Mary everything she could think of to take up time. She explained how she had worked part-time at a travel agency while in high school. After she graduated they offered her a full-time position. She worked there during the day and at night attended college. When the agency's owners retired, they helped her buy it by allowing her to pay out the sales price at a rate she could afford. Lydia tried to talk fast enough so Mary couldn't get an opening to ask questions. When Lydia shifted her monologue to explaining how she got to travel a lot and places she'd visited, Mary lifted her hand with palm out fingers up signaling Lydia to stop. Lydia paused.

Mary quickly inserted, "You must enjoy being able to visit interesting places. You mentioned last time we talked that you recently traveled to San Francisco and that you took part in a debate on Evolution vs. Creation. You defended the creationist viewpoint, right?

Lydia responded quickly, "Of course."

"I see," continued Mary, "Are you currently affiliated with a church family?"

"Yes, I'm a member of the Crossroads Bible Church and attend services every week. I often seek my pastor's advice. I wouldn't be here if I hadn't discussed with him my doctor's recommendation to see you."

"I'm curious. What was your pastor's opinion of psychotherapists?" Mary risked.

"Well, he didn't exactly talk about psychotherapists, but he said that God always provides us with what we need when we need it. He reminded me that God works in many ways and that one of God's greatest gifts is the knowledge and skill of doctors and other health care professionals. He also said that Jesus was a healer and counselor. I hadn't thought of that. Anyway, he and I prayed that I would recognize and accept guidance from whatever source it came. He is a man that follows the word of God and he knows how to lead his flock."

"Wow!" Mary exclaimed. "I see why you like him. After I catch my breath, let's see if I can live up to that." She reached for a sip of her Coke. "There's something I want to tell you about myself. I try to be objective and open to my clients' values and religious beliefs, but I need you to know that I'm Catholic and I, too, value my priest's support. I don't attend Mass much anymore except, of course, on Christmas," she grinned. "Is that going to be a problem for you in working with me?"

Lydia smiled. "I also try not to be prejudice or judge others' beliefs. Thank you for telling me; but if you believe in God and our Lord Jesus Christ, I think we'll be okay."

"Good. I feel better," Mary let out the breath she'd been holding. "Now...what I'd like to know is have you felt any better since we last talked?"

"Perhaps a little bit better, but I don't know if I'm feeling sad or mostly bored," Lydia reflected not being able to recognize the difference.

"Hmm...," Mary went on, glancing at Lydia's file. "So all of this started at a debate." Lydia got a scared look in her eyes and nodded affirmatively as she began to squirm a little on the couch. Without responding in any way to Lydia's quick mood shift Mary continued, "If you'll hang with me for a moment, we'll see if you remember exactly when those feelings began—before, during, or after the debate? First relax your muscles and get comfortable. Lydia let out a nervous giggle and slumped. Close your eyes and take a deep breath. Now let it out slowly as you imagine yourself back in San Francisco. When was the first moment you felt afraid or angry?"

Lydia opened her eyes, grabbed a pillow hugging it her stomach, and whispered without much hesitation, "At the end. When the judge announced that I had lost. I was *so angry.*" Her eyes filled up and tears slowly trickled down her cheeks. Mary handed her a tissue.

Both of them were silent for a minute or so. "What else," Mary prompted.

"Then during Chester's acceptance speech he called me forward, but to be honest, I don't know exactly what he said. I remember starting to feel dizzy. I was afraid I couldn't get offstage without crashing. I made it to through the door at the back entrance to the stage when my friend, Tina, caught up with me and put her arms around me. If she hadn't helped me get to the elevator and up to my room, I don't know if I'd have made it. When the door closed behind me in my room, I ran straight to the bed and collapsed. My heart felt like it was breaking and I was shaking all over. Tina tried to help. She gave me water, put a blanket around me, and tried to comfort me; but I wanted to be alone so I asked her to leave. I don't know how long I stayed crunched up on the bed crying. I felt so tired and hopeless. I guess I finally fell asleep from exhaustion."

Carefully, Mary asked, "Did you know Chester before the debate?"

"No," Lydia stated.

"Think carefully and take your time. Did Chester remind you of anyone in your past that hurt you?"

Lydia sat still as she stared out of the window. Mary didn't break the silence. She just waited.

Finally, a nervous laugh erupted and Lydia answered, "My father, I think."

Treading lightly, Mary inquired, "Tell me about your father."

Lydia's head was down. Her mouth opened to continue but no sound came out at first; then she choked out, "When I was six years old, I remember waking up one morning and he was gone. The night before he left, he whipped me real hard because I was bad and locked me in my bedroom without dinner. Mama and Daddy yelled at each other all night, but I couldn't make out what they said. Sometimes I could hear my dad yell my name at her. What is so weird is that I can't remember what I did to make him so mad. He was gone when I got up, and I didn't see him again until after my eighth birthday. Mama said he had left to find work, but I knew it was something about me. I found out later the reason I saw him when I was eight was because he had come to sign the divorce papers."

Mary leaned back surprised. She hadn't expected to hit pay dirt so quickly. After Lydia regained her composure, she asked, "Does Chester look, sound, or act like your father?"

Lydia slowly answered like she was trying hard to remember. "I don't know but it felt like I was with my father. During the debate, Chester kept making fun of everything I said. He convinced everyone I was lying about the codes in the Torah, but they are true!"

Mary reflected her words, "Chester made fun of you and accused you of lying. Is that what your father did?"

Lydia took a deep breath, shook her head, and retreated back into her shell. "I don't know. I can't remember much of anything else about him. I suppose my mother knows, but she always got upset when anyone mentioned his name. I didn't want to hurt her so I never asked questions."

Mary knew if she pushed now on the lying issue, this scared little rabbit might bolt and never return. She decided to err on the side of caution and come at it another way. "If you told your mother how important it is for you to find out about your early years, do you think she might tell you? Does she know you're in therapy?"

Lydia looked horrified. "I can't tell her I'm in *therapy*.... But she might talk with me now that I'm an adult. I'll ask her. I have to admit I've always been curious."

"All you can do is ask."

Lydia nodded. "Okay, I'll ask." Feeling drained, she looked at her watch and sighed with relief. Her session time was almost over.

Mary also noticed the time and wanted to end the session on a positive note so moved to something safer, "Were you able to get in the exercise and quiet moments we talked about last week?"

"Just a little bit," admitted Lydia sheepishly. "I got up each morning and walked three times around my townhouse complex. I think that's about a mile and a half. I found out that I'm out of shape, but I did feel better afterward. I wasn't able to stop for lunch, though. I was just too busy."

Mary rewarded Lydia with a big smile as she said, "But you made a start. That's what's important. Has your sleep improved any?"

Lydia laughed, "If I force myself to stay up later, I can sleep about 5 or 6 hours without waking. The exercise must be helping.

"I bet if you'll continue walking and make room for a little quiet time during the day, you will begin to feel much better physically before too long," encouraged Mary. "You're doing great."

The Glint of Gold

The next morning Chester was in a foul mood while he ate the breakfast of fruit and sweet bread that Sanjiv served him. They were in an alcove off from the main kitchen. Chester grumped, "Where am I and where is the guy who drew those pictures of me?"

Sanjiv bobbed and smiled, "Oh, you mean Master? He go to contemplation garden for morning meditation." Sanjiv spoke slowly and carefully. After finishing a sentence he would stop, nod his head, smile, and then wait for a response.

Chester mumbled around a mouthful of fruit. "What is he, some Zen master? Or is he one of those so-called holy men always begging for money like I see in the city?"

Sanjiv's smile got bigger and his eyes got wider. "Master have plenty of money and he knows much about everything. You will see. You will see." Sanjiv cocked his head. "Master come now."

Shortly the Master strolled into the room looking serene and pleased. "Ah, my friend on my donkey. I am so glad you are here. Did you enjoy your breakfast?" The Master nodded to Sanjiv who bowed and left. "He is a good servant, but he seldom gets to practice his English. Don't let his broken English fool you. He is a smart young man. Now before I answer your questions, I must show you something. You see, I have been waiting for you for a long time."

Chester spluttered, "Now wait a minute. What do you mean you've been waiting for me? Where am I? When can I leave? I know I'm probably going to miss my plane anyway, but I need to leave soon. Can you help me get back to Mahe?" Chester paused and looked around, trying to think of what else to say.

The Master held up his hand for silence and said, "Let me show you what I have to show you. If you still want to leave, I will have Sanjiv take you back to the city." The Master disappeared down a hall motioning him to follow.

Chester shrugged and followed him to a large room, "Suit yourself. Thanks for sending your servant after me and all, but I need to go. First I have a score to settle with a bus driver for leaving me on the side of the road. Then I have to get my bags and catch a plane so I can get out of this..." His nervous commentary faded away as he stopped dead in his tracks and stared at the paintings and drawings covering the walls. Everyone one of them was of him, some going all the way back to when he was a child. *What the hell have I gotten myself into? Am I dead and this is my life flashing before my eyes?* There had to be at least two dozen paintings covering every major event in his life. There was even one of when he was a young boy with his pet duck. Chester whirled and blurted out, "This is impossible. Something doesn't smell right. I...I have to leave."

The Master called out in a loud voice, "Sanjiv, get the donkey. You are taking our friend to the city."

Chester eyes were open wide and his hands shook. "No wait!" He stumbled then nearly fell before sitting in a nearby chair. With his face in his hands Chester groaned, "What is happening to me?"

The Master moved over to sit next to Chester and put his hand on his shoulder. "My friend, this is also happening to me. For I have been waiting for today a long time. We have much to learn from each other. This moment has been long in coming and now it is here."

Chester couldn't move. He looked up with tears involuntary streaming down his face. There was a strong sense that somehow this had happened before. He had a heightened ability to focus. Everything was happening slowly and deliberately. The moment had a familiar quality about it that wouldn't go away. "What could you possibly learn from me?" Chester squinted and slowly turned his head to look around.

The Master stood up and walked over to a table in the center of the room. He opened a bag lying on it and took out a gold coin. He walked over to Chester and handed it to him. "For every truth we teach each other, I will give you a gold coin like this. I earned this gold from my Master in much the same way, and now I offer it to you."

Chester hefted the old coin in his hand and estimated it was at least an ounce. Even if this strange man didn't teach him anything, it might be worth his time. He suspected these were rare, antique coins and worth multiple times their weight. He could possibly make more money this way than programming for the Torah Codes project. There had to be a catch, but his curiosity pulled at him. Chester put on his poker face and used his casual bored voice to avoid appearing too eager. "Let me see if I've got this straight. If I learn something from you, you will give me a gold coin. If you learn something from me, I get a gold coin. As long as somebody around here is learning something, I come out like a consultant." In Chester's business, sometimes his clients didn't realize he was staying just one white paper ahead of them and then teaching it to them a few days later. The deal the Master was making was the same but with on-the-job training bonuses out in the open. "I don't know which is weirder, those paintings of me or you paying me in gold to hang around. I have to admit I've always been a sucker for mysteries, booze and women. I guess I can add gold to that list now."

The Master replied, "Many mysteries will be unraveled in time. Many mysteries…"

Chester felt triumphant and held out his hand. "Deal. Plus I get an extra gold coin when I figure out how you did the picture painting trick."

The Master mirrored Chester's grin and shook his hand. "So you can stay for awhile?"

Chester shrugged and replied, "The people I was working with think I've flown to the United States and my folks in the U.S. were not expecting me. I'm probably going to lose everything in my bag back at the hotel, but it was mostly just clothes. Yeah, I can stay awhile if the gold holds out. I hate to be that way, but business is business."

The Master said, "Then keep the one you are holding as a way to pay for losing your belongings." Chester started to protest, but the Master held up his hand and said, "I insist. But do not let me forget to tell you the story that goes with that one."

Chester opened his mouth to ask another question, but the Master was no longer there.

Lydia's Baby Book

A thin rectangle box made of old cardboard lay across Lydia's knees as she sat erect on a chair in the corner. She kept one hand on the box as if she thought someone might snatch it from her. There was no one else in the room, but her fear of someone seeing the contents was overwhelming. She felt shame at what was in it. It took all the strength she had to sit there until Mary came to get her. Finally, the door to the back offices opened suddenly. Lydia jerked at the sound, almost dislodging the package she was protecting. She fumbled quickly to secure it. Out of the door came a couple holding hands. They didn't even notice her as they made their way out the door to the parking lot. Mary appeared in the hall doorway behind them and motioned for Lydia to follow her to her office. It was an effort for Lydia to get up and slowly walk toward Mary's office.

* * * *

Mary smiled remembering the session that just ended. As she put away the couple's file, she thought about how fulfilling it was when a session worked out well. The couple that had just left had been through some big problems, but it looked like they had finally worked them out. Lydia came in and sat down on the couch as usual and clutched a box in front of her. Mary turned to get her file from the corner desk. When Mary turned around and saw Lydia's despondent face, she knew something bad had happened to her. She sat down across from Lydia and observed, "You don't look so good. What's wrong?"

Lydia was hesitant to answer and struggled to start. Quietly, she said with her eyes downcast, "I'm okay, I guess."

Mary frowned and looked concerned, "You don't seem okay. Please tell me why you have such a sad face?"

Lydia glanced up and hung her head again. Mary knew that she was crying softly. Lydia extended the box she held out toward her. Mary took it with questioning eyes. Lydia dabbed at the tears with a tissue she'd picked up from the coffee table that separated her and Mary. Finally she was able to croak, "Just open the box. It's my baby book. There're some pages in the back that you'll probably want to read."

Mary did as Lydia requested. She lifted the box top trying to keep from tearing the fragile carton. She took out what looked like a normal baby book for twenty or thirty years ago. She flipped through the pages starting at the front. It had the usual collection of pictures, locks of hair, and milestones of the first few years of a small child's life. As Lydia had said, there were about a dozen yellowed sheets that someone had slipped inside the back cover. Their tattered edges showed that they were once in a spiral notebook. A beautiful flowing script covered both sides of the sheets. "Do you know who wrote these?" Mary asked.

"My mother said she did. I only read the first page but couldn't go any further. I tried but my head starting hurting; I got dizzy and sick at my stomach. I don't know what's happening to me. It's like I don't even know myself anymore."

"Please describe what happened when you went to see your mother," urged Mary.

Lydia collected herself. "Well, my mother didn't want to tell me anything. She kept saying the past was the past and needed to stay the past. I told her I couldn't remember anything but being a bad girl, and

I begged her to tell me why." Lydia's bottom lip quivered. Finally, she did and I wish she hadn't. It's all too horrible."

"What's so horrible?" Mary whispered.

"Mama said that Daddy thought I had the Devil in me. She said that what made Daddy the maddest was when things I said sounded more like an adult instead of like a child." Tears flowed down Lydia's cheeks as she looked up at the ceiling.

Mary didn't know what to think, but it was important that she move forward gently. She decided to read what Lydia's mother had written; maybe it would yield some clues about what this was all about. As she read a few pages, she began to see why Lydia was upset. It appeared that when Lydia had first started to talk in sentences, she talked about when she was big like her parents. Mary poured over pages and pages that recorded Lydia's words from the time she was three years old to almost six. It looked like a diary of what Lydia had talked about when she was just a toddler. At first Mary just wrote it off as a child's fantasies, but as she read further she began to see that it was more than that. This was unusual. It recorded Lydia's detailed descriptions of a time when she was a young woman living in India. Lydia's mother had done a good job of capturing her child's exact words or something close to them. They had a matter-of-fact tone that was consistent over time. The other striking feature was the knowledge of the world that was beyond the experience of a young child. Mary looked up at Lydia and exclaimed, "This is remarkable. Your mother has written down your conversations when you were little girl. Your grasp of language and the experiences you speak of are astonishing. I don't know what to make of it, but your mother did a great job of recording what she heard. It says here that your mother thought you sounded like someone who had been an adult."

Lydia looked scared, "Daddy never knew that Mama wrote down what I said. Before she'd let me take the book, she made me promise never to tell him. She said Daddy thought what I said was the work of the Devil. It's not Christian." Lydia's tone was emphatic and unyielding.

Mary queried, "Did you know before your mother showed you the baby book that you had these thoughts when you were a child?"

Lydia shook her head and clutched one of the pillows on the couch.

Mary decided to continue carefully. "Do you know why your father thought what you said was the work of the Devil?"

"It's in the Bible."

Mary rubbed her face and chin. "Tell me more about that."

"Well," Lydia settled back and looked up. "There is no way I was ever an adult before I was a baby. In Hebrews it says man only dies once. Only pagans believe they live over and over."

Mary frowned, "What do you mean living over and over?"

With disgust she spewed, "Pagan religions teach that we die more than once and live more than once. They teach you just keep getting bodies over and over."

Mary didn't realize she was frowning as she asked, "So how does that translate into you having the Devil in you?"

Lydia had a look of pity on her face as she tried to explain, "It's easy. People who think they have lived more than once aren't remembering a past life. Like when hypnotized people talk about a past life, that's just a demon talking through them while they are under hypnosis. The demon was alive back then and makes them think it's their memories, but it's just the demon remembering what it saw years ago."

Mary tried to interject, "But, you weren't hypnotized when you were a little girl. That is…"

Lydia interrupted. "It's the same thing. The only way I could have had talked about what Mama said I did was if a demon was inside me making me say it. That's what's wrong with me. *I'm possessed.*" Lydia bobbed her head and said it emphatically as if there was no other possible explanation.

Mary cocked her head slightly and made a rolling motion with her hand for Lydia to keep talking.

Lydia continued, "The Bible plainly says, *just as man is destined to die once, and after that to face judgment, so Christ was sacrificed once to take away the sins of many people.* That's in Hebrews 9 something. If you live more than once then you die more than once, see?"

"I'm not sure I follow you but I know a bit about what is called 'demon possession'. I did a field study on the subject when I was in college. Even the people that appeared to be demon possessed showed severe emotional and behavioral symptoms. I've also read the Bible and every single time that a person was said to be demon possessed that person couldn't function normally. Let me assure you, Lydia, you show absolutely no signs of demon possession or even mental illness. You are confused and frustrated, but that is a far cry from demon possession. At least take that with you when you leave today, okay?"

Lydia pursed her lips and finally reluctantly nodded her head. "Well, maybe I'm not now; but I must have been when I was a little girl."

Mary decided to take her concession as a positive and end the session on it. She looked at her watch and realized she was close to running over into the next session. As she made some notes she commented, "Lydia, I need to do some research; and I need to see you for sure next week. May I keep your baby book for awhile?"

Lydia nodded her head. "Sure, I don't want it. It's evil!"

Mary didn't know what to say. She was positive Lydia was not demon possessed. The turn of events dismayed her, but at least significant issues were beginning to come out. She hoped she could help Lydia, but if they didn't make some headway quickly Lydia would bury her past again. After Lydia left, Mary made a note to consult with Dr. Crystal Gibson, a friend and colleague who had done extensive psychological research on paranormal experiences. Getting another viewpoint was always helpful in deciphering complicated information. She didn't want to overlook significant factors in Lydia's treatment planning.

Master's Cottage

The Master's cottage was a beautiful sprawling design with an oriental flavor to the décor. Before breakfast Sanjiv showed Chester around the place. Sanjiv seemed proud as he explained every room they entered. He showed Chester the porch and explained it was his favorite place during the heat of the day because it offered shade and a breeze. It was enclosed with black mosquito netting that looked almost invisible. The tour included the property, too. The roof was lined with solar panels. This Master was no jungle scrounger. He had money and advanced technology disguised as a simple cottage living off the land. Sanjiv's arm swept across several gardens proudly saying, "Master help Sanjiv with garden so have much to eat and see."

Clustered around small ponds were fruit trees, rows of carrots, celery, was well as some plants Chester didn't recognize. Spidery channels radiated out allowing the pond water to irrigate the plants in the dry season and to route water to the ponds for storage when rains came. The last stop on the tour was the modern kitchen. Sanjiv excused himself to prepare a breakfast from the fruits they had gathered. Chester wandered out onto the porch to ponder his situation. "What am I doing here?" He said out loud.

"Doing what you are supposed to."

Chester whirled. He hadn't heard the Master approach. "Good morning."

"Good morning to you, my long-awaited friend. Please join me for breakfast." Sanjiv arrived with breakfast. They sat on pillows around a low table. As they ate there was a sense of connection that was hauntingly pleasant. Each moment echoed with peaceful familiar feelings. They hovered just outside the range of logic. Finally, Chester broke the spell with the question. "Have I been here before?"

The Master paused and said, "You tell me."

Chester blinked. "Obviously I haven't, but it feels like I have."

Sanjiv got up and cleared away the remnants of breakfast. The Master reached under the table and pulled out a chessboard and a leather bag bulging with pieces. "Can you think of something logical we could discuss while you show me how well you play chess?" The Master pointed at a painting leaning against the wall behind them. It depicted Chester winning the Atlanta City Chess Club yearly tournament. The Master had painted him holding a golden knight-shaped statue. Chester was a 'golden knight' in chess and went on to play in the Georgia state finals. Chester still couldn't understand the painting trick. *Had some lifelong stalker been sending this guy photos?* He shook it off and decided to see how good the guy was. *I wonder if this so-called Master can handle a debate and a chess game at the same time.*

Sanjiv served his Master hot tea and Chester coffee. Chester grinned. "I challenge you to a debate on Evolution vs. Creation."

The Master nodded in agreement. He had a jovial air about him and a look of excitement in his eyes. The Master appeared to be in excellent spirits and eager for a conversation. "I would like to take both sides of the argument at the same time."

"You can't have it both ways. Evolution and Creation are not compatible ideas. You have to pick one or the other. There is all of the scientific evidence for evolution. You can't have it both ways."

The Master grinned. "Of course you can. You can have both if you know the missing piece of information."

"Wait. You can't take both sides at the same time. It's not allowed. Pick a side." Chester was getting a bit steamed. He felt like the Master was cheating somehow.

The Master sipped his tea and leaned back. "So you are saying you don't want to hear what I've learned from Masters past that can solve your little puzzle?" Grinning he waited.

Chester eyed the Master as he finished his coffee. After tilting the mug back for the last drop, he leaned forward and said, "You're on, but it had better be logically consistent." Chester was so confident in his debate skills that he felt he could take on anyone.

The Master acted unconcerned as he set up the chess set. "Both the evolutionists and the theologians are missing the meaning of the first two verses of Genesis. The whole mystery is hidden in *one word*."

The Master's conversation didn't interest him as much as the chess set did. His lifelong passion about chess began when he was just a child. He collected chessboards from around the world. The old and intricate Chinese chess pieces fascinated him. He handled each piece carefully as he helped set up the chessboard. "I get white. Besides you have a long tale to tell."

Laughing, Chester moved out the pawn in front of his King's Knight to the fourth square. Chester and the Master played quietly for a dozen moves or so. The Master's ability to easily adapt to his strange opening impressed Chester. In fact, the Master was putting pressure on Chester's position. After about four more moves, Chester had reached a position where he felt he wasn't in danger of losing a piece. Slowly he looked up at the Master and asked, "What word?"

The Master replied, "Word?" A joy seeped into the room.

Chester wasn't looking at the board. Instead, he focused on the Master. "How can one word solve the debate of evolution versus creation? That is a paradox."

The Master got up from his chair and declared. "It doesn't solve the debate it joins them. They are both part of the story." The Master left the porch and when he came back he was carrying a *King James Version* of the Bible and a large, thick concordance. "Read out loud the first two verses of this Bible and then stop."

Chester took the leather book and flipped pages until he found Genesis. Reading he said, "*In the beginning God created the heavens and the earth. And the earth was without form and void; and darkness was upon the face of the deep. And the Spirit of God moved upon the face of the waters.*" Looking up Chester shrugged and said, "So?"

The Master said, "If you look it up in the concordance, you will see the Hebrew word *hayah* which the King James translates as *was* is more accurately translated as *it came to pass.* Or if you insist on a word for word translation, *became* instead of *was.* My Master told me the original Hebrew meant, *and it came to pass that the earth became a lifeless wasteland empty and chaotic.*"

Chester challenged, "You can't just rewrite Genesis."

The Master pointed to the second verse. "I'm showing you the full meaning of verse two in the original Hebrew not as it was translated into English. Look up what the original Hebrew meant for the phrase *without form and void.* The English is from the Hebrew words *tohuw* and *bohuw.* An equally accurate translation is the phrase *chaotic and empty.* If you look all of this up, you will see there is no word for word equivalence in English for the Hebrew words. Taking their full meaning, it becomes clear that a lot of time must have passed between Genesis 1:1 and Genesis 1:2."

It took Chester a moment to figure out how to use the thick heavy concordance. The Master waited patiently for Chester to verify that what he had said was indeed true. After a few minutes of cross-referencing all the words, Chester looked up and said, "Let me see if I have this straight. You're saying the second verse in Genesis is describing something that happened many years later than what is described in the first verse?"

The Master replied, "Billions of years later according to the ancient teachings handed down through the ages."

Chester grinned. "That means the fossil records that say that life has been on this planet for billions years are correct. Genesis 1:1 states God created the heavens and the earth and that doesn't necessarily contradict the Big Bang Theory." Chester clapped his hands and tilted his head back and chortled, "I knew it. I knew it. I knew it. The fossil record doesn't lie."

The Master repeated, "The definition of *was*, in Genesis 1:2 could better be translated as the phrase *it came to pass*. My Master taught the original Hebrew should have been translated *and it came to pass that the earth became a lifeless wasteland empty and chaotic*."

Chester eyed the Master suspiciously. "But Genesis plainly says that God created the Sun and Moon on the fourth day. Explain that, O Wise One." Chester rubbed his hands together.

The Master sat back. "Why would God put plants on the earth on the third day before creating the Sun on the fourth day? Genesis does not contradict science. I can clear it up but hear me out before you start your debate." The Master looked relaxed and unconcerned.

Chester nodded. "Go ahead."

"Let me explain it to you the way my Master explained it to me. He went through Genesis verse by verse and his explanation made perfect sense. Imagine the world as frozen and covered with a dark atmosphere choked with smoke and clouds, its air so thick with corruption that no light could glimmer through. Sunlight was blocked so completely that only a few deep-sea creatures were still alive. In fact the seas were close to freezing up and if the Spirit of God hadn't intervened, then eventually even the deep-sea creatures would have died. Genesis 1:2 begins with the Spirit of God hovering over the water. Obviously science understands the universe was not created from water. By believing both science and Genesis, we can have understanding. You see, from Genesis 1:2 on, you're *not* reading how God created the Heavens and the Earth. You are reading a description of the steps needed to repair the Earth."

Chester nodded his head in understanding. So far it was logically consistent. "Hmmm…What you are describing sounds almost like a nuclear winter. In fact, your theory might explain why the mammoths froze so quickly that many had food still in their mouths. That has always been a puzzle to me as to how or why they became frozen so quickly and suddenly. Research points to many species that disappeared overnight geologically speaking. Somewhere between 10,000 and 6,000 years ago, we lost mammoths, saber-toothed tigers, giant armadillos and such. The best current scientific theory is violent climate changes caused them to become extinct. If the weather change was a severe as you say then…" His voiced trailed off as he pondered this new approach.

The Master coached. "Now pay attention to the words in Genesis and notice they match your nuclear winter scenario perfectly. It says that God divided the light from the darkness. On the first day, God cleared the atmosphere enough for light to penetrate. And afterwards, God called the light 'Day', and the darkness he called 'Night'."

Chester followed in the Bible trying to spot any error in the Master's story. "So you are saying that where the Bible says *let there be light,* it was talking about God clearing the atmosphere of our planet enough to let light through?"

The Master nodded and continued to explain the real meaning of Genesis. Now notice what happens next." Reciting, the Master continued, "*Let there be a firmament in the midst of the waters, and let it divide the waters from the waters. And God called the firmament Heaven. And the evening and the morning were the second day.*" The Master explained, "The temperature of the Earth was so cold that the seas were frozen, at least on the surface, and the land was covered in deep ice and snow. God warmed the earth so water separated from the ice to become water below and clouds above. Most school children know the composition of a cloud is water vapor."

Chester quickly looked up the word *heaven* in the concordance and read out loud the definition as referenced in Genesis 1:8, "*Visible heav-*

ens, sky." Chester motioned for the Master to continue as he had no challenge yet.

The Master recited from memory, "*Let the waters under the heaven be gathered together unto one place, and let the dry land appear. And God called the dry land Earth; and the gathering together of the waters called he Seas.*" The Master explained further. "Warming the Earth and melting the ice caused massive flooding."

Even Chester could see the obvious meaning of Genesis 1:10. "So, the water finally settled in the low areas revealing the land. Funny, I had never seen that possible meaning but it makes sense. Go on."

The Master closed his eyes as if he was remembering something. "*And God said, Let the earth bring forth grass, the herb yielding seed, and the fruit tree yielding fruit after his kind, whose seed is in itself, upon the earth: and it was so.…And the evening and the morning were the third day.*" The Master offered more commentary, "The cold had killed all the plants. Plus God needed the plants to be in place before he could put animals on the Earth. After all they had to have something to eat."

Chester said, "So far so good, but you still can't explain why God is creating the Sun and Moon and stars on the fourth day." Chester was excited for he was sure he had found the flaw in the Master's story.

The Master seemed unconcerned as he replied, "You forget the atmosphere. On day two the ice had just been melted into water and clouds, but the atmosphere wasn't clear yet. Clouds still covered the Earth heavily on day three. God brought the water-loving plants back into the world, but the cloudy steamy atmosphere prevented a clear view of the celestial heavens."

Stumped, Chester flipped back to Genesis and said, "The tense is *present* on day four not *past*. It doesn't say '*God had made*'. It says '*God made*'."

The Master simply smiled and recited, "*And God said, Let the lights in the firmament of the heaven divide the day from the night for they are the signs of days, seasons, and years. The lights in the firmament of the heaven will give light upon the earth. And God made the heavens shine with two great lights; the greater light to rule the day, and the lesser light to rule the night. The stars also were seen in their glory shining from the heavens. For God set the sun and stars in the firmament of the heaven to give light upon the earth, to rule over the day and over the night, and to divide the light from the darkness. And the evening and the morning were the fourth day.*"

Chester looked puzzled, "It doesn't make sense that the Sun and stars were created after the Earth." Chester ran his hands through his hair. "I want to make sure that I understand what you are saying. What God did on the fourth day was finish cleaning up the air and break up the cloud cover? Ahhhh…The Sun, Moon and stars were hidden because the atmosphere had become so polluted and dark. Your theory at least matches the scientific record. Obviously, the Sun wasn't formed a day after plants were on the Earth."

The Master said, "Genesis 1:1 plainly says God created the heavens and the earth. The Sun, Moon and stars are part of the heavens. At the beginning of this conversation, I told you God created the heavens and earth. Verse two is *later* in the timeline. It is not a detailed commentary of verse one. Verse one stands alone. God created the heavens and the earth, *period.* We see the heavens mentioned again in verse four, billions of years later than verse one in the timeline. The Sun, Moon and stars existed for billions of years before they were hidden by the dense black clouds. God cleared the air for the plants restored on day three so they could have sunshine. Genesis 1 is a record of God repairing a badly damaged and frozen Earth. The fourth day was the day the clouds were cleared by God so that the Sun, Moon and stars could be seen. Maybe it will help if you understood that there is no such thing as 'tense' in Biblical Hebrew because it is not a 'tense' language. Modern grammarians recognize that it is an 'aspectual' language. This means that the same form of a verb can be translated as past, present, or future depending on the context and various grammatical cues. So when it refers to the Sun and stars, the original Hebrew does not indicate when the Sun and stars were made but is simply a statement that God made them to be for times, seasons and so forth."

Chester turned and stared out the window thinking, *that would explain why the Bible didn't mention dinosaurs—they were already gone when it was written. Sure hope Lydia doesn't hear about this viewpoint.* Grinning and looking sheepish, he turned back to the Master and finally said, "I'll look into this further, but go ahead."

The Master recited again. "*And God said, let the waters bring forth abundantly the moving creature that hath life, and fowl that may fly above the earth in the open firmament of heaven. And God created great whales, and every living creature that moveth in the waters did God create. And every winged fowl after his kind did God place for his pleasure.*"

Chester realized there were no new challenges so he let the Master continue his recitation.

The Master took a deep breath and said, "*And the evening and the morning were the fifth day. And God said, Let the earth bring forth the living creature after his kind, cattle, and creeping thing, and beast of the earth after his kind: and it was so. And God made the beast of the earth after his kind, and cattle after their kind, and every thing that creepeth upon the earth after his kind: and God saw that it was good. And God said, Let us make man in our image, after our likeness: and let them have dominion over the fish of the sea, and over the fowl of the air, and over the cattle, and over all the earth, and over every creeping thing that creepeth upon the earth. So God created man in his own image, in the image of God created he him; male and female created he them.*"

Holding up both hands as in surrender, Chester conceded. "Don't recite the rest. I get the point. But how did this destruction come about? There is no known evidence of major volcanic activity or a meteor strike 6,000 years ago that could explain what you have described. It couldn't have been a nuclear war or there would still be radioactive hot spots."

The Master stood up. "Yes, indeed. It is a mystery; but before you leave here, you will know this and many other secrets. But I'm not going describe it to you. I will show you as my Master showed me. But first I must train you to be aware. Without the training you can't…"

Chester interrupted. "What are you going to do, show me a movie?"

The Master laughed and walked toward the door. "Not exactly. After I have taught you the ancient arts, you will be able to see the past much better than any movie. That is all for today. We will begin your training tomorrow. Leave the chessboard set up. We can finish it after our evening meal." Farther away Chester heard. "Remember it is your move."

Chester scratched his ear. *Why does he always just leave like that? There has to be something wrong with his theory.*

Lydia and Tina Girl Talk

It had been so hectic the last few months that Lydia and Tina had not been able to find a time that both of them could meet for a few hours. Tina had been looking for another job and had been busy going on interviews. Some of them had been out of town. She didn't want to move, but some of the local opportunities required her to travel because their headquarters were out of town. Lydia's business had also picked up so all she did was eat, sleep, and work. That left her feeling tired and irritable.

But tonight, Tina was coming over. They had agreed to turn off the pagers and telephones and relax by catching up. Lydia wiped the already spotless end table again and adjusted the magazines so they would line up just right. Her apartment reflected her ordered life. Sparsely furnished in light tones of beige and cream, the only color was in the soft peach and moss green pillows neatly placed on the sofa. Looking around, there was nothing else to do. She had already stocked the refrigerator with Dr. Pepper, Tina's favorite soft drink. She sat down, picked up a magazine and absently thumbed through it while she waited.

She was looking forward to seeing Tina. She didn't know yet if she would tell her about being in therapy. Lydia couldn't say she exactly enjoyed her sessions with Mary, but she was gaining some insight into herself and why she acted like she did sometimes. The feeling part was hard, though. There wasn't much she could get past Mary. It impressed her that Mary could catch her trying to divert the conversation when she started to feel emotional discomfort. Mary would have this amused look on her face and hold up her hand and say, "Stop." It'd become a game and Lydia was losing it seemed. Each time they met, Lydia was able to tell her a little more about herself. There was still something hidden deep down that she couldn't or wouldn't face. A couple of times, she almost let her guard down but the anxiety prevented her from continuing. Those were the times that she tried to change the dialog to anything or anyone but herself. Lydia was still having moments of feeling afraid for no clear reason. Her sleep had improved but her dreams were disturbing.

Tina's knock startled Lydia and she dropped the magazine she had been staring at for the past five minutes. She quickly picked it up and lined it up with the others. She was all smiles as she opened the door and saw Tina standing there with a sack from the gourmet shop around the corner. They hugged and Tina almost dropped her package. Lydia exclaimed, "Just what do you have there?"

"Three kinds of cheese, grapes, apples and an assortment of crackers. Even you can't refuse health food and..." Tina grinned impishly, "in case we have a moment of weakness, two fresh baked cookies with the big chocolate chunks. I think they're still warm."

"You're something, you know," laughed Lydia, "I've missed you. If you'll spread these out on the coffee table, I'll get the drinks. Dr. Pepper?"

"Of course, thanks for getting some for me. I know you don't usually keep it around."

Tina snuggled into the deep cushions of the sofa as Lydia settled in the matching chair. Lydia let out a deep breath and said, "Now. Let's catch up. You go first."

Tina smiled slyly as she said, "You remember Paul, Chester's friend at the debate in San Francisco?

"Yeah, sure," Lydia responded raising an eyebrow.

Tina giggled. "Remember I told you on the plane that it wasn't the first time I'd seen him.'

"Didn't you say that you had met him a year or so ago at a debate in his hometown of Atlanta?"

"Yeah, we beat the socks off his team, but they were good sports and invited us to join them in a drink afterward. I liked him then but didn't get a chance to talk much with him because of the crowd. Well, what I didn't tell you was that while you were asleep the last night in San Francisco, he asked me to get with him for a drink. We ended up going dancing. I sneaked back into the hotel room about 3:00 a.m. Remember fussing at me because I had a hard time waking up to catch the plane the next day?"

"I guess," sighed Lydia, "but I was in a fog too, remember. I still can't figure out why I reacted so strongly to losing the debate. In fact, I still haven't returned to my old self." Tina was so caught up in her memories of being with Paul those few hours that she didn't even hear Lydia's comment about her distress.

"Anyway," Tina continued, "Paul and I have been talking a lot by phone since we returned. He's *so* wonderful. I see that look on your face. Don't even say it. I know I lead with my heart too much and get hurt; but I don't think he's like my past boyfriends." Nodding her head slightly, pinching her lips together to keep from speaking, Lydia settled in to listen. "The biggest problem is that he's so far away. He said he might have a job coming up in Dallas so it *could* work. Seeing the twinkle in Lydia's eyes Tina pleaded, "Don't be so skeptical. Oh, the big news I have for you. Guess who's in India?

"Indians?" laughed Lydia.

"Probably. But who do you, Paul, and I know in common?" Tina teased.

"Not Chester? What's he doing in India?"

"Trying to disprove the Torah Codes!" Tina exploded with laughter almost falling out of her chair.

"*No...way*!" Lydia burst out, stunned.

"Yes, *way*." Tina grinned. "Seems he's an internationally known computer geek. According to Paul, Chester had been putting out feelers for overseas work because it pays so much better. "And," she teased, "He probably wanted to put an ocean between you and him. What's so funny is that Paul thinks that Chester was bummed out like you were after the debate. I think Paul mentioned that Chester had received several contract proposals, but the one that interested him most came in not long after your debate. Paul said it was from a headhunter representing some rich Swami in India. The Swami had read about the Torah Codes and was intrigued by them. He wanted someone to find out if the ancient Hindu texts also contain hidden messages from God. That was not exactly what Chester had imagined doing, but it was close enough. Paul said if he finds that they are also encrypted it would disprove the Bible was special. I don't know if it would prove or disprove anything since the Bible and the Hindu texts are all religious documents. But anyway, that is what I was dying to tell."

"Why would they hire Chester of all people? He doesn't even believe the codes in the Bible exist," Lydia frowned.

"Who better than a skeptic?" Tina continued, "The Swami wanted the best computer programmer available and has deep pockets to fund the project. Paul also said there's no one better than Chester in that field. And, Paul says Chester's meticulous and has a reputation of being objective when it comes to his research. He apparently jumped at the chance to earn big bucks writing a software program that would pick up and interpret any encryption contained in large texts. He's going to try to reproduce the work of those Jewish guys you mentioned at the debate. Paul says Chester's working theory is there is no encryption in the Bible or that computer manipulation can reveal similar patterns in all big texts. His goal, of course, is to prove beyond a doubt the Torah Codes are fake or, at best, a skewed data interpretation."

"Skewed data?" Lydia parroted back.

"Sure," Tina ran on, "Remember, Chester claimed the Jewish scientists had a vested interest in the outcome of their research. If he finds similar patterns in other books, especially nonreligious writings, it'll negate their claim that God's hand wrote the Bible as you presented in the debate."

"Huh…What does Paul think of all of this?"

"Oh," Tina shrugged, "He says he's used to Chester's moods and knows the guy likes to solve complicated puzzles. Says when he gets set on doing something, he won't stop until he conquers it. Paul says Chester has a Mensa IQ to go with his drive. He thinks that Chester intends to test his software first on large literary works like *Gone with the Wind* and *War and Peace* before applying it to religious texts. Should be interesting. I told Paul he'll be sorry if he doesn't let me know what happens. You want to be in the loop?"

"Why not?" Lydia said quietly. Inside she felt the walls closing in on her. *What if I'm wrong about the Torah Codes?* she thought, sinking deeper into despair.

Tina saw her friend shrink into the chair and put a hand to her head. "You just got pale, are you sick?"

"Oh, I've got a headache. That's all. Been getting them a lot lately," Lydia sighed.

"Have you seen a doctor about that?" Tina asked.

"Yeah, he checked me over from head to toe and did some blood work. He couldn't find anything physically wrong so suggested that it might be stress related. I'm working on slowing down, but it's hard. I'm even seeing a psychologist he recommended."

Tina grinned, "That's great! I'm so proud of you. You know how important you are to me, and I've worried about you since that night you collapsed after the debate. How's it going with the counseling sessions?"

"Fine," Lydia commented without energy, "I'm learning how to recognize what I do that isn't healthy. Mary, that's the name of my shrink, has me walking for 30 minutes every morning and night to 'stimulate the endorphins,' she says. Don't worry. I'm taking care of myself, but the best stress management is seeing you. Before we forget it, let's set a date to get together again soon, what do you say?"

"Of course," Tina eagerly replied, "I'll be in Houston in a couple of weeks. I'm going on a job interview." She raised her hand to let Lydia know she didn't want her to inquire deeper. "Oh, it's nothing. I don't want to jinx it and talk it up and get all excited. If it's meant to be it will happen. If I get the job I'll tell you about it. Besides I want to visit Galveston while I'm down there anyway. If you need me while I'm away, you have my pager. Beep me anytime, day or night; and you know I mean it. What are best friends for, huh? How about dinner together Saturday after next…meet at Pappadeaux at 7:00? We'll eat lots of boiled shrimp out in the fresh air of their patio garden and lose our troubles in live Cajun music. Better make that 6:00. They don't take reservations, and it's always crowded on the weekend. I'll even buy."

"You're on," Lydia said as she compulsively reached for her date book. After penciling in the dinner date, place, and time, she tried to lighten up the mood. "Now where are those cookies?"

Chester's Mystic Day

The Master waved his hands in exasperation. Chester looked up from the blackboard with his face in a classic puzzled response. The Master tried to explain, "You don't have to spend all your time trying to prove your conclusions to me. If I don't accept your conclusions, I'll ask questions. Otherwise, just give me the conclusions." The Master smiled and gestured for Chester to continue. He paced back and forth as he played with a gold coin. He made it appear and disappear from one hand to the other.

Chester said, "Your slight of hand doesn't impress me. I have a couple of card tricks I can show you. So, you want conclusions and skip the logic behind it? I can do that. Let me lay this one on you. Infinity makes reality possible. Quantum Reality describes our physical universe by allowing an infinite number of parallel universes to be part of the solution set. Science calls it the Many Worlds Solution."

The Master grinned and said, "I agree. An ancient Hindu Master taught us that Brahma contained the infinities and all possibilities in his heart. One of the Seven Wisdoms is the infinite nature of God makes all possible. I am not going to give you a gold coin for what my Master taught me many years ago. Please, I'm waiting for new truth."

It shocked Chester that the Master quickly agreed with one of the most profound discoveries of Quantum Science. "It gets weirder than that. Unless you observe something, it isn't real. It is only a potential set of probabilities that are not resolved unless observed."

The Master laughed. "My Master taught me long ago that what I call reality is just my awareness choosing one of the infinite paths that is before me. He taught me that all life sprang from the Absolute Awareness and discovers its place in the Infinite. That sounds much like your Quantum Reality. I want you to tell me something I don't know."

Chester bulled on. "The entire material physical universe is a balance of forces. You see, it is just positive and negative energy in balance in an infinite array of forms and patterns. In fact, all of reality is a zero-sum game."

The Master nodded and said. "The Wisdom of Balance; you know much already. Please…" His voice trailed off as he played with the gold coin and watched Chester think.

Undaunted, Chester quickly shot back. "At the subatomic layer all reality is nonlocal."

The Master paused and asked, "What do you mean by nonlocal?"

Chester smiled and said, "At the most basic level of reality there is no separateness. Everything is connected to everything else. I barely believe it myself."

The Master pushed his index fingers together and pressed them to his lips. His eyes lit up and he exclaimed, "Oneness. You describe Oneness. You are sharing with me some of the Seven Wisdoms. But, I understand the nonseparateness of this world for nothing is separate from God."

Chester licked his lips. This was harder than he thought. He watched the Master play with the ancient gold coin. "How about time is an illusion. It is relative to the motion of the observer."

The Master held out his hands palm up and said, "Science is wise. You have shared with me five Wisdoms. I am impressed you know these. You lack but two Wisdoms to be a Master such as I. That you know time is an illusion is most perceptive of you. For time is the opposite of eternity. Eternity is one of the Absolute Aspects of God. All there is and always will be the eternal ever changing *now*."

"Now wait a minute. Are you saying that *now* and *eternity* are the same thing?"

The Master looked at Chester with a grin. "What is your definition of eternity?"

Chester thought a moment. "It means no beginning and no end."

The Master laughed. "That's not a definition of what eternity is. That is a definition of what it isn't. If you have no beginning and you have no end then all you have is whatever is in the middle. What we call the middle is *Now*. Have you ever experienced not-now? Isn't it always *Now*?"

Chester struggled with the concept. "So what is time? Wait, before you answer. I know that time is relative to motion and all of that, but what do you define time as?"

The Master played with the gold coin as he answered. "Time is how we measure change. Reality is an ever changing pattern that is projected upon the canvas we call *The Now*. The past is the memory of the pattern before. The future is the anticipation of the pattern to come. There is no time, there is just *Now*. If there was no change, there would be no time; but there would still be *Now*." The Master pushed the coin into his pocket. "We'll talk again later. It is time for lunch."

Chester couldn't help himself. "If there is no time, how can it be *time* for lunch?"

* * * *

Chester argued all the way back to the kitchen. "What does God have to do with the five Wisdoms? They are part of nature. Science has proven all this through centuries of experimentation and observation. No religion has had these five truths buried in its mysterious past. And none of this proves God exists, at least not to me. If God exists he must give me a sign. But a sign from God would have to be damned significant to make me believe." Chester had the grin of a confident man.

"There are always signs. Even if you don't recognize them, they are still there. You have to learn to tune in." The Master grabbed a lunch basket. Chester assumed Sanjiv had made it earlier. He followed the Master to the back porch. Looking around he saw a small table with a digital clock on it. Clustered around the table were several pillows. Up against the wall a cloth covered several paintings. The Master motioned for Chester to sit. As he laid out the lunch, he explained. "God is a personal experience. And it occurs in your heart, not in your brain. God has been showing you a sign for over 30 years. He is about to show it to you again." The Master paused for a few seconds. "Chester, what time is it?"

Chester quit reaching for the warm rolls with a start. Glancing at the digital clock he did a double-take. It read 12:34 p.m. Chester felt a rising disbelief as he watched the Master uncover a painting depicting his 7th grade science project. It was a mechanical clock that had wheels with numbers on it that peeked through holes to show a digital time. It didn't work well and for some reason, at 12:34, it always quit. Chester felt a sense of awe and fear as he watched the Master pull out several more paintings, each with Chester at various ages looking at a digital clock with the numerals 12:34 as the time of day. The Master looked at Chester. "All I know is this is your sign from God, but I don't understand exactly what it means. Would you please solve this mystery for me? For several years I have made these paintings with 12:34 being a theme and you looking at a clock in surprise. Please explain this mystery to me."

Chester's head swam. 12:34 was Chester's most private secret. He had never told anyone of the little head game he had played with himself since he was a boy. Chester's voice was hoarse as he tried to get the words out. "When I was a boy I read all about Merlin the Magician and fancied myself as a powerful wizard. And since my mom taught me that our religion hated anything that resembled magic, I liked it even better. So I invented my own special secret magic. I came up with it at the same time I was doing my science project. I decided I was an all-powerful wizard at exactly 12:34, am or pm, and any wish I made while it was 12:34 would come true. So I started playing a game of trying to notice exactly when a digital clock said it was 12:34. All the clocks in my house were the old fashion analog kind with second hands and such. So I invented a digital clock made of two wheels that turned behind two holes in a cardboard box. It was the source of my magic power. Only I knew the secret of seeing 12:34 on digital clocks before they were even commonplace. Years later when they outnumbered analog clocks and wristwatches, I remembered my childish game of magic. However, weird events started happening. I would absentmindedly look up to see what time it was, and it seemed that for several weeks at a time, almost every night and every day, I would just glance up and see 12:34 on a clock. Then I started trying to catch the clock at 12:34 on purpose and would miss it every time. I've played this game for years. It still drives me nuts. The harder I try to catch the clock at 12:34, the more I miss it. When I finally give up and leave it alone, it plays the game with me. I start seeing 12:34 in the weirdest places. On buses, on billboards, on clocks, but never when I am looking for it. I've never told anyone about this because I'm sure they would think I'm crazy. It's the only irrational part of my life that I know of. Tell me, please, how does this prove God exists?"

The Master looked at Chester and sighed. "All I can say is that I asked God for a sign many years ago when I realized I was a Master of the true knowledge. You see a Master must pass on his or her knowledge to others. This is how it done. I asked God to show me a sign so I could recognize my next student, and he showed me 12:34 as glowing numbers. About ten years ago, my meditations showed me I should learn how to paint. About five years ago, I started having visions that would nag at me until I painted them. The most persistent ones have always been of you."

Chester was feeling strange. Tears formed in his eyes as he felt distant and detached. He started experiencing a powerful *I've been here before feeling.* He was unable to control his emotions so he got up and hurriedly walked off the porch and down a well-kept path. As he left, Chester shouted something inaudible. The Master watched him leave without trying to stop him.

The Master waited patiently for Chester to come back. About three hours later, Chester returned. His face was different from the shocked expression he had when he stormed off the porch. The Master waited patiently. Chester looked like he desperately wanted to say something but just didn't know what to say or how to begin. After running his hands through his hair Chester spoke slowly and precisely, "I've argued with myself about whether to tell you what happened to me these last few hours. I guess I must have snapped. I remember walking off the porch and screaming at you to leave me alone. I'm not sure who I was talking to, you or God. The last two days have been too strange, and I couldn't take it anymore."

"Where did you go?"

"I found myself on a clean well-kept path that wandered through your oriental garden. I felt so angry, and I couldn't find any outlet for it. I stomped down the path until it came to a dead end. I found a pond, flowers, shrubs and an expanse of sweet smelling emerald green grass."

The Master nodded and said, "You went to my contemplation glade." He motioned for Chester to continue.

"I was mad and I felt all crazy inside. I remember sitting down and looking up into the sky and screaming, 'I hate you God' while I shook my fist. Then I started crying…just bawling like a baby. As I cried I closed my eyes and remembered the first time I ever said the words, 'I hate you God.' I was eight years old, and I had just discovered my pet duck was dead. I was devastated for days. My mom tried to console me and told me that even though we don't understand why, everything happens for a purpose. She held me and told me that my duck was with God. I remember telling her that God can have all the ducks in the world, why did he have to have mine, too? I jumped off her lap and screamed, 'I hate God! I hate him!' I ran into my room and locked my door. I decided at that moment there was no God because if there was, he wouldn't have let my duck die. As I sat by your contemplation pond, I remembered the incident in such vivid detail that it felt like I was a small boy again. I sat there quietly and tried to collect my thoughts. What happened next is the part that is hard for me to talk about. An eerie calm settled over me. I was intensely aware of all the sounds around me. The only way to describe it is that I felt at peace and a sense of knowing filled me. An extreme clarity of mind and feeling swept through my being. Abruptly my viewpoint changed. I could see myself cross-legged on the grass. It was as if I was looking down from a vantage point of about ten feet above my head at my body. I no longer felt confined to a body. Instead I was the air, the ground, the trees, the garden, and even the birds. Then it was like I remembered something I had forgotten long ago. In an instant I knew everything. I don't know any other way to describe it. I felt overwhelming joy, and I started snickering and laughing. I watched as I lay back on the grass and roared with laughter. It was as if I had reached a place I had been striving for forever. I don't know how else to put it. I was remembering and knowing everything at once and the experience of joy and ecstasy was overwhelming."

"You felt the joy of God."

"My perspective changed again and the sky became a projection screen, and I started watching my life. Every significant event I had ever experienced played out before me, only I knew that I was guiding and shaping my life for a purpose. What I'm about to say is going to sound crazy. As I watched my life I realized that I was God. I wasn't all of God, yet I knew I was a slice of God. It felt as stupid to not believe God existed as it did to believe I didn't exist. For a brief moment I knew everything. I was everybody and I was everything. I don't know how long I lay in the grass watching and knowing and feeling merged with God, but while I did time felt suspended. When it ended it felt like a mental rubber band snapped me back into my body. One second I was a part of God and all of creation and the next second I was Chester lying on the grass with tears streaming out of my eyes. It was such a deep impossible moment. For a time, an hour maybe even a couple of hours, there was nothing separating me from God. I knew why I existed and what my destiny was. When it was gone, it was like trying to remember something important, but for some reason I couldn't remember exactly what it was. I decided to accept whatever was happening, and I got up and walked back here. I didn't know whether I would tell you or not, but deep down inside I knew you could help me make sense of what had happened." Chester looked embarrassed and drained. "By the way, may I have something to eat? I am starved."

The Master motioned toward the table. Chester's posture sagged and his hands trembled as reached for the bowl of fruits and vegetables. The Master waited for Chester to regain his strength and his ability to focus. The Master settled comfortably into his chair and started munching on the carrots and celery in the bowl near his armrest. "You experienced for a brief moment your true nature, your God Consciousness, your real self. You saw yourself as who you think you are and who you really are at the same time. You were blessed to see past the illusion and experience your eternal divine self. Remember you told me science has discovered that everything is connected? God connects everything because everything is part of God. Our separateness from God is an illusion and our true purpose for being is to see past the deception and experience our oneness with God."

Chester shook his head and stammered, "Can I be that way again?"

The Master replied, "When you sat down and screamed you hated God. You, for the second time, believed in God enough to hate whatever God is to you. If God did not exist, why would you hate Him so much?"

Chester seemed puzzled, "Well, I guess, well...because...you're right. Why would I hate something that doesn't exist? My hatred betrayed me. I hated God because I know He exists but He doesn't always do what I want him to do."

The Master reached into his pocket then held up what he had retrieved. It was a gold coin. "Tell me why you had the experience in my contemplation glade, and I will give you this gold coin." Chester's face drained of color. The Master reminded him, "You told me for a brief instant you knew everything. 'Everything' includes why you had the experience."

Chester sat up, "Not fair. I can't remember anything but feeling overwhelmed and full of intense joy." The Master seemed unconcerned and played with the gold coin, making sure it sparkled in the sunlight streaming over the porch. Chester stopped mentally fighting and said, "I give up." He looked up as if he was remembering something, "Wait. I remember. I experienced for a brief moment who I truly am so I would strive to achieve it again. I want it again."

The Master stretched out the coin, "Tell me who you are, and I will give you this."

Chester started with, "I'm Chessss…No. I'm God."

The Master pulled the coin back a bit. "How can you be God?"

Chester licked his lips and closed his eyes. Straining he whispered, "I can't believe I know this. I'm the part of God that is experiencing this universe through me as me. I've been trying to remember this since I was first aware I was me."

The Master laughed and handed the gold coin to Chester. "You have spoken a truth. You have danced the Dance of Shiva."

Chester turned the coin over. On one side was a single raised dot in the center. On the second side was a large raised disk. The Master explained. "The coin represents the Wisdom of Oneness. The symbol of the dot is the ancient symbol of the soul in man. The large raised circle on the other side represents our soul at one with the supreme soul."

"What is the Dance of Shiva?"

"When my Master gave me this coin, he had me memorize an ancient secret of self. I will translate it into English for you. Repeat after me. Immediately repeating it will help you remember it. Then you tell me the secret back. With every coin, I will tell you what you must memorize."

Chester licked his lips then began repeating after the Master: *"Lord Shiva danced with his creation yet hid his glory from it. The external world is the expansion of his glory. Yet his creation is not separate from him. For God gave his creation the joy of discovering God Consciousness. God and his creation are One. Yet God hides himself from his creation to give himself the joy of discovering God. God is both Creator and the Created. The Uncreated God and the Creator God are One, yet the creation is attached to the grand illusion of separateness. Whenever God's creation discovers God, God discovers God's Glory all over again. God delights in the dance of hiding and discovering his glory."*

"Good. Repeat it again and again until you can say it by yourself."

"May I write it down?"

"No, not until you have it memorized. If you lose what you wrote how can you recover it? You won't lose what is remembered. Trust the oral transmission practice of our line of masters that has worked for thousands of years."

Chester nodded his head in surrender. "Let's repeat it."

* * * *

Later that day the Master showed Chester his library. The largest room in his house had several ceiling-high bookcases with sacred texts and books on religion. He motioned for Chester to sit at the large table, near the door, that had a reading lamp with a green shade. The chair was comfortable and the table's height was ideal for reading without straining the eyes or the back. Chester looked around nodding his head in awe. "This is some set up. You must have a fortune tied up in these old books."

"Much wisdom is in these pages. I don't have many books in English, but I have enough for the start of your studies. My Master had me travel for seven years to learn about the cultures and religions of the world. I bought many of these books when I traveled and had them sent back to my Master. At the end of each year, I would go back and tell of my travels and what I had learned. You do not have time to travel as I did but I have some books that will give you the background you need."

"I learned speed-reading back in college. It comes in handy in my line of work because research is a big part of what I do. In fact, it is my favorite part of any project." Chester grinned and rubbed his hands together. "Let's start."

The Master disappeared behind a row of bookshelves and came back with a stack of books. "Here read these. Do not discuss them with me or ask any questions. This is for getting you grounded in what people believe around the world. My Master taught me to take in the information but not judge the information, at least not right away. Do not accept or reject what you read. My Master had a saying for this. In English it would be 'Facts before judgment and knowledge before wisdom.'"

Chester looked through the stack. Represented were Eastern and Western religions in equal numbers. "Do you have a recommendation on what I should start with?"

The Master pointed to a large book with a yellow cover. Its title read, *World Scripture: A Comparative Anthology of Sacred Texts.* "Next read *Tao Teh Ching,* then *The Bhagavad-Gita* then *The Gospel of Buddha.* After you finish those, I will tell you which parts of the Bible to read. After that you will read some of the writings of Rumi, the Sufi mystic. I don't have any of the Sikh scripture in English, but I do have a book about the life of Guru Nanak. Once you have read all of that, I will begin the next phase of your training." The Master waited to see if Chester had any questions. His student was already engrossed in the book on world scripture so he left him to his studies.

Mary Examines the Baby Book

That's strange, thought Mary as she came to the last page Lydia's mother had inserted in her baby book. It ends so abruptly. She wondered if something happened that kept Lydia's mother from continuing. Scanning back through the pages she'd read, a frown came on her face. The contents were troubling. Could Lydia have said all that when she was four or five years old? But if she hadn't, why would her mother have written this?

According to the document, Lydia's descriptions of someone other than herself began when she and her mother made plans to travel by rail to visit her grandparents. When her mother started talking about how exciting it was going to be to ride the train, Lydia looked frightened. When her mother tried to encourage her about the trip, Lydia became more distraught. Her mother clearly started writing the journal shortly after that incident. Mary flipped back to the first page and read it again to see what clues she could discover. Lydia's mother had written:

Saturday
I don't know what to do and have no one to talk to. Something is wrong with Lydia but I don't know what it is or how to help her. When I told her that we were going to see grandma and grandpa and ride on a train, she seemed scared. I tried to explain how much fun we'd have. She begged me not to make her go and started crying. She choked out, "The train is going crash!" Why in the world would she think and say that? I tried to assure her that trains were safe but it didn't help. She kept shaking her head saying, "No, No, No." I finally told her we would drive instead and she calmed down.

Tuesday
Something else happened last night; Lydia started talking at the supper table about being in a large restaurant with her family. She said there were lots of candles and the food was spicy. She called the dishes by foreign names that I couldn't understand. I asked her where she heard this. She said she remembered it from when she was big like me. My husband jumped up from the table and grabbed Lydia by the back of the neck and shook her. He told her to stop lying. She said she wasn't lying which made him madder. He jerked off his belt and started whipping her. I tried to stop him, but he pushed me down threatening to kill me if I moved. He grabbed Lydia's arm and dragged her toward her room. She was begging him to stop, but he told her he would beat the Devil out of her if it was the last thing he did. He said she was going to Hell for lying. In her room, he forced her to get down on her knees and ask God's forgiveness. He locked her in her room and dared her to come out. It was hours before he got drunk enough to pass out and I could get to her. She didn't know what she'd done. I told her that her daddy was sick and didn't mean what he did to her. I didn't know what else to do. I thought about leaving with Lydia but where would we go. I don't have a job or any money.

Mary looked through the yellowed pages. The baby book also included drawings Lydia had created using crayons. She was getting a better idea of why Lydia had blocked out her early childhood memories. She knew it often happens when young children are abused. She hated to admit it but the scene described was pretty typical of an alcoholic's family dynamics. She would be just guessing but Lydia's father probably went to work the next day as usual and everyone pretended nothing had happened. What was unusual, Mary mulled over, was Lydia describing life as an adult in another place and time. She shrugged and thought that maybe it was just Lydia's way of mentally escaping a reality that was too painful to endure. Whatever happened back then, she knew this was going to take some time to puzzle out.

Paul Gets a Letter

Paul had a surprise when he checked his mail that night. He had a letter from Chester. He had begun to worry about not hearing from his buddy. Chester usually called at least once a month when he was overseas, sometimes more often. Paul hadn't been able to reach him at either of the numbers Chester had given him. The company he had contracted with thought he had flown back home. The hotel he was in claimed Chester had checked out almost two months ago. Maybe this letter would clear up the mystery. Before opening it, he went into his kitchen and got a beer. He decided to leave the TV off and just relax and find out what Chester was up to. He slit the envelope cleanly with a carved ivory letter opener his sister had given him. Chester's scrawl was small. He fumbled in a drawer of the side table that held his reading glasses. Fortunately, they were clean. He hated smudged or dirty glasses.

Dear Paul:

I'm sorry I haven't called. I have a new client who is paying me to do some collaborative research. I'm not sure if he is for real or if this is some scam. He claims to be a master of an ancient understanding that solves paradoxes among science and various religions. It's a long story about how I found him. And since this is a letter I'm not going to reveal right now what all we negotiated for payment. I'm taking a chance, but this could fund my research for at least a couple of years. This guy also plays a mean game of chess. It helps with the boredom and it is keeping me sharp. I hope I will be able to go to some tournaments with you when I get back.

I've seen and heard some strange things while I've been in India but this guy either has to be one hell of a con artist or the real deal. Check out some of the stuff he claims about himself. I'm not saying I buy any of it, but I'm staying around as long as the funding does. To me it's business but this guy acts like this is some cosmic destiny coming to pass.

He described an incident recorded in Genesis called the Tower of Babel. He claims that up to the time of the Tower of Babel incident the information he is sharing with me was common knowledge. He said that was because there was a common language. Much the culture was based on magic and idol worship and some followed a religion that went back to before the Flood. The first prophet Enoch taught something back then called "The Understanding."

This big project came up where they decided to build a tower to heaven. God came down and checked it out and decided humanity was making progress a little too fast. Somehow from this project God decided that whatever man wanted to do they would do it. This guy claims that God foresaw that nothing humankind planned would be impossible for them. To slow humanity's progress down, God decided to confuse our ancestors' language so we could not understand one another. This had a scattering effect. Seven Mysteries or Seven Wisdoms made up "The Understanding." As time went on, each tribe or nation focused only on one or two of the Seven Wisdoms. This split the original religion into seven sacred paths to God and kept the Wisdoms alive, but how they fit together was lost. This guy claims this is the reason the planet has so many different types of religion. You can see why I'm skeptical. How could this guy know what happened thousands of years ago?

When God supposedly did the language confusing mumbo jumbo, "The Understanding" was spread over the earth and become what he calls the Seven Mystic Wisdoms. Some of these Seven Wisdoms are supposed to be found in the different religions on earth, but until they are brought back together the original "Understanding" can't be achieved. He claims that no religion has all of them, but every religion has at least two. Here is the part that makes me the right guy for the job according to him. It turns out that I already knew five of the Wisdoms because of my knowledge of science. Science through experimentation has already discovered five of the Wisdoms. That's better than any religion on the planet. After hearing that, I had to stay around.

This is the part that I haven't swallowed yet. He says that beginning with the Tower of Babel, masters kept the original information that tied the Seven Wisdoms together so they could be revealed at the proper time. There is supposed to be a prophecy about the Seven Wisdoms being revealed when the time is right. Of course no one knows about the prophecy but him. Convenient, huh?

For thousands of years, these teachings have been secretly passed along from master to student using oral transmission, memorization, and some secret technique he says he will teach me. I'm allowed to write down what I've learned if I have satisfied this Master fellow that I have memorized it. It's the craziest project I have ever been on.

My work Visa will expire in the late fall. Since it is late spring as I write this, it means I will stay at least three more months. At least until August. I'm not sure how quick this will get to you. He has a servant who rides a donkey into a village for supplies about once a month. It has a place to post mail. Considering how slow international mail is, I hope you get this before I fly back home.

Don't worry I'm fine and making money. The Torah Project is on hold for now, but I haven't forgotten that either.

Your friend,

Chester

P.S. As soon as I crawl back to civilization, I'll give you a call.

Mary Meets With Crystal

Candlelight flickered in oriental holders on the tables covered with white linen cloths as the wait staff skillfully dodged one another in patterns that looked choreographed. Soft music was coming from the speakers in the corners. She relaxed as she stepped inside the restaurant. For once, she wasn't late. In fact, her patient just before noon had called to reschedule for another day so she was about fifteen minutes early for her lunch meeting with Crystal. It had been a couple of months since they had visited face-to-face but they kept in touch by phone. If Crystal followed her usual habit, she'd breeze in right on time looking like she didn't have a care in the world. Mary thought, *maybe I should have joined a college faculty like Crystal did.* That thought lasted about ten seconds before she shook her head. She liked helping patients reach their goals. Normally, negative behavior patterns were easy to spot and fix, but sometimes puzzling cases popped up like Lydia's where she needed to consult with someone. She'd asked Crystal to lunch to try to pick her brain.

Mary decided to go ahead and ask the hostess to seat her at a table because the noon crowd would be converging on this small place in a few minutes. She ordered water and hot jasmine tea then sat back thinking about why she had chosen to be a clinical psychologist instead going into research. Fact was she didn't think she chose it but instead just drifted with the current. As she had tried to figure out what she wanted to do with her life, opportunities kept opening up and she merely followed them. She always enjoyed new challenges but Lydia's case was getting to be way more than just interesting; it was spooky.

The waitress was refilling her water glass when Crystal strolled in and followed the hostess to the corner table that Mary had requested. She never hurried. Her dress today was of an almost see-through gauze fabric with bright flowers dancing around her as she floated down the restaurant aisle. Crystal accepted life on its terms. When Crystal arrived at their table, Mary almost giggled like she used to do in college. She knew she could count on her friend to put a smile on her face. Crystal's eyes always danced with mischief like she knew a secret that no one else did. *Maybe there was something to be said for being a 70's flower child.* Looking her up and down, Mary teased, "You look like a spring bouquet. And so thin I hope a strong wind doesn't come up. How do you do it?"

Crystal hugged her and laughed, "I gave up everything that tasted good long ago." She noted, "You're one to talk. Looks like you still jog."

"No, I've taken up golf and that helps me get some exercise."

"When did you take up golf?" From the look on Mary's face she took a guess, "Is it a man?"

Mary blushed, "Yes, and I took up golf so I could meet him."

Crystal put her hand on Mary's and pushed it way, "Trolling for a man, huh? Not the *Virgin Mary*! She teased using Mary's old college nickname.

Mary laughed, "I don't see him any more, but I decided I like to play golf. Don't know why, though. It's *hard* work. All that effort just to get a little white ball into a hole in the ground. Maybe I need therapy."

Crystal chuckled as she looked over the menu, “Oh, we all do. So why the sudden need to do lunch? I haven’t seen you since last Christmas. If it isn’t to lord over me that you’ve found the man of your dreams, what is it?”

Before Mary could answer, their waitress showed up. Crystal already knew what she wanted. Mary scanned the menu hoping to find something with low calories that she could convince herself to eat. She winced as Crystal ordered Moo Shi Vegetables without rice and egg drop soup and finally decided on the Cashew Chicken combo plate promising to take most of it home. As if she had to explain, “I’m really hungry, and I’m going to play golf all day Sunday, I promise. I wish I had your willpower.”

The waitress tried to help, “No calories in food on Fridays.” Everyone laughed as the waitress left to turn in their order.

Crystal decided to tease her friend one more time. “I thought Friday rules were only for fish?” Crystal knew Mary used to eat fish every Friday like a good Catholic.

Mary countered, “You know that doesn’t matter any more. But you’re a vegetarian, so it’s all bad for you. Now I’m not going to tell you about my new patient. Besides she’s not your type. She hasn’t died and come back so her background will probably bore you. In fact, this particular case might be too weird for even for a *New Age Alice* like you.” Crystal was an expert in paranormal psychology. Her peers respected her research and specialized clinical skills. Most of the patients she accepted now were referrals from other medical professionals.

Crystal grinned as Mary pretended to be absorbed in drinking her tea. “Hey, studying near-death experiences is not *Alice in Wonderland.* It’s serious science.”

Mary smiled as the waitress brought soup to the table, “I’m not talking about near-death experience, I’m talking about something stranger. Mary tried to look mysterious as the waitress brought their entrees. “Anyway, her presenting problem was rapid onset depression and something interesting cropped up during our exploration of her family history." Mary stopped talking and bit into her egg roll dripping with sweet and sour sauce. "The calories don't count, right?"

Without waiting for Mary to continue, Crystal inserted, "Try this for unusual and unique. I interviewed an NDE[1] who claims he isn't the guy that died." She leaned back, crossed her legs and watched Mary to see how she would react. "If you can top that for weird, I'm in the wrong research field."

Mary groaned as she pushed her plate away. "I'm stuffed, I'm going to need a nap."

"Not so fast. Besides if you tell me your weird, I'll tell you about my weird.

"I was going to tell you anyway. I'm way over my head on this one. I have a woman whose parents divorced when she was about six or seven. She says she doesn't remember much about her father, but she recently met a man whom she thinks might have reminded her at the subconscious level of her father. This triggered an emotional response of depression, anxiety, and a feeling of low self-esteem. I started to assume it was another child abuse post traumatic stress situation and that it wouldn't take long to help her using EMDR[2] or TFT[3]. Boy, was I wrong."

"So what was so weird about her father? Was he an alien?"

Mary shook her head and tried to sound politically correct. "No, a strict Christian fundamentalist whom I'm sure had no way to handle what he heard his daughter saying. Remember this was over 20 years ago."

Crystal leaned on her elbow and propped her head on her palm. "I'm all ears."

Mary dropped her voice so only Crystal could hear." From the time she was two or three to the time she was six, her dad whipped her

1. Near-Death Experience
2. Eye Movement Desensitization & Reprocessing
3. Thought Field Therapy

whenever she talked about what it was like when she was a grownup. In fact, she claimed her name was Kamna and that she had lived in India and had died on a train. Her mom kept a secret record of everything her child talked about and hid it from her husband. I guess she thought he would destroy it. They are divorced now. Otherwise, I don't think my patient's mother would have shown it to her. What I read was fascinating. My patient refuses to read it. She read just the first page and lost emotional control. I'm surprised but glad that she let me keep it."

Crystal leaned back and tried to absorb what she had just been told, "What does she think is in it, embarrassing fantasies?"

Mary waited for the waitress to refill their glasses before leaning forward and whispering, "She thinks that it means that when she was a little girl she was possessed by the Devil. Since then she has been subconsciously trying to prove that she is a good Christian girl. What she doesn't remember but what her mother noted was that when she was six years old her dad abused her so much that her mother finally kicked the S.O.B. out. My patient has few memories between the ages of two and six and no recall at all of her conversations of 'being an adult.' Like I said, it's weird. Got any suggestions?"

Crystal looked pensive and hesitated before saying, "Mine is that weird, but I want to finish this conversation at my house. Do you have time?" Mary nodded making a rolling hand sign for Crystal to continue, "I have some interesting notes there that you might find helpful. Did you drive? I had a friend drop me off instead of walking to my place to get my car."

Mary held up her cell phone and showed Crystal the keys to her Accord hanging on the antenna. "Don't worry about the lunch or the tip. It's on me, and I'll be your limo driver."

* * * *

Crystal shifted in the passenger seat so she was turned toward Mary as she drove. "Since I live so close to the college, I seldom drive my car."

Mary looked over and said, "Is that why you bought that fixer-upper townhouse, to be close to the college?"

Crystal looked out the window and watched the traffic. "Partly, and since it was a HUD repossession, it was cheap. Park next to my Mazda over there, I have two parking spaces."

Mary pulled into the carport and blinked her eyes. "The last time I was here you were still getting it repaired, and there were husky guys everywhere wearing tight jeans and T-shirts. House looks great, but I miss the scenery."

Crystal laughed and shook her head as she got out of the car. "My upstairs is a mess so we won't go there." She unlocked the gate to the patio and let Mary in.

"Wow. This is pretty," Mary complimented. "I like the new carpet. And look at your new kitchen. You put in drawers instead of doors on the bottom cabinets. How do you like them?"

"I love'm and thanks. I've worked hard on this place. If you hear any screeching, it's Peaches. I'm teaching her to whistle instead of scream whenever she wants to communicate. If she starts whistling, I'll have to get her out of her cage. Want something to drink? Coffee, coke, iced tea?"

"Iced tea sounds good."

From the kitchen Crystal whistled loud enough for it to carry upstairs only to hear a demanding screech in reply. Handing Mary her tea she suggested, "Sit on the couch if you want. I'll go get my laptop and see if I can find my notes." A wavering wolf whistle drifted down the stairs. "Oops, make that a laptop and a good bird." Crystal whistled up the stairs. Mary could hear her friend talking baby talk as she walked up the stairs. "Peaches is a good bird, yeah, such a good bird."

Mary hollered up the stairs, "I have to be back to my office at three so I only have about and hour and a half before I need to go."

Crystal's voice sounded muffled and far away. Mary couldn't hear what she said but she sounded frustrated. When she finally came down the stairs she had a large white parrot on one arm and a thin silver laptop under the other. "Here take the laptop."

Mary reached over the parrot gym Crystal had in her living room. Once Peaches was on her play station, she looked over at Mary and spread the crest of feathers on her head. In a lilting high-pitched voice Peaches squawked, "Mary had a little lamb." Peaches bobbed her head and spread her crest even wider and mimicked Crystal's laugh.

Mary giggled, "She remembered."

Crystal looked proud. "You know, she never says that unless you're here. She's a smart bird. Now let me see if I can find that file." As she balanced the laptop on her knees, she explained to Mary about her new case. "I got to interview this young boy from Mexico a couple of weeks ago who is only six years old and whose heart had stopped briefly when he was four because of a near drowning. In fact, his heart had stopped when paramedics found him. After they got his heart to beating, he was rushed to a nearby hospital where he was in a coma for a week. When he finally came to, it was like he was a different person with different memories and a different personality."

Mary teased, "That *is* weird. But if it is so recent, why can't you find your own interview notes?"

Crystal wrinkled her nose at Mary. "Silly, I'm not looking for that; I'm looking for some notes I took at the library about near-death experiences with children. I bought a book that had a similar case. I put the footnotes and credits in my research folder, but I forgot the directory name. Okay, here it is. Now listen to this. In 1954, in India, a three and a half year old boy named Jasbir supposedly died of smallpox. Just before they buried him the next day he came back to life. When he could speak again he had the memories of a twenty-two year old man. He claimed he had died during a wedding procession when he ate poisoned sweets. Here is what I consider an amazing coincidence. The book isn't about near-death experiences. It's about reincarnation. This was just one of 20 cases. The other 19 were about young children who had spontaneous memories of a previous life while very young. A man named Dr. Ian Stephenson did the research, and it's published in a book called *Twenty Cases Suggestive of Reincarnation.* We might be both researching the same paranormal phenomena from two different angles."

Mary stiffened and took a deep breath. A shiver went up and down her spine. Finally, she responded, "Is there someway I could have a copy of the notes about all this?"

Crystal got up. "I have a notepad and a pen." Crystal disappeared around the corner and came back with a fresh legal pad and a couple of pens. She was also holding a book. She handed them to Mary as she slumped on the couch. "You can borrow the book if you want to?"

Mary thanked her as she flipped through the pages. "Is there anything in here that sounds like my patient's story?"

"I know of an account in there of a girl from India who had memories just like you said. Her name is Swarnlata. Her memories started when she was three. She gave enough information to enable Stevenson to find the family of the person she claimed she used to be. He was able to verify over 50 specific facts that would have been impossible for a little girl to know about, such as intimate details of her family from a previous life."

Mary closed the book and shot back, "*Supposed previous life!*"

Crystal clucked back, "Are you being skeptical?"

"You know Catholics don't believe in reincarnation."

Crystal sat up. "Hand me my computer. I have something that will make you want to say a million Hail Mary's."

Mary handed Crystal her laptop with a challenging look, "What do you mean 'make me say a million Hail Mary's'?"

Crystal only smirked as she bent over the laptop. "I've been doing research into reincarnation. But you won't ever guess what I found." Crystal flipped the laptop over into Mary's lap and waited for her reaction.

Mary fussed with the controls. "How do you make the mouse move on this thing? Okay, I got it." Mary read the notes slowly over and over. Her face started turning red as she leaned closer to the monitor. Then she looked up and raised one eyebrow. "Can I have a print out of this?"

Crystal took the laptop and headed toward the stairs. "It will be my pleasure. The printer is upstairs. I'll be right back." Before she took the first step she stopped and looked back at Mary. "I thought that would ring your chime." Laughing, Crystal hurried upstairs leaving Mary staring into space.

Chester's Training Begins

Master said to Chester, "It's time you learned how to clear your mind of thoughts. Have you ever done that before?"

Chester's frowned. "Are you asking me to turn off my brain?"

Master laughed and commented, "Not turn off your brain but control your mind. As part of your training it's important you learn to sit still and clear away distracting thoughts. We will start slowly but you need to practice every day. You will also need to memorize *The Yoga Sutras of Patanjali*. Its poetry contains the wisdom of soul awareness."

Chester sounded frustrated, "What good is sitting still for an hour or so?"

Master paused as if trying to find the right words. He held up one hand, which had become his way of telling Chester to listen. "Meditation is the science of reuniting your soul with God. The soul, descending from God into flesh, reveals its consciousness and life force through the sevenfold spirit. While the soul borrows the body, it borrows its viewpoint with its negative and positive experiences. Thus, soul awareness and life energies become identified with the physical body and its mortal pleasures and pains. With proper training the soul will remember its God nature and origin. The various progressive states of soul awakening are with an ever-increasing accession of inner peace and serenity. In the most exalted states, soul and the Supreme Spirit become reunited in ecstatic, blissful communion, called *samadhi*. I will teach you how to connect the little joy of the soul with the vast bliss of God."

Chester rubbed his face slowly and said, "Sounds a lot like concentration to me."

Master shook his head. "Don't confuse meditation with ordinary concentration. Concentration consists in freeing the attention from distractions and in focusing it on a particular thought. Meditation is a special form of concentration in which one releases attention from restlessness. Meditation is to know God by focusing on God."

"Doing nothing or just sitting can't be that hard."

"Can you place your hand in your lap and control it enough that it is still and without movement?"

"Of course I can."

"Then do it. Let me watch."

Chester rolled his eyes. With a restrained smirk on his face, he placed his hand in his lap with the palm up and the fingers slightly curled. It lay motionless. The Master waited for almost a minute. "Do you have as much control over your thoughts as you do your hand?"

Chester snorted. "I have a high I.Q. My brain is under my control."

"So you have control of your mind? As much control as you have over your hand? Sit still, close your eyes and make your mind as motionless as your hand. If you can control your mind for just five minutes by not thinking of anything for that brief span, then we can skip the meditation lesson and continue at a much faster pace."

Chester rolled his eyes again before closing them. *He thinks I can't calm my mind.* He adjusted his back and rear into a comfortable position then sighed. He closed his eyes and slowed his breathing. *When I count to three, no thoughts. Now I'm not thinking. Wait, I'm thinking about not thinking but that is still thinking. This is easy. How can he tell I'm having thoughts? I can't cheat. One, two, three, now—no thoughts.*

How will I know it has been five minutes? Where do these thoughts come from? I'll count backwards in my mind from ten and then zero will be no thoughts and I stay at zero. Ten, nine, eight, seven, six, five, four, three, two, one, zero. Did the Arabs or the Hindus invent the zero? I think it was the Arabs. Thinking about zero is still a thought. I don't have an off-switch for my thoughts! Chester opened his eyes. He played cool. "I think I could concentrate better if I had a beer. But right now I guess you can go ahead and show me how to meditate. I mean, I'm open to a paradigm shift." Chester went into consultant mode. "What's the protocol for getting started?"

The Master grinned. "The first skill is how to align the posture. The second skill is aligning the breath. The third skill is to align the mind. The spine should be erect. If your legs are flexible enough you may prefer to sit cross-legged on a cushion on the floor or on a firm bed. However, you might want to begin by sitting on a straight armless chair with your feet resting flat on the floor. Regardless of how you sit, you should hold your spine erect, abdomen in, chest out, shoulders back, and your chin parallel to the ground. Place your palms upturned, resting on your legs at the juncture of the thighs and belly to prevent the body from bending forward. With the correct posture, your body will be stable yet relaxed, making it easy to remain still without moving a muscle."

The Master signaled to Chester that he should try one of the postures. Chester sat on a pillow and used a simple cross-legged position. The Master helped him form the proper posture. "When you are in this position, inhale slowly and deeply through your nose to a count of seven. Hold the breath to a count of seven. Breathe out slowly through the mouth to a count of seven. Practice this seven times. Do this every day until you can work up to a count of 21. As you gain mastery of your breath, you gain mastery of your mind."

Chester found the exercise relaxing.

The Master continued his instruction. "Now forget the breath. Let it flow in and out naturally as in ordinary breathing. With your eyes closed look upward, focusing the gaze and the attention as if looking out between the eyebrows. Do not cross your eyes or strain them; the upward gaze comes naturally when relaxed and calmly concentrating. What is important is fixing your whole attention at the point between the eyebrows. This is the Christ-Consciousness center, the seat of the single eye spoken of by Christ: '*The light of the body is the eye: if therefore thine eye be single, thy whole body shall be full of light.*[1]'"

Chester found seven was an easy number to use for timed breathing. The breathing was easy but finding the mystical Christ eye was impossible he was sure. The Master waited as Chester practiced the skill of seven breaths. Chester felt stress melt away as he took deep controlled breaths.

The Master taught further. "Keep your eyes closed, once you are focusing your attention between the eyebrows, try to stop thinking. It is much harder than you think." Both Chester and Master laughed at the pun. "Let me give you three techniques that will help you to calm your thoughts and discover how to keep a mind free from thoughts. First, every time you breathe out, focus on the balance between the 'out' breath and the 'in' breath. At this perfect point of balance your awareness can stay undisturbed by thoughts. Once you find you can calm your thoughts for just a moment, you can work on keeping the mind free of thoughts for longer and longer stretches of time. You can do the same for the moment of balance between the 'out' breath and the 'in' breath."

Chester asked while keeping his eyes closed, "What were the other techniques?"

Master smiled at Chester's impatience to learn. "When a thought comes unbidden, just watch it like you would watch a bubble disturb the surface of a lake or pond. Become aware of the gap between your thoughts. When one thought ends, just before another thought begins, there is a brief but distinct emptiness that is your true nature. Try to

---

1. Matthew 6:22

find it and hold it. Here is another technique. Once a thought has started, try to slow it down until you never finish it. Just let it trail off and die because you give it no energy. Every time you achieve the thoughtless state, hold it as long as you can."

Chester started to get up. The Master waved him back down. "You stay here and practice. I'm going to take a walk before I begin my nightly meditation." Chester slumped back down and got back into position. Feeling silly, he started practicing what he had just learned.

Paul Calls Tina

Paul walked down the hall to his office cubicle. The Atlanta skyline filled the windows on one side of it. The city bustled below. He wasn't at headquarters often enough to justify having an office. His tiny workspace had a phone and a network connection for his laptop and that was it. His tenure there was the only reason he rated a window view. He didn't care. He had good news for Tina. He sat down and used the speed dial button to call the Hertz office at the DFW airport down in Texas. Calling her hadn't become a daily part of his life, but it was often enough for her to deserve a speed dial button on his work and home phones. He propped his feet on the edge of the walnut table that he used for paperwork. Three rings and he had an answer.

"*Hertz Rent-A-Car can you hold please?*"

Before Paul could say, "Yes," a click told him he was on hold. He had heard the canned spiel so many times he had it memorized. Was he glad to hear it again, not exactly.

"*Hello, Hertz Rent-A-Car how can I help you*".

"May I speak with Tina?"

"*Hold please.*"

"*Hello, this is Tina may I help you?*"

Paul lowered his voice. "Yes, I will need to rent a car in September."

"I'm sorry, sir, we can't reserve that far in advance. You can call our 800 number, and they can put you in the reservation system there. Do you have that number, sir?"

"I didn't expect your leg to come off in my hand."

"Is this Paul?"

"Yes ma'am, I'm calling from the great state of Georgia." Paul exaggerated his southern drawl and heard muffled laughter.

"I'm sorry. I didn't recognize your voice."

"I was using my work voice," he quipped before shifting gears. "But for you, ma'am, I can be downright friendly. How ya'll doing? They feeding ya purty good down there?

"I've been so busy I haven't even had time to eat. It's called the workaholic diet."

"Well, we'll have to get ya'll some chitlins and grits when I be down there in September."

"Oh? What's going on?"

Paul shifted back to his regular voice. "I'm going to California for the summer to work with a company that is ramping up to provide Internet access all over the country."

"Internet? What's that?"

"It's only the hottest technology since the telephone and the personal computer, darlin'. Anyway, our company is switching from mainframe and minicomputer projects to focus only on Internet projects. We think it will be a billion-dollar industry by 1996. In September, I'm scheduled to work with a new hub they are building in Dallas. It's all hush-hush or I would tell you who *they* are."

"Sounds exciting and technical. How long will you be in Dallas?"

Paul launched back into his southern drawl. "Well, ma'am, it all depends on how much I enjoy the scenery. I just might be able to arrange to be there permanently if the stars align just so." The pause at the end of the phone was beginning to encroach on uncomfortable territory when Paul asked, "What is it?"

"I just accepted a new job offer that might move me down to Houston. Even if I don't move, I'll be there at least half of the time. I wish I had known."

Paul felt a sinking sensation but put on his most encouraging voice. "I'm sure it's a great opportunity for you. Besides, I just found out myself about the new plans. There was a company-wide meeting this morning announcing our new shift in technologies. Is Hertz giving you a promotion?"

"No. I'm managing a limousine service that is expanding from Houston to Dallas, San Antonio and Austin. I'll run the Houston and Dallas offices, and the owner will focus on the San Antonio and Austin area. It's a great career opportunity and the salary is much more than I'm now making. My last day here is in a little over a week. I tried to call but…"

"Don't worry. It's going to be all right. The timing is all wrong for me here in Atlanta, too."

"Why's that?"

"I got a letter from Chester and he thinks he won't be back home until September. I'll probably have to renew the lease on our condo in July even though neither one of us will be there. I guess that's one reason I'm trying to find a way to quit all this traveling. If the Internet is the new frontier they say it is, it looks like there will be enough work for me to stay in one spot. Dallas and Chicago will be the places to be outside California and New York."

"You sure it's not just a fad? Hertz just spent a zillion dollars upgrading their mainframes."

"Mainframes are not going anywhere, but they will connect to the Internet." A loud beep sounded as his other line lit up.

"Is that your phone?"

"Yeah, I have to take this call. I'll call you tonight, and we can talk about all of this. September is a few months away. A lot can happen between now and then." *Beep.* "Sorry, I have to go."

"Me, too. It's a madhouse in here. Take care."

"Bye," Paul answered. He didn't have time to think about Tina right then. He punched the flashing button on the phone. "Hello, this is Paul."

Wisdom of Holiness

The Master and Chester watched the sunset's reflection on the contemplation pond. In the last month, Chester had noticed the Master did this every week on Friday night. He decided to mimic the Master as he knelt and sat on his heels. The Master timed it so he could watch the setting sun. Every week the position would shift a little. He always found the one angle where the red ball of the sun reflected on the cool still water as its reflection made the symbol eight, like one round ball balanced on the other. The red balls touched and started merging as the sun slowly set. At the exact time the sun was halfway down, Chester watched as a red round sun floated in a reflected sky. The Master whispered, "The two become one."

Chester recognized the same presence that was so subtle yet blissful during his mystic experience at this pond the first time. He asked in a voice drenched with awe, "What is happening?"

The Master's voice vibrated deeply in harmony with his words, "To understand the Wisdom of Holiness, one must experience closeness to God. After God repaired the earth, God made it easier for His creation to draw close to him by resting on the seventh day. A day filled with Holy Presence. A gift so God's children can easily connect with the Divine Supreme Soul by resting, praying and meditating. Right now you are feeling God's Holy Presence and you can continue to feel a Divine Oneness for the next 24 hours by simply keeping the Sabbath Holy."

Chester kept silent as the stress of the day faded and the peace of the stillness bathed him. The moment was gone once they got up to go back. But the memory lingered in the dusk.

As they walked back to the Master's house, Chester started probing. "I thought only Jews kept the Sabbath."

The Master shook his head in the fading twilight. "God created the Sabbath thousands of years before he commanded the Hebrews to remember it. Jesus said God made the Sabbath for mankind as a special blessing."

"To understand holiness, one must experience closeness to God. It is only when a soul becomes pure that it can join God for eternity. There are many paths but one goal—Oneness with God. Buddha walked one path when he began his journey of poverty and of begging for food. He dedicated every waking moment to achieving enlightenment. He achieved his goal by meditating and a vow of total nonattachment. His soul lived many physical lifetimes of pain and suffering before it became an advanced soul capable of reaching enlightenment."

"What about us not-so-advanced souls."

"That is the heart of the matter," the Master responded. "As God watched mankind interacting in the universe, it was obvious there were many distractions and temptations which made it difficult to stay on a spiritual path. So God created an extra way to reach purity of spirit. In Genesis, God modeled working for six days and resting on the seventh. God called the day of rest the Sabbath. This is an easier path to enlightenment or holiness. Enlightenment and holiness are the same. The day of rest is not only for the needs of the body but also the needs of the spirit. During your time here you have learned to take a few minutes at the beginning and end of each day to pause, clear your mind of worldly issues, and be one with God through meditation. We use the weekdays as the time to produce food, shelter, and other material needs. Ending all work at sunset each Friday is to follow God's model of keeping the Sabbath Holy. For 24 hours, we dedicate all thoughts and actions to communing with God."

"My mother always kept Sunday holy by going to church." Chester remembered. "She wasn't happy that I didn't want to go to church anymore after my duck died." Breaking free from his childhood memories, Chester focused on what had become to him another debate. "Can't you commune with God on Sunday?"

"Every day is a perfect day for communing with God. My Master taught that a true disciple of the spirit meditates every day. But if one can only stop to completely rest once a week, the seventh day of the week was modeled by God for that purpose."

"What about going to church on Sunday? What's wrong with that?" Chester poked at any opening he could find.

The Master paused a moment to find the words to guide his student in charting his own course. He finally continued, "God's presence is available all the time; but to grow spiritually, one must take time to allow the soul to commune with the Divine Supreme Soul. Fellowship is fitting on Sunday and meditation is effective on Saturday. The early Christians came together for worship and fellowship on Sunday; but called it the eighth day, the day that Christ rose from the dead. Another reason the early Christians gathered on Sunday was to allow the Sabbath to remain a true day of rest. Many had to walk a long way to reach the church so they waited until the eighth day to hold worship services."

Chester shook his head. "Why are all of your answers yes and no at the same time?"

Sanjiv was waiting for them as they as they entered the porch. The Master ignored Chester's last remark as Sanjiv lit some candles. All three sat on one of several pillows scattered about the porch. The Sabbath and its peace hung in the air with the sound of the insects as Chester, Sanjiv and Master basked in their inner stillness.

Mary Challenges Lydia

Lydia glared at Mary. "Why are you doing this? I just want to stop feeling depressed, and you want to talk about reincarnation." Biting her tongue, Lydia didn't finish the rest...*besides, you're a Catholic. You don't even believe in reincarnation.*

Mary sat quietly until Lydia recovered from the emotional outburst before she continued. "I'm looking at my notes from your session on the 5th. You brought up the subject. The notes also state that your mother told you that when you were young you had conversations with both your mother and father where you claimed you remembered living in India and remembered traveling on a train. Is this correct?

Lydia sat up and started to protest. "Yes, but..."

Mary held up her hand. Lydia closed her mouth and slumped back in disgust. Crossing her arms, she listened with a frown. Mary tried to explain it again. "I have been doing some research and have found out that your experiences as a young child are not unique. There are scientists who have studied this and found it to be suggestive of reincarnation. Previous Life Memories or PLM is the clinical term. It's considered to be even more credible than hypnotic past life regression. But, hey, I'm just following up on something you mentioned earlier."

Lydia jerked her shoulders up, tightened her arms around her like a shield, and spat out her next sentence. "Scientists are just atheists deceived by Satan!"

Mary waited for Lydia to calm down. "I have some research notes on it that you might find interesting. I also brought two books for you to borrow and read if you like." She walked over to her bookcase and pulled down two books written by Dr. Ian Stevenson. One had the title, *Twenty Cases Suggestive of Reincarnation*, and the other, *Where Reincarnation and Biology Intersect.* The only reason I'm even telling you about them is that some of the events documented as described by others are chillingly similar to what your mother recorded in your baby book. She placed the books on the coffee table in front of where Lydia was sitting.

Lydia didn't pick up the books. Instead she looked hard into Mary's eyes and said. "It wouldn't be Christian to entertain such mendacities as that." Lydia tried to clamp down on her doubts. *I mustn't let myself become deceived. I must guard my mind from false doctrine.* "Thank you for your offer, but I'm not interested in reading scientific heresy." Lydia nodded her head as if that made it irrevocably settled. She focused her eyes on her hands. If the hands were steady then she was steady.

Mary kept a calm straight face, but she paused a little longer than before. "If you won't read research will you read history? I have some information that shocked me so much that I almost didn't share it with you."

Lydia looked up carefully. "Something historic shocked you?"

"Yeah. It looks like history records the early Christian church believed in reincarnation. She handed Lydia about a half dozen pages. As Lydia read the first page, she explained further. "I looked it up in the Catholic Encyclopedia. It didn't go into much detail, but it did describe a big battle over the subject. I guess there wouldn't have been a disagreement if some of the top leaders didn't believe in it. Here's something passed by the Holy Church in 545 A.D. to try to stop the belief. In essence, it says that anyone who believes that souls come from God and return to God will be banished from the Church.

Lydia read it out loud. "*If anyone asserts the fabulous preexistence of souls, and shall assert the monstrous restoration which follows from it: let him be anathema.* (The Anathemas against Origen), attached to the decrees of the Fifth Ecumenical Council, A.D. 553 in *Nicene and Post-Nicene Fathers*, 2d ser., 14: 318)." She looked up and asked, "What does it mean when it says monstrous restoration?"

Mary pointed to the sheaf of papers in Lydia's hand. "A prominent theologian named Origen wrote around 250 A.D. about the preexistence of the soul. He taught the soul's source was God and the soul was traveling back to oneness with God by the lessons learned in multiple lives. He taught that Christ came to show us what we can become. The Christians of that time respected him and followed his teachings. But 300 years later it became a huge issue."

"Why?"

"In the sixth century A.D., Emperor Justinian and Pope Vigilius disagreed on whether the teachings of Origen were heresy. The Pope supported the teaching as being consistent with the teachings of Jesus the Messiah. The Emperor determined to wipe out the belief and wanted Origen's writings condemned."

Lydia interrupted. "Wait a minute. You are saying there was a Pope who believed in reincarnation?"

Mary hesitated. "I'm not a historian but my colleague's research says that Emperor Justinian ordered Pope Vigilius to sign a papal decree condemning Origen's teachings, as well as others, referred to as The Three Chapters. The Pope refused. According to the *Liber pontificalis*, on 22 November, 545 Justinian ordered the Pope to immediately start on a journey to Constantinople to settle the matter. He was taken under guard to a ship waiting in the Tiber. The Pope diverted the ship to Sicily where he remained for several years. He finally signed the decree in order to be permitted to return to Rome but died aboard ship on his journey home." Mary stopped and gestured toward the papers in Lydia's lap, "Those are Dr. Gibson's research notes you are holding. It's all there."

Lydia shook her head slowly but looked down at the papers. She took a deep breath and read one of the pages marked 'history.' Lydia silently read as Mary quietly watched and waited.

> *"The Encyclopedia Britannica states that Origen was 'the most prominent of all the Church Fathers with the possible exception of Augustine', while St. Jerome at one time considered him as 'the greatest teacher of the Church after the apostles'. St. Gregory of Nyssa called him 'the prince of Christian learning in the third century.' Indeed, Origen's scriptural expertise was unequaled. In his writing, Origen comments on every book, almost every word, of scripture. First and foremost a Christian philosopher, Origen synthesized his scriptural analyzes and was the first to form a system of Christian doctrine. And his system includes the doctrine of reincarnation. In his book, On First Principles, one finds expression of his belief in reincarnation and the law of karma: "Every soul…comes into this world strengthened by the victories or weakened by the defeats of its previous life…"*
>
> *Emperor Justinian assembled the Fifth General Council of the Church and ordered Pope Vigilius to sign an official church order condemning The Three Chapters. The Pope refused to recognize the order. He was taken from Rome by guards while he was celebrating the feast of St. Cecilia in Trastevere. He was ordered by the imperial official Anthimus to journey to Constantinople to settle the matter there with the synod. A ship was waiting for him on the Tiber to transport him to the eastern capital. When aboard, the Pope ordered the ship to go to Sicily instead of Constantinople. The Emperor commanded the Council to continue despite the Pope's refusal to attend. Emperor Justinian opposed the idea that all of mankind originally came from God and was returning to God by the cycle of birth and death. High ranking cardinals convinced him that it was not in the best interest of the Empire to allow Origen's teachings to be taught. A powerful group of cardinals and bishops explained that if every soul had once preexisted with God, then why worship Christ? These cardinals convinced the Emperor that if people thought they were the children of God they might begin to believe they no longer needed an Emperor. They also*

> *worried the masses might begin to think that they shouldn't pay taxes, or that it wasn't necessary to obey the Holy Church. They reasoned that only Christ had come from God. Only Christ preexisted with God and the souls of humans only came into existence at conception. Only the Holy Church could bring these souls to God. Without the Empire and the Church, all people would be doomed to be forever cut off from God in Hell. This doctrine was acceptable to Emperor Justinian. Once he understood the political danger inherent in the belief in reincarnation, the rest is history.*

Lydia looked up from the paper. "This is hard to believe."

"I know. I've been struggling with it all week," conceded Mary.

Lydia gently laid the pages on top of the two books Mary had offered to her. She looked up at Mary and took a deep breath. "I won't be taking any books or notes home. I appreciate all that you have done but…"

Mary cocked her head at Lydia. "What?"

Lydia let out a slow sigh. She sat up straight and folded her hands into her lap. Looking calm and composed she evenly said, "Nothing you could say would make me change my religious beliefs. I came here to get help for my depression. My religion does *not* need an overhaul." *My eternal life is at stake. I must get out of here.*

Mary was caught off guard. "You still think the Devil controlled you when you were a child? Is that why you said what you did to your parents?"

"I must admit that reincarnation does sound less wicked, but I can't buy it. I believe in the resurrection to life and my savior Jesus Christ and that is good enough for me. I'm not sure if I should keep doing this. I want to take a break and pray about all of this. This is happening too fast for me." She got up and started toward the door.

"You look uncomfortable," remarked Mary. "Can you describe what you're feeling right now?"

"I'm going to visit my doctor again and see if he can prescribe something. I'm not sleeping well. I'm fine, *really!* I'll call you."

"Okay, you have my card with my phone numbers, including my pager. Call anytime for whatever reason."

Lydia thanked her and was out of the door before Mary could digest what had just happened.

The Mountain of God

Chester and Master were sitting on the porch watching the rain and listening to its steady rhythm on the roof. The rainy season had begun in India. The next few months would be damp and humid. Chester frowned as he tried to work out a problem. He blew out a deep breath and exclaimed, "It doesn't make sense. They should work together. Why don't they see it?"

The Master looked over at Chester and asked, "What are you referring to?"

Chester continued mostly to himself, "Science has several disciplines, biology, physics, astronomy, geology and such; but they are all a study of nature in one way or another." Turning to the Master he directed a question at him. "Why does each religion act like it knows the only right way. Why do they regard the other religions as wrong, foolishness, or worse—blasphemy?"

The Master rubbed his jaw in thought. "Perhaps an old story my Master once told me will help. It is a story about mountain climbers, road builders, horse trainers and wagon builders." Chester smiled and slowly shook his head as he looked down at his feet but waited to see how the Master tied this to the subject he mentioned.

The Master looked up as if the details of the story were in the rain clouds. "Oh yes, they lived at the base of a mountain, these people. An ancient legend claimed that they would find God when they made it to the top of the mountain. The reward would be peace and prosperity for everyone. It also said that a great temple dedicated to the God of Love and Peace would be built by the followers of the way."

Chester watched an ant crawling on the porch but listened intently to the Master.

"Four separate groups lived at the base of the mountain: Mountain Climbers, Road Builders, Horse Trainers, and Wagon Builders. Each was full of pride and thought its work was superior to the others. All believed in a God that was love and responsible for peace. But each sect also believed that it was unique in the fact that only it knew how to reach the top of the mountain. The Mountain Climbers argued that they were the true way for only by climbing the mountain could one ascend up to God. The Road Builders were equally strong in their faith. They taught to all that would listen that only a road built by them would get the people to the top of the mountain to enjoy the eternal pleasures of being with God. Master was smiling as he remembered the story.

Chester got tired of watching the ant and commented, "I guess the Horse Trainers and Wagon Builders felt the same way."

Master nodded, "Of course. The Horse Trainers recited the portion of the prophecy that the top of the mountain would be brought low. They taught that only those that had a fast and well trained horse would be able to quickly ride to God and experience the love and peace of God."

"How did the Wagon Builders get so confident they knew the one true way?" Chester prompted.

The Master paused to watch a bird taking a bath in a puddle near the front steps. "The Wagon Makers spread the story of a great prophet from God that came down from the mountain and proclaimed that some day a wagon would transport them to God. So the Wagon Makers taught that other beliefs were based on falsehoods and that all had to get on their wagon to make it to God."

Chester laughed, "I've heard of a few churches that sound like that. Of course, the Wagon Makers had to make the wagon and no one else, right?"

The Master held up a finger and said. "Right. The Mountain Climbers made fun of the others for the road up the mountain was never finished, the mountain top never came down, and the prophet died as the wagons got bigger and more ornate yet no miracle ever lifted them to God. The Road Builders had contempt for the Mountain Climbers because all of the climbers fell trying to make it to God."

Chester joined in, "I guess the Horse Trainers were confident that only they were right because until the top of the mountain came down no one would find God and, of course, they had the horses."

"Correct," Master sounded pleased, "Then one day a man was digging a well and found a tablet of stone. Carved on it was a temple surrounded by inscriptions in a language long forgotten and no longer spoken. All of the great scholars from the four ways to God each claimed it was the ancient instructions spoken of in the legend explaining how to get to God. Each group was sure that once the writing was deciphered, it would prove once and for all that their way was right. The legend spoke of the great temple that would be built by the true way and only by the true way. They were all convinced that finding the stone was the long sought sign that the temple was to be built."

"Then what happened?" Chester was getting into the story.

"A terrible war broke out over the tablet and much blood was spilled over who would build the temple. The conflict raged for years but none could win. Finally peace was declared and a compromise was made." The Master paused for effect. "The people grew tired of war and conflict. They decided to join together to build the great temple spoken of in the prophecy of old."

Chester cocked his head and said, "Did they quit believing their way was right?"

The Master smiled. "Secretly they held to their own beliefs; but in the spirit of compromise and peace, they came together to build the temple. Quickly all of the artisans of the four ways to God started on the great work of temple building. The carving of the temple was used as the overall design. The stone the carving was on could be found only up on the mountain itself. They agreed that no other type of stone would be worthy for the Temple of God."

"Come on; come on. Did they build it?" Chester was getting impatient.

The Master held up a hand. Chester settled down. "The Mountain Climbers were skilled at finding the stones needed for the temple. The Road Builders constructed roads that spiraled up the mountain so workers could reach and quarry the stone. The Wagon Makers made strong wagons to haul the stone and the Horse Trainers taught the horses to pull the wagons. As the work on the temple continued, they had to go higher and higher up the mountain to find the right type of stone. The roads could be built only because the Mountain Climbers were able to find the best places to safely extend the road. As the road got higher and higher, it took fast horses to make the trips up and down the mountain in less than a day. Without wagons, no stone could be delivered to the bottom for the temple."

"So by working together they built the temple. Then what?" Chester was frowning again.

"As the temple neared completion the search for more stones of the right type took them to the top of the mountain. At the top was plenty of stone to finish the temple. Just as the ancient prophecy had stated, the top of the mountain was brought down and the way to the top was found."

"Was God on the mountain?" Chester cocked his head.

"The prophecy had always stated that they would find God when they made it to the top of the mountain, and the reward would be peace and prosperity for everyone. They learned that to find the God of Peace and Love, they had to first become a people who were peaceful and loving." The Master waited for Chester.

"So until people learn that the religions of today each have something to teach about the journey to God, they will be like the people living at the base of the mountain!" Chester beamed.

The Master stood up and said, "Exactly." Chester was left to ponder what he had just learned.

Lydia and Her Minister

For the next few days after her meeting with Mary, Lydia cried and prayed. Prayed and cried. She'd been in bed all weekend. *What is wrong with me? Why can't I just trust God and get on with my life. I don't know what to believe anymore. Stop! There is no such thing as reincarnation. Any Christian knows that. I wish I'd never seen my baby book. I'll forget about it, that's what I'll do. Fat chance. I'm a mess! Lydia, what do you need to do? I've got to talk to my minister. He's the only one that might understand.*

Lydia made an appointment to meet with her pastor that afternoon. Arriving at the Crossroads Bible Church made Lydia feel better. She parked her car so the afternoon sun was blocked by the shade of several large trees lining the church parking lot. There was no one around on the first floor of the church. She took the stairs that led up to the church offices. She could hear her pastor on the phone. His door was open. He motioned for her to come in as he wrapped up his telephone call. "Thanks. Talk to you later." He hung up the phone and stood up so he could walk around his desk and give Lydia a hug. "Hello, Lydia, how are you doing?"

Lydia returned the hug before answering. "I'm fine Reverend Biggs, but I need some advice, and I didn't know anywhere else to go."

He motioned for her to sit down on the couch. He sat in leather lounger that groaned as he settled in. Biggs was a large man with gray hair and a graying beard. He reminded Lydia of a giant teddy bear. If he couldn't help her navigate through dangerous waters, she didn't know what she would do.

"I don't know where to start. Remember when I asked your opinion of me getting professional help for depression?" Biggs nodded. "Well, it's not working or maybe it's working too well. I'm not making any sense, am I? I've learned a lot about myself and I don't like what I learned. Instead of continuing, Lydia stopped as her eyes filled with tears. Biggs handed her a box of tissue sitting near his chair. She dried her eyes and composed herself a little. Lydia held the wet tissue in her lap. Her shoulders slumped and her head bowed.

"Lydia, you are going to have to tell me what is wrong or I can't help you."

Lydia looked up, her face a mixture of fear and shame. "I think I'm demon possessed."

Biggs wasn't able to disguise his shock at first. Shaking his head, he lowered his already low voice to a rumble, "*Demon possessed?*"

"I must be. It's the only explanation that makes sense.

"Let's back up, can we? I'm going to need a lot more information before I can make heads or tails of this." He gently listened as she related the story of the debate, her reaction to Chester, and of her depression afterwards, getting the baby book and its contents. "Wait. Tell me about the baby book?"

Lydia stopped her breathless chatter. She took a deep breath. "My mom wrote down stories I told about being a grown up lady living in India. She wrote on the top of the first page that sometimes I talked more like an adult than a little girl. My daddy always insisted that I had the Devil in me. Now I know why."

Biggs leaned forward in the lounger and shook his head. "Did your mother think you were demon possessed?"

"Well not exactly, I think she just thought what I said was odd and funny. Of course, I've never been to India. She did tell me that sometimes I sounded grownup for my age. She told me Daddy would whip me if I talked about India or being a grown up."

Lydia paused. She started to say something then stopped. Biggs encouraged her to speak up. "Well, uh, never mind. I can't say it.

Puzzled, the pastor took her hand and gently prodded her to say whatever she was thinking. Lydia finally blurted out, "There are only two possible explanations for me saying what I did and both scare me to death."

"You mentioned demon possession. What's the other choice?"

"Reincarnation," Lydia whispered as she covered her face sobbing.

Biggs nodded. "Reincarnation is a pagan belief that came to the Christians via the teachings of Plato. You know the Bible teaches that paganism is as bad as idolatry. We mustn't listen to paganism no matter how sweet it is to the ears. You did right to come to me."

Lydia straightened up and looked proud. *I'm putting on the armor of God and resisting Satan. I knew Brother Biggs would help me understand.* "I remember your sermon on holding fast to the truth. What should I do now?"

Biggs stood up and looked for a moment as if he was a soldier instead of a minister. He looked at Lydia with compassion. "You can't help what happened when you were a child. God is using this crisis to bring you closer to our Lord Jesus." He strode across his room and opened a file drawer. He pulled out a blue directory and closed the cabinet. Once at his desk he sat down and flipped through the pages until he found what he was looking for. He took out his pen and circled one of the entries. He looked up and his tone was one of determination. "Lydia, there are many of us who are part of God's army against wickedness in high places. We have our gifts. Some of us are called to battle the wicked ones directly. I can give you the name and number of a preacher who is willing to enter the gates of hell and fight the good fight."

Lydia sat straight. "Do you think I'm demon possessed?"

Biggs took a deep breath. "What science likes to call personality disorders we know from the miracles of Jesus to be in fact demon possession. It possible that your depression and your feelings of fear are both the result of a spiritual attack on your soul."

Lydia sat still and softly asked. "Why me?"

Biggs came around and sat on the edge of his desk. "Lydia, some people are identified at birth. Just as the angels know who we are and protect us, the demons know who we are and attack us. When you told me that you used to talk and act like an adult as a child, it was clearly a case of demons attacking God's chosen when you were young and vulnerable. You should feel proud the demons are so afraid of you that they tried to harm you when you were young. They did the same to our Savior when he was a baby. That is why Joseph and Mary had to flee into Egypt."

Lydia nodded her head. *It all makes sense. I'm a soldier of God.* She sat up straighter. "It's an honor to suffer for the Lord's sake."

Biggs nodded his head. "Lydia, I'm proud of you. Christ didn't promise his disciples a wide and easy path. He promised that all of his true followers would experience trials and tribulations. He also promised we wouldn't experience more than we can handle. It wasn't that long ago that you were baptized into the family of God. You received the Holy Spirit at your baptism and now it is at war with the evil spirits trying to drag you with them to hell."

"What are you trying to tell me?"

"Just as Jesus exorcised evil spirits, so can his ministers today. I'm afraid I have no experience with exorcisms but Brother Meriwether in Kentucky does. I'm going to give you his number. I urge you to call him and set up a time to visit him."

He walked around his desk and got a pen and paper out. As he wrote down the information that Lydia would need, she asked. "How does an exorcism happen?"

Biggs looked up. "You can forget all about the movie *The Exorcist*. That's all Hollywood. Some exorcisms like ones performed in the Catholic Church are full of ritual and long prayers. I've heard that Brother Meriwether has cast out demons with a short prayer and a laying on of hands." He ripped the paper from the tablet and handed it to Lydia. "If you want, I can go with you?"

Lydia shook her head. She folded the paper in half and held it to her heart. "No, something I can do well is travel. I'm ready to walk the path that God has set before me." She stood up and hugged her minister. "Thank you so much." With her head held high, Lydia left ready and willing to go fight her demon with the help of her Lord and Savior.

Visions

The Master, Sanjiv, and Chester were just finishing dinner. It was Friday night, so the Sabbath had begun. During the rainy season the Master kept the Sabbath indoors instead of meditating at the contemplation pond. As Sanjiv lit some incense, the Master became quiet and serene. Chester had come to look forward to the Sabbath and to listening to the Master teach. Sometimes the Master would sit motionless with his eyes closed for up to an hour before teaching Chester. Somehow during that still time the Master would come to know exactly what his student needed for further spiritual progress. Chester crossed his legs, closed his eyes, and began the relaxing exercise. He focused on slowing his breathing so it would be easier to avoid distracting thoughts. He pictured a wide lake disturbed by wind, unable to reflect the large full moon just above the lake. He tried to calm the waves on the lake. Even when he imagined the air as being windless, the calmness of the lake eluded him. Mild ripples made the reflected moon dance and wiggle. *Why can't I still the lake and see two motionless moons? The picture in my mind of the moon and sky above the lake are motionless. The same mind is creating both images.* Then he remembered a trick the Master had taught him. *Rotate the image in my mind until the sky becomes the lake.* Chester rotated the picture in his mind until the sky was on the bottom. What was the sky was still calm and motionless. What had been the lake was now motionless like the sky. Instantly, the image became two full moons—mirror opposite, both without movement. The stars in the lake looked like the ones in the sky. At that perfect moment, the vision began.

The Master waited for Chester to finish his meditation. It had been over an hour since he had begun. After Chester completed the breathing exercise for returning to full wakefulness, he opened his eyes. The Master waited for Chester to look at him before asking a question. The vision was still vivid in Chester's memory, and he didn't hear what the Master was asking him. "I'm sorry. What?"

"Tell me what you saw."

Chester took a deep breath and stared into space. "I saw the throne of God surrounded by angels. Seven Candlesticks with Seven Candles stood before it. An angel was speaking in a language I had never heard before, yet I understood. It told me the Seven Candlesticks were the Seven Wisdoms and the Seven Candles were the Seven Spiritual paths to God. The Seven Flames represented the sevenfold spirit that burns in the hearts of every true believer."

The Master exclaimed. "So you saw the Seven Wisdoms. This is good news. Please continue."

"There was a pause in heaven. After this pause, seven saints from seven different paths lined with silver and other precious jewels approached the throne of God. The host of the angels around the throne bowed toward the Holy Eternal. Yet the seven saints did not. As the saints got closer, my vision became clearer and larger. It reminded me of a TV close-up but with perfect resolution. I didn't hear what the first four saints said, but I watched as each one approached the throne, dropped on one knee, and spoke. Each of them received a glowing white stone. On the throne of God was the shape of a man that glowed brightly like polished brass or copper. The face shone so incredibly bright and pure that no one could look into the utter brilliance. The best I could do was look away just to the left or right of the piercing light. For some reason, no matter how hard I tried, I couldn't look directly at the face of God. The radiant rainbow surrounding God's throne was much easier to look at, and I found myself gazing at it in wonder, unable to take in all that was happening at once. I did get to hear and watch what happened to the last three saints. The fifth one approached the throne. As he knelt, I heard him say,

> *'Holy Father, I come as your son to claim my inheritance.'*
> *God asked. 'And what is your inheritance?'*
> *'My place in your eternal kingdom.'*
> *'Welcome my son, this is your new name, known only to you and me. Dwell forever in my paradise.'*

The stone glowed as it passed from the hand of God to the saint's. Bowing further, he took his leave. The sixth saint also knelt and asked for his inheritance. I watched the shimmering hue of the rainbow again as the stone was passed in my peripheral sight. The seventh saint came forward and knelt. Spellbound by the splendor, I barely heard the request for the inheritance. There was sudden quiet. The entire hosts of God watched with focused attention. I was glad I noticed in time to hear God ask.

> *'What is your inheritance?' The seventh saint stood. The suspense felt both intense and awesome. 'My inheritance is the inheritance of one who has found the truest path of all.'*
> *'What is that?'*
> *'To look into the face of God.'*
> *'You cannot gaze into my face and live.'*
> *'I can because I know who I am and I know what I will see. I will see my face for I know myself fully and it is time I take my place.'*

With that bold statement, the saint walked forward. For the briefest moment, the entire host saw the face of God was now the face of the saint and the face of the saint had become the face of God. It shined so brightly that no one could gaze at it fully. The saint turned around and sat on the throne. Both images merged instantly, indistinguishable from the other. In deafening unison the entire angelic host said, 'The two become one!' Before the sound faded, the throne was brighter than before, and the seventh saint was gone."

Chester tilted his head upward but kept his eyes closed because he was so focused on remembering. He hadn't realized he had been talking the whole time with his eyes closed. He opened them as he took a deep breath and shook his head. He let out a whistle and said. "Wow, I can't believe I just relived that as if I were there."

The Master praised Chester. "This is a sign of divine blessing. You have progressed fast. The *Sutras of Patanjali* that you have memorized are helping you maximize your meditation practice." The Master paused as Chester tilted and nodded his head in thanks. Chester beamed further as he winked at the Master. "Everything you saw was in symbols. As you progress, the visions will be less symbolic, and it will be easier to understand them."

"You witnessed two memory visions, the second after the first in timeline order. Soon it will be possible for you to see up to a dozen visions in a row. The angel explained what the seven candlesticks meant. Each candlestick represents one of the Seven Wisdoms that together bring total understanding. As you know these seven are: Eternity, Infinity, Awareness, Oneness, Balance, Faith and Holiness. At least two wisdoms are in each of the seven paths that lead to sainthood."

"So that's why I saw seven saints on seven paths."

The Master nodded. "In the vision of the seven saints, you watched a symbolic scene of the saints arriving at the supreme destination their path took them. Six received a brilliantly glowing stone. On each one was a name known only to God and the saint forever."

Chester laughed. "I get it. God was handing out unlisted phone numbers. No wait, I have better one. He was handing out IP addresses. In a way it sounds like God's security system of unique passwords."

The Master chuckled briefly at the cleverness of his student. "The glowing rock represents a set of infinities that make up a universe given to the saint to be its king and high priest."

"You mean the saint becomes a god of a whole universe?" Chester was intently concentrating on the Master's next words.

"Yes. And since only the Holy Eternal knows the saint's sacred name, only the Holy Eternal can contact the god dwelling in that universe. You can think of it as a way to prevent any being or god from ever masquerading as the Most High."

Chester shook his head. "You have gone way out there. Just for the sake of curiosity, what was the deal about the seventh saint?"

The Master smiled. "My astute observer, one can choose not to spend eternity in the created realms. The only way to achieve what the seventh saint called the truest path is to shed all attachments, desires, ego and the sense of a separate self, and become one with the Eternal Uncreated Awareness. This can only be achieved if the individual self is seen as the illusion it really is. Yet paradoxically, nothing is lost but all is gained. For your level of advancement, you were presented symbols you could understand. What you watched was symbolic of total oneness with God."

Chester blinked and narrowed his eyes. "How do you know what my visions mean and don't mean? How do I know you aren't just making this up?"

The Master waggled his finger at him. "I had many symbolic visions before my Master taught me how to let him guide me to important ancient information. Now it is time for me to guide you."

Kentucky

The view from her plane window was breathtaking. They were flying in a valley between two large mountains covered with various shades of vibrant green foliage. The trees looked miniature from her lofty vantage point. Below, when the plane turned just right, she could see a stream meandering between the bases of the mountains. Every once in a while, color peaked out that must be native wild flowers. For a moment Lydia forgot why she was making this trip. How could anything be wrong when God's world was so beautiful? The ride was a little bumpy as the pilot maneuvered around the mountains, but Lydia was a seasoned traveler and easily swayed with the movement. She had boarded the small prop plane after landing in Nashville. It was surprising the pilot flew through the mountains instead of over them. When she had landed at the Blue Grass Airport in Lexington, the only rent cars left were a large Lincoln and several tiny subcompacts. She had reserved a midsize so they upgraded her to the Lincoln. She would at least get to drive in style and comfort to her appointment with Reverend Meriwether.

Trying to focus on the drive instead of what waited at her destination was difficult. Most of the route headed south on Interstate 75 so the hour's drive was uneventful. Lydia followed the directions given to her and a map which showed a small town about five miles east of the interstate. The exit was clearly marked. She turned right at the stop sign onto Kingwood as directed which led straight to the center of town. She spotted the little church immediately. Knowing the parsonage was behind the church, she circled to find the best place to park the tank of a car without smashing into something. The curb was open along the side of the church so she carefully parked and sat there finally realizing the big step she was taking. For a moment she panicked and reached down to start the car and just drive off but forced herself to get out and walk up the long drive. She again hesitated before meekly tapping on the front door. It opened almost immediately which startled Lydia and she jumped back. Embarrassed, she stammered as she introduced herself. "Hi, I'm…um…Lydia Masters. I think we talked on the phone."

"Of course, please come in. We've been looking forward to meeting you. How was your trip? I'm Kim a.k.a. the pastor's wife." Her blue eyes sparkled as her short honey blonde curls bounced in every direction. She looked a little like Meg Ryan. *So much for the stereotypical matronly country preacher's wife,* thought Lydia, trying to grasp for anything to distract her mind from the real reason she was there.

Kim smiled and motioned Lydia to enter. Her jitters started settling down a bit since this woman was acting like there was nothing out of the ordinary. Maybe everything would be okay. Kim seemed genuinely happy to have a visitor and led her into the house's large living room. Several groups of couches and chairs formed intimate conversation pits. The room had several low tables scattered around, probably to hold refreshments. It even smelled welcoming as she got a whiff of cinnamon and apples. She wondered if a pie had just come out of the oven. It looked like the Meriwethers often entertained and enjoyed it. She could easily imagine a dozen or so people fitting comfortably into the room. The faint sound of man's voice drifted into the room. The one-sided conversation suggested that he was on the phone. "May I get you something to drink—ice tea, juice, coke, water?" offered Kim.

Lydia shook her head and tried to calm herself by making idle conversation. "No thanks, I'm fine. I like this room. It feels so warm and inviting. Have you lived here a long time?" As Kim was about to reply, a man with hazel eyes and short dark hair sprinkled with gray walked in from the adjoining room. There was a distinguished air about him and a subtle confidence in how he looked straight into Lydia's eyes as he slowly approached her. He smiled and stuck out his hand.

"Welcome. I see you've met my wife. I'm Philip Meriwether. Please sit down." He pointed out a large chair across from the sofa nearest the front door. The couple sat side by side on the sofa.

"Should I call you Reverend or Brother or Mr. Meriwether?" Lydia queried.

Chuckling, he responded, "I'm more comfortable with plain 'Philip.' We're all brothers and sisters in the Lord, neither higher nor lower."

Lydia blurted out a verse she had learned as a child in Vacation Bible School. "*For there is no difference between the Jew and the Greek: for the same Lord over all is rich unto all that call upon him.* Romans 10:12." She didn't know why she did that; it just fell out of her mouth.

Philip's eyes twinkled as he grinned. "Good, I'm impressed. Now…you came a long way to be here with us." He folded his hands in front of him and sat silently as if waiting for her to speak.

Lydia appreciated him being patient with her. "As I told you on the phone, I think I am possessed by a demon; and I heard you were an exorcist…." Lydia had on her *in control* debate face but inside she was crumbling. She had never been so anxious. Flushing slightly as she paused and inhaled a deep breath, she began, "A seminary colleague of my pastor recommended you. He said you helped his nephew, Brandon, about a year ago. Do you remember?" Philip nodded but didn't speak. She looked at Philip's peaceful face and her voice quivered, "What should I do?"

Both Philip and Kim looked concerned yet understanding. "Why do you think you are possessed?" asked Philip.

"Well, for the last few months I have felt scared much of the time and I can't figure out why. My life is normal. I own a small travel agency and business is good. I like my work and customers, but I can't get a lot done. I don't think I've made any huge mistakes at the office yet, but I can't concentrate and am afraid if I don't stop this daydreaming or whatever it is happening to me, I'll lose everything I've worked so hard for."

"Being distracted doesn't fit with demon possession. Is there more?" Philip prompted.

"I don't know exactly how to describe what I think about…or maybe it's not thinking…it's more like quick flashes of images and a feeling of danger. But I don't remember ever being in any real danger. And the dream…sometimes at night I think a heavy weight is crushing my chest. I can't get it off me. I wake up struggling to push it away. It's so real; I'm exhausted when I awaken. I do fine during the day while it is hectic but when I go home and try to relax I get panicky. This is just not like me! I've been to my doctor and had a thorough checkup. I thought I might be having a heart attack, but all tests were clear and nothing is physically wrong with me. I've tried getting therapy for stress management, and I do feel a little better. The exercise is helping. Maybe I'm weaker when I'm asleep so a demon can control me and that's why the dreams don't make sense. In them, I interact with people I can't remember when I'm awake. I sense that they are somehow real, though; and I'm scared. My heart races and I'm covered with sweat. Of course, then I can't get back to sleep," explained Lydia. "Oh, I'm sorry. I chatter when I'm nervous."

"How did you get the idea this was a demon messing with you?" Philip asked.

Lydia tried to find a way to put it into words without sounding too psycho. She hung her head, shaking it slowly. "I don't know what those images could be except demons. There's nothing *real* to be scared of, but I am. I guess it might help if you knew there's always been something wrong with me." A tear rolled down her cheek. "My father saw it when I was little. I don't know exactly what went on back then because apparently I've forgotten it. Even *that* is weird. But…I'll tell you what my mother reluctantly revealed to me recently. She said that when I was about three or four years old, I tried over and over to tell about stuff I had done when I was big, you know, taller. She said that at times I'd look in a mirror and act puzzled. I'd ask when my skin turned white and my hair got light. I guess I thought it should be darker and my hair black. She said she asked me to show her what color skin I was talking about and all I could find to compare it with was a sweet potato skin that was on the cabinet. Sort of a tan color. Mama said she thought it was interesting, but I guess all mothers think their kids are cute and funny. She said that sometimes when I talked about this stuff that I'd act happy and excited. Other times I seemed angry or sad. She wrote down much of what I said and put the tablet pages in my baby book. I didn't know this until recently when my therapist asked me to talk with her about my early years that I'd blanked out. Mama said the strangest part was that I'd use adult words or phrases. When I asked for an example, she said, 'Oh, I don't know. It's been a long time. Just read your baby book.' I tried but got sick at my stomach before I finished the first page." Lydia glanced up to see their reactions. All she saw was two concerned faces looking at her with compassion.

"Sounds to me like you had an active imagination. Maybe you have a talent for creative writing," Philip smiled. "But this was *not* the end of your mother's story, was it?"

"No, it's not, but this part is so hard to tell. She told me that my daddy said the Devil was in me and he was trying to beat him out of me. He'd whip me with a belt anytime I talked about once being a grown up or asked adult questions he didn't understand. Mama said he would say over and over, 'I am going to run Satan out of this house if it's the last thing I do.' He'd put me in my room on my knees and make me beg the Lord's forgiveness for my lying." Lydia sank deeper into the cushions and hung her head. In almost a whisper, she continued, "I must have *tried* to keep from talking to him. I guess the Devil had too much influence on me. Why else would I keep making my Daddy mad?" Lydia hid her face in her hands; her shoulders slumped as they silently shook with shame.

No one said a word. Finally, Lydia glanced up to see her new friends quietly praying. This gave her the strength to continue. "When it was just Mama and me alone, she said that she would let me tell her whatever I wanted. She only tried to hush me up when Daddy was nearby. She said she didn't understand what I was talking about half of the time, but it seemed important to me so she listened and wrote down much of it. She won't say, but I *know* I was the cause of their divorce. There was a big fight one night with Mama crying and Daddy yelling. The next morning he was gone. I know I was the reason that he left and didn't return. Lydia was sobbing as she admitted this secret sin. Kim handed her a wad of tissues and knelt on the floor beside the chair gently holding Lydia's hand.

"So you think your father was right about you having the Devil in you?" Philip whispered softly.

"What else could it be?" Lydia answered as she looked up at him with overflowing eyes. Without her knowing that it was a screening test, Philip asked her if she would join him in a prayer to help guide them. Lydia readily agreed. They bowed their heads as Philip led the prayer. At one point, he asked Lydia to repeat what he said. He glanced up at her to see how she was reacting. There was no outward sign of distress as she said the words 'God,' 'Jesus,' 'Christ,' 'Savior,' 'Lord'.

When the prayer was finished, Philip and Kim left Lydia reading a Bible passage while they conferred in the adjoining room. When they returned, Philip gently told Lydia that after interacting with her, he could see no sign of demon possession. He must have thought that this would relieve Lydia but instead it upset her more. She thought he didn't want to help her. She told him that this might just be one of the demon's attempts to deceive so it could stay inside her.

Philip sat quietly thinking for a few minutes. He was struggling with the idea of conducting the exorcism ritual on someone whom he was sure was not possessed. But Lydia had traveled a long way for his guidance. Finally, he thought she probably couldn't be harmed by the cleansing prayers; and on the slight chance she was possessed, he wanted to err on the safe side. He sighed and softly clapped his hands together, finally making a decision. "Well…the next step is to call some folks that are strong in the Lord to help us. But before I do that I want you to watch a tape of an exorcism and then tell me if you are still willing to continue. Does that sound reasonable?"

Lydia nodded her head. Kim got up and took a video out of the bookcase and walked over to the large TV at the other end of the room and put it in the VCR. She turned on the TV and pushed the "play" button. When the picture appeared, Philip commented as the tape showed a group of people kneeling down to pray. "Our exorcisms are straightforward and may not appear much different from an ordinary prayer service."

One man was sitting in a chair and the other people were kneeling around him with their Bibles. Some held crosses. They all began to pray softly. Occasionally, they would pause and Philip would read a passage of scripture. At one point, they all quieted and Philip directed the man sitting in the center of the circle to repeat after him the phrase, 'Jesus is my Lord.' Instead of repeating it, the man's face became inflamed and distorted. Cold hatred stared through his squinted eyes as he screamed, "NO!"

Lydia watched as Philip's voice rang out. "By the power of the Almighty God and his Son Jesus Christ I command all evil spirits to leave this man alone and to go at once!" Philip repeated this over and over. As he did, the others around him chanted the same phrase in unison. "By the power of the Almighty God and his Son Jesus Christ I command all evil spirits to leave this man alone and to go at once!" Philip stopped the tape. Lydia knew he was watching her for a reaction. She just waited. He slightly nodded his head toward her. "Let me show you how it ends. This lasted over two hours." As if gauging that Lydia was hanging in there so far, he fast-forwarded the tape. "Ah, here we are."

The tape showed Philip holding a cross and commanding the demon to leave. Everyone behind him was praying for God to give Brother Philip strength. The man sitting down suddenly leaned forward and violently vomited. The liquid spewed in a straight line just missing one of the people kneeling in front of him. Lydia drew back covering her mouth with her hand and almost gagged. Philip paid no attention to her and continued narrating. "He's spitting out the poison and all evil is leaving his body." At this point, the man slumped back into the chair. His face was wet with perspiration. All the defiance was gone from his eyes as he closed them. Someone rubbed a wet washcloth over his face. Philip softly continued, "Billy Joe, who is your Lord and Master?" An exhausted Billy Joe smiled weakly and said. "Jesus is my Lord. God is my Master." The whole room erupted in celebration. Everyone in the room took turns hugging Billy Joe. Philip turned off the TV and the VCR as Kim got up to put the tape back in the cabinet.

Philip turned to Lydia and asked, "How do you feel about what you just watched?"

Lydia lifted her chin and showed no emotion as she answered. She seemed resigned to whatever was to happen to her. "I have to know that I'm free from demonic spirits. Seemingly I've battled them all of my life. I admit I'm scared, but I can't quit now. Please help me."

Philip looked at his wife and nodded his head. "I'm going to go see when the others can come over." He walked into the adjacent room. Lydia figured it was his office. They could hear him on the phone. Kim asked, "Do we have your permission to record this on a tape? We will give it to you and you can watch it or not. We won't make a copy for us unless you want to share your experience as a witness for others."

"Do I have to sign anything?"

"No, as soon as I get the camera set up, I'll record you giving consent. Then I'll stop the recorder until it's time to get started." Kim opened a closet near the back of the room and got out a large video recorder. "It feeds directly to a VHS tape so you can watch it in any VCR. We never know how long a session will last so it's set on extended play so a full six hours can be taped." Kim attached the camera to a tall tripod using a screw that was on the small platform attached to the handle. She extended the legs to their farthest so the lens looked down on the braided oval rug that covered half of the room. She held the remote control. "Lydia, please look up a little bit towards the camera."

Lydia did as requested and met the glassy eye staring at her. A tiny red light glowed. "Lydia Masters, do you give your consent to be recorded as we pray for you?"

Lydia nodded her head said, "Yes, I do."

"If at anytime you want the recording stopped, just let us know," Kim assured her.

Lydia said, "Thank you." The red light went off just before Kim let the remote control dangle and swing. She sat down near Lydia waiting. Lydia asked, "How did your husband get started with this special ministry?"

"I guess we had been married about four years when a mother brought her young daughter to him for guidance. This was a normal part of his regular pastoral duties. The woman was at her wit's end on how to get control of her 12-year old. The child had slipped out of a window the night before and had been brought home by a police officer about 2:00 in the morning. Her mother had searched her room and found drawings of violent acts. After what was a simple counseling session, the girl agreed to follow rules and respect her mother. She denied any thoughts of ever harming others. Philip asked if he could lead them in prayer. She and her mother bowed their heads as he began praying. I was in another room. Suddenly I heard this bloodcurdling scream come from his office. I rushed in to see what was wrong and this young girl was standing up and yelling at Philip that Jesus was not her Lord that she was Lord and Master. Her mother was trying to prevent her from hurting herself or harming Philip. She had her hands out in front of her like claws that could scratch his eyes out. Of course, it was obvious to us that a demon controlled her. We had never seen it in person before, but we had studied cases in seminary. Like he had been doing it all of his life, my husband rebuked the demon in the name of the Holy Father God, Jesus Christ and the Holy Spirit."

"I watched the girl suddenly shut up and this incredible look of surprise came across her face. Philip repeated over and over, 'I command by the power and authority of the Holy Father God, Jesus Christ and the Holy Spirit for all demonic spirits to leave this child and release her from their evil power.' Next, she got on her knees and begged. I remember it like it was yesterday. She said '*Please* don't make me go. Let me stay a little while longer.' My husband rebuked the demon again. She screamed really loud then collapsed. I ran for the phone in case we needed to call 911. When I came back her mother was helping her to sit up. She looked bewildered. I gave her a glass of water. My husband stayed focused on her, never glancing away from her face. He again asked her if she would join him in prayer. She simply nodded and bowed her head. Philip started out the prayer just like he always did. 'Heavenly Father, we humbly come before your throne seeking your guidance.' This time the girl repeated it easily and had no problem asking God to guide her through life."

Lydia was amazed at the story. "So what happened to her after that?"

"Her mother told us several months later that she was behaving wonderfully. She acted like a typical child her age. She still did what most kids do as far as getting in trouble, but it was the usual like talking or chewing gum in class, resisting homework, wanting to sleep late, stuff like that."

Philip came back and whispered something in his wife's ear. Kim nodded and they both looked at Lydia. "A deacon of our church who has helped with several exorcisms this year will be here in a few minutes. Kim and I will also be here to support you in any way we can. Do you have any questions while we wait for David?

Lydia shook her head slowly. She felt compelled to follow this through. A peace came over her, and she welcomed in her heart the help of these fine Christian warriors. A knock at the door caused Kim to scurry down the hall to the front door. She came back with a big, round, kind-looking fellow who carried a Bible and a cross. The compassion that flowed out from him dwarfed his size. He reminded Lydia of Santa Claus coming to her rescue. She was so nervous she had to stifle a giggle. His beard was gray and his head was shiny and suntanned. He gently went to her and gave her a hug. "I'm Brother David. I'm here to fight the lion." As David made his acquaintance, Kim turned the video recorder on.

Philip directed traffic. His wife was at his right side and David was at his left. Lydia finished the box by kneeling across from Philip. "Please bow your heads," instructed Philip. "Dear God, we beg you to be with us today as we give ourselves to you as instruments of goodness. Help us to be tools of your love and forgiveness. Please give us power over all evil spirits. Amen"

Lydia mouthed "Amen" and looked to Philip for guidance. He pointed to a large overstuffed chair. Please take that chair, Sister Lydia. The battle will not be with our bodies but with our spirit. Lydia got as comfortable as her mounting anticipation would let her. "Make sure you are sitting up straight. Try to block out all sounds but our voices. Lydia nodded her head. Philip continued in a slow, steady low voice, "Close your eyes so your mind can let go your surroundings. Slow your breathing down to help you relax. Are you comfortable?"

Lydia's eyes stayed closed but she answered in a clear voice, "Yes."

"Do you feel anything inside you putting pressure on you to leave here?"

"No."

"Is any entity pressuring you to keep its identity secret?"

"No."

"Lydia, I want you to pray with me. Repeat after me. "Jesus is my Lord, and God is my Master."

Lydia smiled calmly and said without hesitation, "Jesus is my Lord, and God is my Master."

All three spectators looked at one another with raised eyebrows. Then they all smiled as Philip continued, "Jesus, I accept you and love you with all my heart and soul. You are my Guiding Light."

Lydia spoke clearly and reverently. "Jesus, I accept you and love you with all my heart and soul. You are my Guiding Light."

"God is all powerful," continued Philip.

Lydia followed easily, "God is all powerful."

Philip's questioning eyes met those of Kim and David. Each nodded in affirmation. He then focused on Lydia. "What do you feel surrounding you right this minute?"

Lydia opened her eyes slowly as a serene smile formed on her lips, "Warmth, love, peace, acceptance and overwhelming joy."

Kim beamed and said. "You don't have demon in you."

"You mean you exorcised the demon already?"

David shook out a booming laugh. "No, Sister, you never had a demon in you. You are following the path to God, your Father."

Philip nodded his head. "If you had truly been possessed, there is no way you could have repeated that prayer and statements after me. If a demon were inside you, it would have appeared while you were in that state of deep relaxation. It's all on tape if you want to see what happened."

Lydia looked incredulous. "Was I possessed when I was little but not now?"

"Demons don't just go away. If you had been possessed when you were a small child, it would still be there. Believe me, Lydia, you have *never* been demon possessed," exclaimed Philip.

Finally she put her hands together and raised them up above her head. Tears streamed down her cheeks as she praised her savior. "Sweet Jesus, thank you. Thank you. Thank you."

David moved his bulk slowly as he got up on one foot then the other. He bowed before Lydia. "My dear sister, it was a pleasure to meet you."

Lydia beamed at him. "You are welcome. Thank *you*!"

Philip escorted his friend to the door as Kim turned off the recorder and took the tape out. After finding its box she peeled a long self-sticking label and pressed it onto the back of the tape. She pulled a pen out of a pocket and wrote. "Lydia Masters August 1995." She handed it to Lydia who clutched it to her heart.

"I am a child of God. I know that now." She whispered it so nobody heard it but her.

Kim hugged Philip when he came back. They both relaxed into the soft leather couch by the fireplace. Philip shook his head. "All these years you have thought you were possessed by evil. Instead you are a temple of God, a child of the Father."

Lydia sat back into the plush chair and narrowed her eyes, "What about what I said and drew as a toddler? What about the strange things I talked about? Why would I think I had dark skin?"

Philip shrugged. "I bet it was just the creation of a little girl with a vivid imagination that wanted to get attention. When I was a young boy I had an invisible friend that my mother swears I always insisted I could see. It was harmless. It just shows how powerful our imagination is when we are a children. As we get older and see the real world and how it works, we lose the foolish daydreams. The Apostle Paul said, '*When I was a child, I spake as a child, I understood as a child, I thought as a child: but when I became a man, I put away childish things.*' 1 Corinthians 13:11."

"Lydia, it's time you put away childish things and grow in grace and knowledge of God. I'm sorry your daddy wasn't patient enough to be kind and understanding, but probably in his own way he was trying his best to help you. Can you forgive him for being wrong about you being possessed by the Devil? I believe the only evil in your heart may be your lack of forgiveness."

Lydia felt a chill run down her back, neck, and arms. She physically paled thinking. *This doesn't feel right. I don't even remember my father.* But out loud she calmly responded, "You think my distress will disappear if I forgive my father for being wrong about me being possessed?" Her heart began to hurt. She felt dizzy and numb as if she were floating. She burrowed deeper in the chair reflecting her need to get away from the guilt his words stirred within her. Philip hesitated like he was trying to think of what to do next. Lydia realized that he must have mistaken her pensiveness for stubbornness when he offered, "Lydia, Christ died for your sins and has forgiven you. Let Jesus guide you into true peace by cleansing your heart of hate and anger. '*Let all bitterness, and wrath, and anger, and clamor, and evil speaking, be put away from you, with all malice: And be ye kind one to another, tenderhearted, forgiving one another, even as God for Christ's sake hath forgiven you.*' Ephesians 4:31 and 32."

For the first time, Lydia realized that she had to face the jumble of emotions that had been subconsciously hidden for so many years. She sat still staring at the wall behind Philip. Her mind was racing in all directions as she tried to sort everything out. *Hate and anger? Is that what I feel? Maybe, but there has to be more to what's going on with me than a mistaken father.* Suddenly she wished she could talk with Mary. *Could my depression be because I hold a grudge against my father? I didn't even know he was wrong until today. At least demon possession has been eliminated.* Finally Lydia responded as best she could, "I don't know if I can do what you're asking. I don't know how."

Philip must have thought that he had cracked her resistance because he tried another scripture. "Jesus taught us by saying, '*Ye have heard that it hath been said, Thou shalt love thy neighbour, and hate thine enemy. But I say unto you, Love your enemies, bless them that curse you, do good to them that hate you, and pray for them which despitefully use you, and persecute you…'* Matthew 5: 43 and 44. There was no response from Lydia. She still sat expressionless staring into space.

Lydia realized she hadn't heard much of what Philip had said from the time she heard him say the only evil in her heart was her inability to forgive. An overwhelming sense of hopelessness had descended like an arrow to her heart at those words. She was that scared little girl again on her knees in the dark room saying, "Daddy, Daddy, I'm sorry. I'm sorry. Please don't hit me again…You're a good daddy, I love you. I love you!" Another image flashed into her mind of a tall, handsome man with olive skin and sad eyes begging her not to get on the train. She was saying, "You're a horrible father. Why won't you let me go? I hate you!" Lydia closed her eyes bringing down the curtain on this painful scene. When she opened them again, she was still in the Meriwethers' living room. All Lydia wanted to do was get to a safe place to think about all she had learned and experienced. *I'll call Mary and set an appointment just as soon as I get back to Dallas.*

Shaking her head slowly, still fighting to stay in the present, Lydia calmly looked straight at Philip then Kim as she honestly requested, "Please pray for me. I want to do whatever is God's will but sometimes it's not easy. I think I may still have a ways to go." Praying was familiar territory for any minister. Philip's shoulders relaxed as he smiled and asked her to kneel as they prayed for her. As Lydia knelt before them, Philip and Kim leaned over her and laid their hands on her head. "Great God in heaven, please give your daughter, Lydia, the gift of your unconditional love. Place in her heart the wisdom to follow your path and show her the way. With this laying on of hands, we ask you to anoint her with the Holy Spirit to support and guide her. Please heal her heart and let your light and love shine there. In the name of Jesus, we pray. Amen."

As Lydia said, "Amen," she slowly rose to her feet. She thanked the couple for their compassion and support. Each hugged her as she reached the door to leave. She glanced around the room one last time and offered a silent prayer: *God, please give me wisdom and strength.* Her eyes stopped at the digital clock sitting on the TV. It said 12:34.

The Absolute Realm

The Master waited for Chester to settle onto the pillow. "You have wanted to know what caused the Earth to become so dark and chaotic that God had to personally repair it. Instead of telling you, I will show you. I am going to reveal to you the technique that has been used for thousands of years to pass this secret knowledge from Master to student. Your training is progressing well, and you are ready for the next phase."

Chester had become skillful at sitting in a balanced relaxed position either on the ground or on a pillow. He was good at clearing his mind of the thoughts that usually sabotaged any useful contemplation. The Master was patient and coached him by explaining logically what he was asking of him.

He had been practicing with the Master for about a week on a new technique. As he relaxed, he could barely hear the Master breathing. "Tonight we will both focus on the light." He had been taught to concentrate on the same image so the Master could lead him slowly and lend support all along the way. He concentrated on seeing a pinpoint of light become brighter inside the darkness of his mind's eye. The Master used a simple one-syllable tone to help his mind focus. The Master began slowly. "Aum, ommm, auoooooommmmmmm."

Chester focused on mimicking Master's exact sound and volume. Note for note, duration for duration, they finally got in perfect sync. When Chester stayed exactly with the Master's sound, the light got brighter. If his tone wandered, the light dimmed. Using that feedback, Chester closed in on the sound and the light until the brightness was complete.

The Master slowly lowered his voice until there was perfect quiet. Chester opened his eyes and said, "Wow!"

The Master opened his eyes and slowly inhaled.

Chester took a deep cleansing breath and whispered, "What exactly did I just experience?"

The Master whispered back, "You tell me what you experienced, and I will answer any questions you have."

"I approached the light like I had all this week. When you started the low tones, the light got so bright I was almost overwhelmed. When I joined you and finally got in sync with your voice, the light was so bright that all I experienced was total joy. There was nothing but peace, happiness and unlimited joy which had no end. What was that?

"The Absolute Realm."

Chester sat remembering that feeling and tried to come up with words to describe what had happened to him. During that moment in time, it was as if extremely bright, overpowering peace went on forever. Chester laughed and shook his head, "I experimented with some psychedelic mushrooms in college, but I never reached a high like that. How did I do that?"

The Master spoke softly but distinctly. "The Absolute Realm exists totally in the *Now*. You were not looking backward or forward but were experiencing being totally connected to God. You were one with the universe. The feeling was a glimpse of God's love and power. Remember the three absolutes of God?"

"I remember what you called them: Awareness, Eternity, and Infinity." Seemed like mumbo jumbo the first time I heard it. I didn't want to look stupid so pretended to understand what you were saying."

The Master grinned, "These make up three of the Seven Wisdoms. Your destiny and that of mankind is to be able to connect and stay connected to that peaceful, joyous awareness. You have the innate ability to access and fully experience unadulterated joy. The ability is called pure soul awareness. In the Absolute Realm, it is always *Now*. It is without beginning or end. That is eternity. There are no limits to how often you can have that feeling. It is unbounded and transcends space and time. When you're one with the universe, you are not only in the presence of God but you are aware of whom you are with. That feeling of complete peace is God's unconditional love protecting, guiding, and nourishing you. It has always been there and will always be there. Infinity is the third absolute of God. The word infinity is inadequate because God is also unbounded and unlimited and so is his love. The third absolute wisdom contains the knowledge that God is unbounded, unlimited and infinite." Sensing that Chester was finally comprehending, the Master continued, "I know you must have of heard of the term 'mystical.' A few moments ago, you found out what it means. It is a transcendent experience with God that goes beyond human emotion or logic. The only way I know how to express it in words is the simple phrase: *IT JUST IS*."

Chester didn't respond. Instead he closed his eyes. Within in a few moments he was once again experiencing the joy of the Absolute Realm.

Lydia's Dreams

Lydia sat up in bed, her heart pounding. Her lungs heaved as she panted in fear. Awakening in such a jarring manner caused her confusion. One hand slowly rubbed her forehead and cheek as she propped up herself with the other. *Another scary dream. Maybe I can remember what it was about this time. I think something heavy fell on top of me and I couldn't get up.* She reached for a pen by the nightstand but found just a pen cap. She blindly felt around the top of the table for the tablet she thought she had put on it last night but it wasn't there either. *I must have left it by the phone in the kitchen.* "Coffee!" She sleepily announced to the silent bedroom. She journeyed down the stairs from her bedroom to the kitchen precisely like a person who was on auto pilot. The coffeepot was still chugging as it cranked out drops of the hot fragrant liquid. Last night she had followed her usual bedtime routine of getting the pot ready and pushing the auto button. *Is the clock on the coffeepot running slow? It says 4:32 a.m.* She waited for the last drops to finish and poured a cup, topping it with a dollop of cream and cinnamon sprinkles. She cupped her hands around the warm container as she carried it into the living room. She slumped into the cushions of her favorite chair and sipped the chocolate-flavored brew. The clock on the VCR read 4:34. *Why am I up already? Did the alarm go off?*

I don't have to be up for another 15 minutes. Oh yeah, I had that crazy dream again. So that's why the coffee was still making. 4:45 am was the setting for her radio to come on, and the annoying buzzer blasted at 5:00 am. The coffeepot was programmed to start at 4:29 am. The caffeine was just kicking in when she heard the radio come on upstairs. *Time for my bath. I'll get to work early and maybe I can get some shopping done later.*

* * * *

"Yes sir. I confirmed your flight for two round tickets to Tokyo. You will get your tickets in the mail. Lydia scribbled a note on legal pad. "I'll make sure they're in the morning pickup. Thank you for letting DFW Travel Partners arrange your vacation. I hope you have a wonderful time." She spent a few minutes preparing the envelope. She relaxed a little after it was addressed, stamped, and ready. She put it in the growing pile in her "out" basket, looked at her watch, and buzzed her receptionist. "While it's quiet, I'm going to lunch. I'll be back in an hour or so." Her office had a door that opened directly into the hall. She liked her office because it was close to the elevators. Today she felt compelled to problem solve. The annoying part of the problem was that she didn't know what needed solving, but the answer must be at the mall. The ultimate mall was the Galleria. She had scheduled a lunch with Tina at the little French bakery near the skating rink. Lydia was a little early as usual and Tina was probably going to be a little late. The place wasn't that big so she knew Tina wouldn't have any trouble finding her.

She was on her second bread stick when Tina called out to her. "There you are. I'm so glad the traffic was kind. I thought I was going to be late." Lydia looked her watch by reflex. *12:34.*

"You're four minutes late and I was four minutes early. I say that makes us even." Before Tina sat down across from Lydia, the waitress was there.

"Do you want something to drink?"

Lydia and Tina chimed together, "Dr. Pepper." The waitress jotted on her pad and disappeared. Tina leaned forward with excitement. "Look, our first mall moment. Remember when we used to do that all the time? You usually don't drink Dr. Pepper. Have you ever had the original recipe? I have an uncle that is making a trip down to Dublin, Texas, where you can still get the original recipe."

"What do you mean 'original recipe?'"

"The company started in Dublin in 1891. For years they made Dr. Pepper with pure cane sugar, not corn sweeteners like you get nowadays. The only place you can still get it made with real sugar is in Dublin. My uncle won't drink anything else so he makes a special trip twice a year to stock up. He has his own antique bottles and everything. This time I asked him to get me a six-pack. I have to find out if it's really better or what. In a few weeks you and I can have a tasting party. Mercy, I'm just on a talking streak. How is it with you?"

"Well," Lydia hesitated. "Have you ever had the same dream over and over but still can't remember it?"

Tina raised her eyebrows. "I didn't see that one coming. My problem is I never have the same dream twice. I've had a few dreams I wouldn't mind putting on auto repeat," Tina chuckled.

"I'm serious. Lately it seems like I'm having the same dream over and over. I tried to remember to put pen and pencil by my bed, but I can't get a pen by the bed as part of my go to bed habits. I try to remember the dream in the morning, but as soon as I have my coffee I don't care anymore."

The waitress arrived with two glasses filled with dark fizzing liquid. Tina and Lydia both took sips before nodding their heads. "Have you decided what you're going to order?"

Both studied the specials scrawled in chalk at the back of the restaurant. Lydia decided first. "Give me the chicken croissant sandwich with French fries."

Tina worried her lower lip for a few seconds. "Hmm. I'm between the soup and the salad."

"We do have a soup and salad special."

"Great, you talked me into it."

As soon as they were alone again, Tina leaned forward and whispered, "Hey dream girl. I have the perfect solution to your problem. But first I have to tell you about Paul. He called and told me he is coming to Dallas for a three-month project about the new Internet. It's supposed to be like dial-up mainframe only it's spread all over the world."

Lydia allowed herself to rejoice with her friend. "I'm so happy. See, I told you that you wouldn't be sorry if you went to San Francisco with me. I hope everything works out. When did he tell you?"

"He called yesterday when I normally go on break and told me. It begins next month in September. He told me Chester had written and was somewhere in the jungle or something like that. He has to keep the lease on their condo since he doesn't know for sure when Chester will get back. The company he works for will pay his rent while he's in Dallas. They have a contract with a place that specializes in visiting executives and consultants. He does get two trips back home a month so he isn't going to be here all the time. The sad part is I'm going to be in Houston half the time with my new job."

"Oh yeah. I forgot about that. I just hope he doesn't zig when you zag. Isn't it weird how everything comes down to timing?"

"I know what you mean."

Their meals arrived. It was a welcome break. As Tina reveled in the soup, Lydia started at the pointed end of the sweet yellow bread. Tomatoes and lettuce hung out generously on both sides.

"Do you want me to give you those tickets to Six Flags? If Paul gets here around Labor Day weekend, you can have them. Both of you could have fun."

Tina shook her head. After a quick sip of Dr. Pepper, she replied. "Paul said it was not going to be by Labor Day. His current project is using Labor Day weekend to do some big computer swap over. You and I are still going to Six Flags."

The rest of the lunch was just the right amount of calories to energize two women for some serious shopping. They paid at their table and left a generous tip.

"I don't know which I liked better, the salad or the soup. Those wonderful croutons were in both."

"I shouldn't have eaten so many French fries, but I love how they make them here. So what is your solution to my dream problem?"

"Follow me. It's up about three levels." Tina chattered on the way. "After we get this, we should check out the bookstore and see if they have anything about interpreting dreams."

"I don't think I need a book like that."

Tina led Lydia into a store that catered to executives. A sharply dressed man walked around the check-out counter and smoothed, "Is there anything I can help you ladies with?"

Tina and Lydia looked at each other just a second before Tina charged on. "Do you have any of those new pocket recorders? You know so you can leave yourself messages while you drive and stuff?"

"Of course; we have several models. Some use tiny cassettes and some are digital which saves on cassette replacement costs, and they take smaller batteries making them slim and stylish."

"$199.00? What makes that one so special?"

The sales clerk laughed. "That's our top-of-the-line digital model. Has enough memory for 15 minutes of recorded sound."

"Do you have anything that is closer to $20.00?"

"Yes ma'am. That price range will use normal cassette tapes and is too large for most pockets. Here's one that is only $19.95."

Lydia discussed it with Tina. "What do you think?"

"I like the fact it uses regular-sized cassettes." Tina turned her attention back to the sales clerk. "Does it come with a cord for the cigarette lighter in the car?"

"That will be an extra $14.00."

Lydia shook her head. "I don't plan to use it in my car. I live close to where I work. I'll just take that one. Does it come with batteries?"

A few minutes later, a flick of a credit card and Lydia was holding a rustling bag filled with technology. Lydia looked at her watch. It read: 1:23. "This has been so much fun. I should get back somewhere around 1:30 to relieve my receptionist."

They hugged after they got off the elevators in the covered parking. "I'll call if I hear anything else about Paul."

"You better." Lydia got into her maroon Mazda Protégé and drove back to the office.

* * * *

That night Lydia was watching Ted Coppell discuss the Internet with Bill Gates. *Windows 95 is the most advanced multi-tasking operating system ever released. It comes standard with TCP/IP which is needed for accessing the Internet.* She turned the TV off. Before she made the coffee she made sure to load the batteries in her new cassette recorder and put it by the bed. Going to bed was easy enough. The last thought she had before falling asleep was wondering if her little company should upgrade from Windows 3.1.

She didn't have any disturbing dreams for the rest of the month. Since she left the tape recorder on the table by her bed, she had forgotten about the dreams. Her daily routine of work, eat, watch TV, and sleep blurred August together until Labor Day appeared. She had agreed to go with Tina to Six Flags. Tina promised to show up on time at nine in the morning. They had decided to go on Monday because they knew it was the slowest day of the three day weekend. It had been a summer ritual for her and Tina going back five years. In all of those years, Tina had never gotten her on the big roller coaster. Every year she tried, but every year she failed. The best she could do was to get Lydia to stand in line with her all the way to the point where Tina got into the coaster. She would cross over and wait on the side everyone exits. Lydia never could figure out why she was so afraid of roller coasters. Tina had told her on the phone that this was going to be the year. Lydia was beginning to think her life of routines and rituals was too limiting. She had been listening to a set of Wayne Dyer's tapes. He encouraged people to get out of their comfort zones. She decided Dr. Dyer was right and this was the year she would expand her horizons and ride the Texas Giant.

Tina knocked on the door. It was 9:04. Lydia grabbed her purse, making sure the tickets and a bottle of sunscreen were inside. They were off to Six Flags once again. Tina drove them in her Toyota Corolla. The longest line they had to deal with was the string of cars waiting to go into the first gate. The tickets she had were only good for the Labor Day weekend but they were free to travel agents around the area as part of Six Flag's marketing routine. Lydia liked to see the shows and Tina wanted to ride the bumper cars and play skeeball. They were able to time it so they saw every show, even the new Batman show. The time had come for the big decision.

Tina stomped her foot. "Come on, just this once ride the Texas Giant with me. I swear you will love it."

Lydia shook her head. "I'll go through the line with you, but I just can't. I don't know why. I just can't."

"You told me you were going to get out of your comfort zone. Come on, your horoscope even told you to do that."

Lydia was regretting she had told Tina about that. "Here's the deal. I'll think about it as we are in line."

Tina grinned. "That won't work this year. Come on girl, live a little."

Lydia stressed about it all the way through the line. When decision time finally arrived, she surrendered to the moment. Tina looked astonished as Lydia buckled into the third car from the front. *The Lord is my shepherd, I shall not want…*

Tina buckled up and held Lydia's hand. "Trust me, this will be so much fun."

Lydia's heartbeat pounded the sound of fear in her ears. Before she could change her mind, the whole coaster jerked a little as it moved forward. Lydia heard the harsh metallic clang of the giant bicycle chain kick in and clank ominously as it dragged six cars up the fourteen-story-high structure. The sound from within the car was like a jangling sound of doom. Slowly, steadily, it pulled her, Tina and twenty-two other people higher and higher. Her heart tried to beat its way out of her chest. She didn't realize how tall it was. When they reached the top, all six cars paused briefly, balanced between ascent and descent. Gravity did its job and the roller coaster plunged almost straight down forever. Forever in this case was almost two seconds. Lydia didn't remember when she started screaming, but she and Tina were in full scream the rest of the terrifying ride. A sharp intake of breath, and it was screaming time again. The sharp turns and unexpected drops made her entire belly, thighs, and groin explode into an almost weightless ecstasy every time they hit the top of a hill or the bottom of a plunge. As they coasted to the point of departure the screams turned into laughter. Lydia felt like she had just experienced the most intense two minutes of her life. Her legs were weak and her hands trembled as she stumbled out of the car. "Oh, my God. I can't believe I just did that."

Tina bubbled with laughter. "See what you have been missing these last five years. She pointed at the line forming at a row of television sets. Come on. Let's see what we looked like. Tina and Lydia crowded with the others around six TV monitors. Each one displayed four people, one for each car of the roller coaster. Tina pointed out that they were in the third car back so they should be on the third screen. Lydia started laughing again. Both of them had their mouths open wide, hair flying and leaning to the left.

Tina pulled Lydia with her to one of the windows. "Let's each get a T-shirt with our picture on it. They are only $16.00 a T-shirt. My treat so you can't say no."

Lydia's cheeks hurt from smiling. "All right, let do it. But I'm going to buy us both a coffee mug with our screaming faces on it. My treat, so you can't say no."

The rest of the day Lydia felt ten feet tall. They both agreed they were too tired to stay after dark. There was an endless supply of kids with an endless supply of energy, but they both had to work the next day. During the ride back, Lydia fell asleep. She yawned and sleepily said good-bye to Tina when she dropped her off. They hugged through the window. She was almost a zombie as she did her nightly routine. All she could think of was going to bed. She was exhausted. All the walking had made her legs sore. She collapsed sprawling onto the bed and fell asleep immediately. The sensations she had experienced all day molded her dreams into series of falls, swings, and the feeling of floating all sleepily woven together. In her dream, people screamed like on the roller coaster. The screams echoed in her head until the images changed from a roller coaster to a train. The train was trying to stop, and the squealing brakes sounded like screams for help. When the train started falling, Lydia jerked awake. Her heart was pounding, and she was terrified. She sat up and saw the tape recorder. Fumbling with the controls, she started describing the still-fresh dream in a sleep-slurred voice. "I was on a train. First it was like I was on a roller coaster but the screams were from people terrified. The train wrecked, and it was dark and wet and I became frightened. Just before I woke up, I realized I was on the train, and I was the one screaming." Lydia clicked off the recorder and sighed. Putting it aside she announced. "Coffee!"

The Dreams of God

The next evening Chester was full of expectations as he approached the meditation glade right before twilight. The Master was already there. Chester heard the grass rustle as he settled in. The Master began a simple repetition of 'Aum, aum...' Chester joined in.

This time, he had to force himself to breathe deeply to slow his heart rate. He was tense with anticipation. He finally accessed an old stress management technique by starting at his toes relaxing each of his muscles and working his way up his body until there was no tension left. As the muscles in his face and neck relaxed, his mind went blank. Slowly he could focus on a pinpoint of light. At first it got brighter and that same peaceful, joyous feeling he had experienced last night engulfed him. Then it retreated until the light was in the distance with nothing but darkness around it. He couldn't figure out why it looked flat and void. As he watched, a white line radiated upward and downward from the original light and pierced the darkness. Then another appeared at a 90-degree angle. When the third one appeared, he realized the view had suddenly gone from flat nothingness to three dimensions. It was like an architect creating the first draft of a complex building project or an artist making white brush strokes on a black canvas. As soon as the three-dimensional canvas appeared, the space filled with intricate vibrating lines, circles, and curls. They became even more animated and danced around like visual music changing form over and over. The patterns became more complex, more beautiful. Colors started appearing. Without preamble, the entire visual space exploded into multiple experiences. It appeared as if he was experiencing everything all at once. The lack of any recognizable patterns made the entire experience confusing and disorienting.

Chester didn't know how long he sat there watching this light show, but he was so fascinated he didn't want to stop. The shifting frames of color and images sped up. The closest thing Chester could relate it to was as if someone had edited a million scenes from a million movies into a random montage and then played it at a superfast speed. He opened his eyes after the images faded to find the Master patiently waiting to hear of his experience.

Chester described it as best he could. "What did I see? What didn't I see. The only way I can explain it is with a joke. I remember this cartoon where an old man was sitting with his index finger point up. The caption said, 'Time is God's way of making sure everything doesn't happen all at once.'" Chester laughed. "It was like time hadn't been invented yet and everything happened at once over and over but in different sequences. I know that doesn't make any sense. What I saw didn't either. Do you know what I mean?" Chester was struggling to find the right words. Before he could launch into another explanation, the Master saved him the trouble.

"Ahhhh…," the Master chuckled. "You saw the beginnings of the Dreams of God. You witnessed the first set of realities. You saw their beginning."

Chester interrupted. "Why do you say realities, plural?"

"Don't forget that one of the absolute aspects of God is infinity. When the first primitive yet infinite realities began, they were without structure or meaning. That's why the earliest realities are known as the Realm of Chaos."

Chester nodded. "Hmmm. Did you know that recently science has uncovered a new mathematical model for describing the dynamics of the universe? It's called chaos theory. In essence, everything in the physical world is based on chaos which is why long-term predictions about anything are essentially impossible."

"The Realm of Chaos is the foundation of all reality. God manifested the space for creation by withdrawing his glory. What you remembered was the beginning of reality based on dimensions, sounds, textures and change but without an organization or a set pattern placed on it."

"What do you mean? *I remembered*?"

"The part of you that is pure awareness has existed for eternity and always will. Your awareness was there at the beginning. I have just shown you how to recall the memory. Soon you will need no help to recall your heritage, your memory of eternity."

* * * *

The next night Chester was eager for his lesson. As a scientist he had the opportunity to know the answers to all the questions ever asked. As soon as the Master began, Chester found himself transported back to the beginning of all realities based on dimension and sound. He watched as God dreamed of reality. He was intensely awed as he watched the cup of dreams spread out like rivers overflowing their banks. God dreamed of infinite possibilities in an instant, and infinity multiplied by infinity as God created indescribable patterns in one awesome instant of the *Now*. The Realm of Chaos was the first of many universes to exist outside the Absolute Realm.

For a long time, God only watched the dreams. The newest delight was when God began to alter their flow and pattern by switching from observer to participant. God purposed to remove from reality confusion by actively taking part in the dreams until they became patterns of incredible complexities that grew with beauty, precision, and majesty.

When God achieved his goal, the time of chaos was over; and the dawn of the Perfect Realm began.

Chester lost his sense of identity as he merged with the beauty. He was remembering his participation in the new Realm of Perfection. Once the Eternal controlled the expanding patterns, he crafted them into greater and grander vistas. The Perfect Realm's changing patterns were joyous to experience. The Perfect Realm resonated in the Eternal Now as a perfect blend of sound, textures and color. Chester gloried in the ecstasy of colors, patterns, and dimensions dancing to the perfect control of the Eternal's Infinite Awareness. God completely erased chaos from the *Now*. Yet there was something chaos had that was desirable. Perfection lacked the new and the unexpected. During the time of chaos, it was continuity and predictability that God sought. Surprise was in every shifting frame of chaos, but surprise had been removed in the search for perfection. God wanted predictability *and* surprise to exist in balance. The seed of a new realm was sown.

As Chester opened his eyes, he breathed out noisily. "Master, I'm overwhelmed. How do I remember so much history in less time than it takes to eat my dinner?"

"It is the nature of memory. Can't you remember your past without regard to the time it took to make the memory?"

Chester nodded his head, but the experiences were becoming more and more difficult to sort out.

Lydia Visits Mary Again

Mary looked through the receptionist window and saw Lydia sitting in the lobby. Until late last week she thought Lydia wouldn't return. Last Friday Lydia had called and scheduled an appointment for 4:00 pm. Mary pushed aside the door leading to the inner office and smiled at Lydia. "It's so good to see you again, Lydia."

"You, too."

"Would you like anything to drink? We have some Gatorade or water."

"Water, please."

"The Gatorade is from my bowling league. We drink it while we bowl. I can't tell if it helps or not but it has become a part of our Thursday night ritual." Mary was hoping to get Lydia talking about anything. She pulled two bottles of spring water out of the freezer section of the mini refrigerator.

Lydia open and sipped one. "It's very cold, I like that."

Mary acted like the water temperature was the real subject of the day. "I guess I keep it that way because when I was a kid I used to eat grape ice cones until I got a brain freeze. Have you ever had a brain freeze?"

Lydia nodded and smiled. "I got my first one from eating orange sherbet too fast. I'll never forget it. I wasn't sure what was happening. I dropped my spoon and held my head with both hands and started crying and screaming. It was so intense I thought my head had exploded. Then it went away. My mother was laughing so hard. She tried to apologize. Then she told me about her first brain freeze at a family reunion where they had homemade ice-cream."

Mary added thoughtfully. "Wouldn't it be nice if all of our problems would go away by just pausing long enough for the pain to go away?"

Lydia sighed and nodded her head. "I thought my problems had gone away."

"Are they back?"

"Not exactly like before. When I first came in here, it was because I was depressed."

"Are you still depressed?"

"No. I take a purple pill in the morning and I'm fine. In some ways I would prefer feeling depressed to what I have been through this last month."

Mary shifted in her chair. "Go on."

Lydia opened her purse and took out a cassette tape and a VHS tape. "I don't think I am having any problems with what is on the VHS tape. If you want you can watch it. It didn't turn out anything like I had expected."

"Is that from Kentucky?"

"Yes. To make a long journey and a long story short and simple, it turns out I wasn't possessed and probably never have been possessed by a demon or the Devil. I guess you knew that all along. It is what is on the cassette tape that is giving me problems now."

Mary held it up. It had no markings and was rewound.

"I don't want to sit and listen to it with you unless you think we should. I can tell you exactly what's on there because it's a recording of me remembering my dreams after I wake up."

Mary queried, "This cassette is a recording of your dreams?"

"Yes. I have been having nightmares almost every night. I started recording what they were about. Before that I could never remember what the dream was. Every time I listened to what I had recorded, I would remember the dream."

"What is so disturbing about these dreams?"

"The most disturbing?" Lydia raised her hands and dropped them and then watched them as if the answer was somehow in the bowl of her palms. Speaking to her hands she confessed, "It turns out it is the same dream every time. I don't even have to go to sleep anymore. It's like the dream is a loop in my head going over and over like one of those pictures of a hurricane you see on the weather channel."

Outwardly Mary nodded as if this was within her scope of experience. Inwardly she marveled at how this seemingly normal individual kept having extraordinary experiences. "Can you describe the dream or would it be too uncomfortable for you."

"I can tell you. Maybe if I knew why I was having it, I could have some peace of mind. At first I thought I was dreaming about something that happened at Six Flags. Labor Day weekend my best friend and I went to Six Flags. I rode the giant wooden roller coaster for the first time. That night I dreamed of the roller coaster, but it turned into a dream of a train having a terrible wreck. Every since that night I have had the same dream about the train wrecking. I'm on the train, and I wake up screaming."

"How long does the dream last?"

"I'm not sure. Sometimes it starts back at home with my mother and father. Sometimes it starts with me and my mother on the train. It always ends with the train falling off a bridge into deep water. The weird part about the dream is that even though I'm with my mother and father, it's not my mother and father."

"What do you mean?"

"Have you ever had a dream where you know everything needed for the dream to make sense? It's like you know where you are and who you are with and you don't question it as long as you have the dream."

Mary nodded slowly.

"It's like that except the people who I know are my mother and father, aren't my mom and dad when I'm awake. Does that make sense?"

Mary nodded. "Yes, at least so far it does. I've had dreams where I'm married and it didn't seem strange even though I have never been married. Maybe it was my subconscious mind telling me I should get married." Mary laughed. "I don't know. Maybe your dream is about something your subconscious wants you to know about." Lydia curled her chin up and considered what she had said. Mary took the silence as permission to continue. "Remember your baby book?" Lydia nodded and focused on Mary, her eyebrows drawn toward each other. "I remember you said you never wanted to see it again or that you would never read it. But..." Mary held up her hand as Lydia sat up and opened her mouth to resist. "Wait. All I want to do is show you a drawing you made as a little girl that your mom kept for you. Not only did she write down what you said, but she kept drawings you made for her. Some of them go with the stories you told your mom. May I show you just one of those drawings right now?"

Lydia remained stiff and erect in the chair. After a pause she relaxed slightly and nodded her head. "Okay."

Mary got up and went to a filing cabinet and opened the second drawer. Near the front, she pulled out a thick folder. A major portion of the folder was a large baby book. The back of the baby book bulged with yellowing paper. One of the large folded items was made of manila paper. Mary examined it briefly to make sure it was the right one before passing it on to Lydia. Lydia's eyes watered immediately. The drawing was obviously a child's. The black and red crayon marks revealed a simple two-dimensional representation of a train broken and lying on its side. Two stick figures laid about with their eyes closed.

Lydia's eyes filled to overflowing. Her distress was in her tears but her voice was under control. "Why is a train wreck so important to me all of a sudden?"

Mary replied. "It also appears that it was an important subject when you were a child."

Lydia's control never wavered but neither did the tears. "I'm crying yet I don't feel sad."

Mary paused, unsure if it was safe to continue. "Is it okay if I read a small portion of your mom's journal about you?"

Lydia didn't answer but dried her tears instead. Finished, she held the tissue in her lap, just in case. "Oh, why not."

Mary cocked her head a little. "Are you sure?"

Lydia took a deep breath and nodded her head as she noisily breathed out.

Mary got up and sat at her desk with the file. She found one that was marked with a yellow tab. From her desk she read out loud. "*Today Lydia waited for her daddy to leave for work. After he left, she wanted to tell me a secret. She told me the secret about the train wreck she was in. The last two times she had tried to tell the story her daddy had threatened to whip her for telling lies. As she told the story of a girl and her mommy riding a train, she drew me a picture. It was of a train wreck. Lydia told me that she and her mother went to visit her grandparents. Before they got there, she and her mother died in a train wreck. This was the third time Lydia wanted to talk about her train ride. Neither of us has ever been on a train. Her father knew that and scolded Lydia for telling lies about trains. She made me promise to keep it a secret.*" Mary looked up from her desk at Lydia. "This is not the only one in here about a train wreck. Do you want me to read some more out of your baby book? It is about trains."

Lydia's leaned forward and drank deeply from the bottle. The cold sweat on the outside ran down her arm and made her shiver a little. "I don't know if I'm ready. If I let you read more, will I stop having the dreams?"

"I wish I knew for sure that it would. All I can do is tell you that it was important to your mother that you had access to this information when the time was right. You tell me when the time is right, Lydia; and I will hand you your baby book so you can read it."

Lydia shook her head. "Go ahead. Read it to me."

Mary picked out another page marked with an adhesive strip of red plastic. "*Today Lydia told me she used to be a grown up girl before she rode the train. In a serious tone she said that her father was mad at her because he didn't want her to go anywhere. I couldn't find out which father she was talking about. Later she admitted to me in her sweet innocent voice, that if she hadn't made her father mad he would have been on the train and died too. She went on playing with her doll as if all four-year-old children talked about dying*"

Lydia raised her hand and pleaded. "That is enough. I have heard enough for today."

Mary dropped the yellowed paper and came around to sit across from the coffee table. Lydia wrapped the tissue over and over around her little finger. She braved eye contact. As Mary sat down, Lydia forced a smile and found a nervous laugh. "I'm not sure what is going on. It looks like I have been dreaming about a story I made up as a child. I had a vivid imagination for a four-year-old. I must have had if I still dream about my train wreck story."

Mary watched Lydia stare into space and talk it out.

"I want to know what the dream is about." She focused on Mary.

Mary paused as if trying to find the right words. "I have a colleague that specializes in death and near-death experiences. This dream about dying on a train is similar to the near-death experiences she has studied for years. Would you be comfortable discussing this with a psychologist that specializes in this?"

Lydia shifted and stroked her hair back. She blinked a few times. "Who is she?"

"She is a research psychologist who has experience helping people who are dealing with extraordinary circumstances. To be honest with you, I think you need a special kind of help I can't give you."

"Where is she?"

"Her offices are in Arlington near the university."

"Do you think she is available?"

Mary nodded. "I will need to call her and set up an appointment. Is that all right with you?"

Mary got up and sat down at her desk. She looked up Crystal's office number and dialed it. Mary looked at Lydia as she talked with the receptionist. "Is she in? Yes, I can hold." Mary held her hand over the mouthpiece and stage-whispered to Lydia. "She is on another line. I'm on hold. The on-hold music is Steely Dan. I don't know why I told you that but it is my favorite band. I'll have to tell you..." Mary dropped her hand. "Hello. Yes. Great." Mary covered the mouthpiece again and whispered. "Her name is Crystal, and she knows we are on the second line and said it wouldn't be long." Mary dropped her hand to respond. "Hi, Crystal. Sounds like you have been busy. I have a patient I would like to refer to you." Mary looked at Lydia as she listened. "How is your calendar for next week?" Mary nodded at Lydia. "Hold on, I'll ask." Mary focused on Lydia. "Next Tuesday at 4:00 good for you?"

Lydia looked at her the pocket calendar she kept in her purse. She nodded quietly.

Mary wrapped it up. "Okay, I understand. I have to go, too. I'll call you later."

Lydia sighed again. "When will this ever end?"

The Angelic Realm

Chester's body was with the Master, but his mind melted into the divine memory. He watched as God purposed to create beings of independence. God began to divide his Awareness into specific roles. God created a reflection of his awareness and gave the reflection purpose. Chester watched the beginning of God's awareness separating into countless viewpoints.

He saw God bring into the dream beings of beauty and intellect with a sense of self. It was as if he watched and joined in at the same time. He found himself unable to tell when he was himself or when he was God. As God separated his awareness into viewpoints, he gave each viewpoint permanent independence and free will. As each viewpoint became fully formed, it would slowly became brighter and brighter.

Somehow he knew that each new being of light would never die nor would it progress or deviate from its newly created purpose. God set their design and role for all eternity. God created the angels to share the dream with him and to help guide the dream. God sent their independent awareness into the infinities. Billions of angels filled the *Now*. They revealed realities for God by discovering the possibilities God had created. God used the angels to carry out his will in the discovered realities. This created memories from many viewpoints. The multiple-viewpoint past began as soon as God created independent minds with awareness. The angels began existence with no individual memory. That which the created views becomes part of the past, and that which is yet unobserved is the future. From the time of the first angel, individual pasts and futures had meaning for the first time.

The evening lesson had ended but Chester wanted to continue. Instead of lying down on his cot, he decided to see if the Master was right about him being able to access the ancient memories without the Master's help. With practiced ease, he sat on his bed and began the deep breathing exercises leading up to the thoughtless state. He soon found himself immersed in the memory of the Angelic Realm. There were three beings of great power and glory that ruled over the other light beings. Each majestic being was a leader over a third of the others. He saw a path paved with stones of fire lead away from the Throne of the Eternal. Some of the stones were bright and others just managed to eek out a dull glow. The beings of light walked up and down the path of fiery stones. If he focused on one particular angel, he could follow it as it went on its journeys. The angels could walk into any stone, and he discovered that he could follow them whenever they entered one. Once inside, the beings' brightness uncovered the marvels within. Each stone contained a universe. He noticed whenever an angel entered one that was dull, the stone glowed brightly after the angel left. An angel could walk into any stone it chose and discover universe after universe. Each stone contained a universe more beautiful and incredible than the last. Some were like gardens and some were like geometric mazes that went on forever in their beauty and complexity. He began to realize that every stone contained a universe that was similar yet slightly different. Some of them looked like universes with stars and planets while others had a completely different makeup. Each stone contained a universe that worked off a set of laws different from the others. The longer he watched the longer it appeared as if the billions of angels were looking for something. He became lost in the splendor and forgot who he was or why he was there as he traveled in memory throughout the universes.

Mary Visits Crystal

Mary pulled into Crystal's driveway. Tonight, Crystal was cooking Italian food for Mary. She made the best meatless lasagna Mary had ever tasted.

Crystal opened the door almost immediately. "You got here just in time. Dinner is almost ready." As they greeted each other, Crystal's cockatoo Peaches whistled from the other room. "She hates to be alone. Why don't you keep her company, and I'll bring dinner out in a minute."

As Mary walked into the room, Peaches bobbed her head and squawked, "Mary had a little lamb."

"I love it when she does that," Mary laughed.

Crystal called from the kitchen, "It wouldn't be Peaches if she didn't do that when she saw you. My dining table is knee-deep with research material. Would you get the TV trays out?"

"Sure. Need any help in there?"

"No, I'm fine. Thanks." Crystal returned carrying forks and napkins. "What do you want to drink?"

"Have any iced tea made?"

"I do and I think you'll love it. It's raspberry flavored. Do you want anything on your salad? I have ranch, thousand island, and Italian."

"I'll take thousand island."

Crystal came in carrying a wide tray. Bread dripping with garlic butter surrounded piles of steaming lasagna. Two large salads were overflowing with shredded lettuce and tomatoes cut into tiny pieces topped with grated parmesan cheese. Tasting the first bite of pasta, Mary moaned, "I love this stuff what do you put in it?"

"It's cottage cheese, fresh vegetables, marinara sauce, *secret* spices, parmesan, Romano, ricotta, and mozzarella cheese. It's mostly flavored cheese wrapped in pasta. The vegetables are always different with each batch I cook. I just raid the fridge and throw in what's there. This time, I used broccoli, carrots, zucchini, mushrooms and, of course, bell pepper and onions."

"I thought vegetarians didn't eat animal products?"

"I keep it simple. I don't eat anything with a face; but I eat eggs, milk and cheese."

The bird frantically paced back and forth on her perch. Mary notice and said, "I bet she's hungry. What can I give her to eat?"

Crystal jumped up. "I'm sorry. I forgot her salad." She hurried into the kitchen and came back with a bowl heaped with raw vegetables and poured it into Peaches' stainless steel cup. Peaches started eating the broccoli, carrots, cauliflower. What she didn't eat, she slung onto the floor."

Mary laughed. "Goodness, she's messy."

Crystal defended her. "Not any messier than I am. You should see my kitchen. I'll put up with the mess if she'll eat right. It took me forever to get her to eat vegetables instead of just nuts."

Mary moaned again. "My…gosh, this is good tea. How many different flavors does it come in?"

"Don't know for sure. My favorite is peach, but I used it all up last Sunday and haven't been to the store."

Both Mary and Crystal sat in silence as they finished their lasagna and salad. Mary finally pushed the TV tray away and held her stomach. "I wish you hadn't made it taste so good. Now I'm miserable."

"I know. Lasagna is my weakness. I try not to have any unless it's a special occasion. Your coming over is a special occasion."

"Thank you. But if I come over too often, I won't fit into any of my clothes." Crystal laughed as Mary got up, grabbed both plates, and stacked the salad bowls on top.

Crystal picked up the silverware and the tea glasses and followed Mary into the kitchen. As Mary went back out and put up the TV trays, Crystal clinked ice into the glasses and filled them up with tea.

Back in the living room Mary was picking up the chunks of vegetables scattered around Peaches' perch. Crystal motioned for her to stop. "Don't worry about that. I have to cleanup around her every night before I go to bed anyway. Just relax."

Mary sat down and sighed. "Thank you so much. That was great!"

Crystal joined her on the couch and turned to face her. "It's going to cost you. What can you tell me about Lydia? I see her tomorrow."

"She took a trip to Kentucky."

"Oh?"

"She told me that she had visited some good Christian people. They helped convince her that she isn't demon possessed. She didn't give me much detail, but it tells me that she has made an important step on her own initiative. That means she isn't a quitter. She's stubborn but not a quitter."

"What about the stuff written in her baby book?"

"As it turns out; she thinks that it was just the imagination of a young child. But now she is having dreams that disturb her. My gut feeling says that her subconscious is trying to tell her something. Unfortunately, I have no experience dealing with what she is up against now. That is why I referred her to you."

Crystal paused. "About those memories of hers, do you think they could have been just something she made up when she was a child?"

Mary shook her head. "I don't know. I gave Lydia her baby book back. She will probably bring it with her when she sees you. Based on what I've read, it doesn't sound like something a child could make up."

Crystal shifted into the couch and got more comfortable. "Slight change of subject? I've had a shift of thinking in my research lately. In fact, it seems I'm always running into reports or research that suggests reincarnation is a valid or even reasonable explanation for otherwise inexplicable circumstances."

Mary stiffened and raised her eyebrows. "What do you mean?"

Crystal leaned forward. "You know how when you buy a new car, after you start driving it, every other car on the road looks like yours. But before you bought it, you never noticed one on the road?"

Mary nodded and waited for Crystal to continue.

"Lately it's been like that about reincarnation. Every time I turn around, it seems I'm either reading or hearing about some strange event where reincarnation is the most logical explanation for what happened."

Mary relaxed a little and nodded her head. "I'm with you. What have you run across?"

Crystal smiled back and said, "I've been reading a book written by S. Robert Tralins who researched incredible, bizarre but factual events."

"I still can't accept that reincarnation is credible, but I'll listen and try to have an open mind."

"I can live with that. There is one story in particular that got my attention. It's a story corroborated by eyewitness accounts. It happened about twenty years ago or so in Florida. There was this teacher who had just started teaching and something strange happened on her first day of school. She was teaching first graders or second graders. Anyway, these kids were about six or seven. After the end of her first day, one of the little girls came up and asked the teacher to give her doll back."

Mary frowned "I'm assuming you're telling me that this was the first time she had ever seen this girl?"

"Right, she told the little girl that she didn't have her doll. But the girl insisted that the teacher had her doll named Rebecca. She even described her doll. She said it had on a pink dress, curly blond hair, and one eye that always stayed closed."

Mary shook her head. "This is strange."

Crystal nodded her head. "It gets stranger. She wasn't sure why, but she felt she had to check it out. That night the teacher went into the attic and found the box of dolls she had saved from her childhood. It turns out she had a doll that did fit the little girl's description, broken eye and all."

Mary smiled and started humming the theme song for *The Twilight Zone.*

Crystal crossed her heart and said, "I swear this is supposed to be a true story."

Peaches wanted to get into the conversation and squawked "I'm a pretty bird, you're a funny bird."

Both of them laughed so hard they almost couldn't catch their breath. Just as they were about to regain control, Peaches sent them into more peals of laughter by mimicking their laughter, guffaws and all. Mary finally caught her breath. "My goodness she's a hoot."

Crystal wiped her tears and took a deep breath. "She always amazes me when she has something to say that fits the context of what is going on. Now where was I? Oh yes, she took the doll she had found to school the next day. When school was over the little girl marched up to the teacher and again asked if she had brought her doll back. The teacher opened her drawer and pulled out a doll that matched the little girl's description. The little girl acted happy and grabbed the doll. The teacher asked her, 'How do you know for sure that is Rebecca? There must be a lot of dolls that have pink dresses and broken eyes.' This is the part that made it sound like *The Twilight Zone.* The little girl told her she could prove it because she had drawn a red heart on the doll's chest. She unbuttoned the doll's dress and there was a red heart outlined in red crayon. To make it even stranger, the little girl acted surprised the teacher hadn't remembered when she drew the heart on Rebecca at a tea party. That was when the teacher remembered something that happened when she was in first grade. Her best friend used to come over and play tea party with her. The doll was left at her house because her friend was supposed to return the next day for another tea party. But before her friend could make it back, she and her mother were in a terrible car crash that killed them both."

Chills were running up and down Mary' spine and her eyes were swimming in unshed tears. "Your story is breaking my heart."

Crystal nodded. "I know. The teacher had blocked it from her memory since she was a little girl because it was so painful."

Mary nodded. "In a twisted way, it sounds a little like Lydia, doesn't it? Speaking of Lydia, I have taken her as far as I can. You are the only one I know who may be able to help her further."

Crystal hugged her friend. "I spent five years as a clinician before branching out into teaching and research. I've had plenty of experience with people experiencing the seemingly inexplicable. Thank you for trusting in me enough to refer her to me. My goal will be to help her; you know that."

"Well, my goal right now is to go home. I have to get up early tomorrow."

The War of the Angels

Chester could hear himself yelling faraway. He woke up to find the Master sitting next to him and shaking him. He tried to talk and found words hard to reach. Finally Chester was able to stammer…"I saw a being of incredible light and beauty become a dragon and start a horrific war. Divine beings fought against other divine beings. One third fought with the dragon and another third fought against the Dragon. The power expended on both sides was mindboggling. It is painful to even remember or to describe it." Chester pressed his fingertips to his temples. "Once again I'm at a loss for words."

The Master was concerned. "How did this happen?"

Chester admitted. "Instead of going to sleep I decided to watch the memories. It was easy to start back up where we left off earlier tonight. But along the way it turned into a nightmare."

The Master sighed. "You are like a child that tries to run before it can walk. You have already walked where angels fear to tread, so I guess I can share the entire story with you. I'll explain the symbol of the dragon. Maybe in the telling you will find peace from the terrible images you saw." Chester just nodded and caught his breath. "Let's go into my study, we can talk there."

Sanjiv was standing in the hallway holding a candle. The Master and Chester followed Sanjiv into the study. Sanjiv left them alone after the Master had turned on a light and nodded that it was okay for him to go. He and the Master settled into the same chairs they had used for countless talks such as these.

The Master began his explanation. "God created three Archangels: Michael, Gabriel, and the one who became the Dragon. These guardian cherubs administered the government of God throughout the Angelic Realm. Each was perfectly crafted and gifted at walking among the stones of fire. Walking among the stones of fire is how angels enter any reality found among the infinities. God gave great power and authority to the three Archangels. They were created to reflect majesty and beauty of the highest quality. The one created as the being of the greatest light and brilliance is sometimes referred to by the Latin word for 'morning star': *Lucifer*. I will use this Latin word as his name. No one knows what his name was before his rebellion, and God has banned its use forever. This brilliant being pleased God because his brightness lit up the infinities thus manifesting the jewels of reality. God created all possibilities; but until they are observed, they are only potential realities. The angels became God's instruments of awareness, peering into the infinite possibilities and manifesting realities. Lucifer brought many beautiful realities before the throne of the Eternal. His awareness was sharp and keen, and Lucifer found many splendors hidden in the infinite possibilities God had set into motion. Then came the time when God brought forth the search for the greatest jewel of all. God created within one of the infinities a realm where the possibility of physical life existed. The pattern of this universe had been expanding for some time, and God declared the time had come for the unveiling of the blue and green jewel. Thus began the Game of Angels. For it was in this new and beautiful expanse called the heavens that God had placed a bright and wonderful jewel, a world where life was growing and changing. The search for the Jewel of God lasted for millions of years."

Chester nodded. "I saw fiery stones that glowed bright within. Each one was a slightly different color. I watched as angels would stand on a stone and enter it. It looked like they were walking down glowing steps."

The Master agreed. "Each stone represented a set of infinities. Within the stone was everything that could or would ever possibly happen within that universe."

Chester reflected. "This sounds a lot like infinite-set theory. Two different sets can both contain an infinite number of objects, but one infinite set isn't necessarily equal to another."

The Master paused in his explanation. "Give me an example. You might be onto a great truth."

"Simple example. Let's say I have a set of infinite odd numbers. And, there is another set of infinite numbers that are even and can be divided by ten. Even though they are both infinite sets, neither set contains what is in the other. Also, one set has only every one out of every ten even numbers. They are both infinite yet not equal."

The Master rubbed his chin. "This is exactly why the angels searched among the infinities. What the infinities contained were just possibilities. The angels had the privilege and the power to unveil realities by observing. God didn't just create one universe. God created an infinite number of potential universes that exist unrealized until seen. Lucifer illuminated the infinite universes of the physical realm until he found the blue and green jewel God promised existed."

Chester was astounded. "You are describing the Many Worlds Solution to Quantum wave functions. I used that in my debate with Lydia."

The Master brought Chester back to the lesson by saying, "I remember when I first accessed the same memory vision you did. Throughout the Angelic Realm the news instantly spread. Lucifer had discovered the jewel God had revealed was waiting to be found. It was waiting in the infinities containing the Physical Realm. The angels gazed in wonder at the miracle jewel before bursting into song."

Chester remembered more of the vision. "I saw a blue and green jewel of incredible complexity dancing to the rhythm of life. The blue was from the ocean that teamed with life. Life was just beginning to discover the land, carpeting it with an emerald green growth. It was a beautiful world full of strange wonders."

The Master was caught up in the memory. "Never before had the patterns of God been so complex or dynamic in their interactions. God allowed every angel to visit the miracle world. The wonder of ever-improving life had been found among the infinities, and God wanted to share his most divine jewel among his eternal angels. All of them loved the new reality, but none loved or wanted it as much as Lucifer. God sensed Lucifer's desire. God had compassion and moved to grant Lucifer his wish and commanded him to occupy the newly discovered world with instructions for him and his angels to help guide the simple souls to their supreme potential. Lucifer felt power and desire for the first time as he took possession and authority of the most beautiful jewel he had ever found for God. Lucifer ruled the Earth for billions of years. God guided the progress on Earth several times by having Lucifer alter the environment to speed up the evolution of life. God had a grand plan that needed evolution to produce ever more intelligent beings. After the age of the great lizards, a new form of life came on the scene with warm blood, hair and intelligence. It was the age of mammals. About 2 million years ago proto-man appeared."

Chester snapped his fingers. "I saw Cro-Magnon man from about 40,000 years ago. Not long after that, I remember seeing the dragon for the first time. The dragon knocked a third of the stars out of the sky. After that the horror began."

The Master nodded. "About 7,000 years ago, Lucifer became jealous of the souls and bodies evolving and living on the Earth because he discovered the souls on this blue and green jewel had a holy and divine purpose."

"He became jealous?" Chester scratched his head. "I thought God told Lucifer his plan from the beginning? You said Lucifer was commanded to help the souls achieve their full potential."

"Lucifer finally realized the full meaning of what a soul's ultimate potential would be. God's plan was to create millions and billions of god beings through soul evolution."

Chester shook his head as if confused. "Why did this upset Lucifer so much?"

The Master paused as if making sure he had Chester's attention, "Lucifer felt betrayed by God. Lucifer thought he would always be the most glorious being in all the Infinite Realities. Instead, he discovered that God was creating His own children by the billions thus making them His heirs to His kingdom, power, and glory. It was Lucifer's pride to always be the highest. Lucifer felt he had to uphold his most high status at all cost.

"What cost?"

"The cost was a War of Angels of such violence that it eventually ended the Jewel of Earth's capacity to sustain life. Lucifer made war against the throne of the Eternal. God commanded Michael to resist Lucifer. What you saw was Michael and his angels battling with Lucifer and his angels. Lucifer tried to overthrow Heaven but was defeated and hurled back to Earth like a bolt of lightening. The angels that rebelled with him were hurled down with him. God had commanded Lucifer to watch over this Earth, and Lucifer had not yet been relieved of his duty. He became enraged at his banishment to the Earth he had once desired and now had come to hate. To add insult to injury, he was still under the command of God to help mankind achieve its destiny. This further enraged Lucifer. It was loathsome to him to be commanded to help beings achieve a station higher than he could achieve. He saw God as holding him back and betraying him. The Mother Earth contained the seed of billions of gods. God seeds that someday would all exist higher, more glorious and more powerful than Lucifer so he devised a plan to destroy the Earth's life-giving properties. This is how the Earth eventually became chaotic and empty of life as described in Genesis 1:2."

"So, when God repaired the earth around 6,000 years ago, it was to undo the damage from the War of the Angels?"

"Lucifer destroyed this world's ability to support life because he wanted to stop the soul evolution. Lucifer discovered that as the souls cycled through many lives that God was making it possible for them to have enough opportunities to discover their God Consciousness. The Rebellion of Lucifer is the missing information that ties evolution and creation together. God changed Lucifer's name to Satan which means 'enemy' or 'adversary.'"

"Let me see if I have the timeline right. God created this universe with the ability for life to evolve. After Lucifer found it, God placed him in charge to help the souls achieve their god destiny. Lucifer didn't figure that out until man evolved. Once he did, he destroyed Earth's life-sustaining properties in an attempt to eliminate God's heirs?"

"Yes, which is why the first chapter of Genesis is about God repairing the Earth. It isn't a description of God creating the entire universe in seven days; it is a description of God restoring the Earth's ability to support life."

"So evolution and Genesis really are both right. That is incredible."

The Master stood up and walked to the door. He turned around and said. "Try to get some sleep. I think we are done with the visions. You have learned what you needed to learn."

"Wait. I'm not done."

The Master didn't raise his voice but it did resonate with authority. "We can talk in the morning. It's quite late, and I am going back to bed."

Lydia meets Crystal

Crystal's office had an academic flavor about it. The chairs were wooden and the hint of mustiness and age peeked out of corners and from under tables. It was as if age had a smell that conquered all attempts at cleanliness. She was in a room that looked like it doubled as storage when no one used it as a waiting room. The fluorescent lights had an annoying hum. Lydia had chosen to dress down. Everybody on campus wore blue jeans and t-shirts. She held her baby book in her lap. Crystal's office door was closed. There was nothing to read but the school newspaper. *I wonder if going back to a therapist means I have no faith in God. Mary said that Dr. Gibson knows how to help people experiencing the paranormal. I'm sure demons are paranormal.* Crystal's door opening broke Lydia from her negative self-talk. She watched as a student shrugged her backpack into place as she headed for the elevators. Crystal looked like a breath of fresh air as she introduced herself to Lydia. Holding out her hand she announced. "I'm Dr. Gibson but everybody calls me Crystal."

Lydia took her hand and stood up at the same time. "Pleased to meet you. I'm Lydia Masters."

Crystal motioned for Lydia to enter her office. The thick wooden door sounded solid as it closed behind her. Plants filled Crystal's office.

The contrast of Crystal's jungle and the stark waiting room caught Lydia by surprise. "I compensate for my office and workrooms being in the basement by giving myself and my students plenty of plants. I have found that they have a calming effect."

Lydia looked around at the ivy and ferns. "This is beautiful."

"This is my office for paperwork. All the real work happens in the next room."

Lydia followed her into a room that had fewer plants because technical equipment was everywhere. A video camera was in the corner. Two soft and comfortable chairs dominated one side of the room. Lydia picked the one nearest her and Crystal the other. "It seems all technical in here."

"Don't worry about that. All we will need is a tape recorder or the video camera. I use both as a backup. Right now, we will use neither. We need to talk and get to know each other."

Lydia felt comfortable. Crystal took control without being bossy. It was a good start. "I guess Mary told you about me?"

"Let me put it this way, enough to convince me that I could help you but not enough to get started." Crystal's confidence permeated the room. "Can I see the baby book?"

Lydia was eager to get rid of it. She still couldn't shake the feeling that it was an indictment against her. As Crystal looked through the book, Lydia volunteered some information just to fill the silence. "The baby book part is normal; it's the papers in the back that freak me out. And those drawings."

Crystal held up about a half dozen sheets covered front and back with beautiful flowing script. She left the drawings in the back of the book. "Mind if I read a couple of pages to get a sense of what we are dealing with?"

Lydia nodded. "I could only read the first page. I don't know why. I just couldn't continue."

Crystal looked up. "In our case this is good. If we are able to corroborate any of this information, especially the stuff you shouldn't know about, the credibility will be higher."

"Why is that?"

"In most cases like this, hypnosis is considered the high percentage route for uncovering suppressed memories." Lydia jerked at the word hypnosis. *I can't let myself be vulnerable to demons.* Crystal reacted to the body language at once. "Mary explained your fear to me. Before you decide one way or another just agree to be open to more information, okay?

Lydia nodded slowly. "I promised Mary I would stay open-minded and be honest."

"Anyway, as I was saying about hypnosis. Many critics of information gathered from hypnosis call it sympathetic storytelling. In other words, you know what the researcher wants to hear and invent a story while in a trance to please the researcher. In your case since you haven't read much of it, there is less danger of you inventing it. Does that make sense?"

Lydia pondered Crystal's words. *I must guard my mind. Don't forget this is still a worldly woman who may be deceived by Satan.* "Can't we do something else instead of hypnosis?"

Crystal nodded thoughtfully. "Of course, but would you tell me why the idea makes you so uncomfortable?"

Lydia sighed. "I mustn't allow myself to become vulnerable to demons."

Crystal asked patiently, "If I were able to convince you that you were safe from demons while under hypnosis, would you be willing to try it?"

Lydia shrugged. "How could you possibly do that?"

"Do you believe in the power of prayer?"

"Of course!"

Crystal spoke softly, "I have had several individuals who felt as you do. We always began the session with a prayer to God to send his angels to protect us while we tried to find the truth. I believe we should focus on the positive and not the negative. We give energy to whatever we focus our thoughts on. I prefer to send all of my energy to God and none to evil."

"How do I know you believe in prayer?"

"How do I know you do?"

Lydia was stunned. For the first time in her life she found herself boxed in by her own beliefs. *Remember, even Satan can appear as a being of light. It is too soon to trust her, but maybe I should give her a chance.* "Fair enough. Let's say I do agree to being hypnotized, how could that possibly help me?"

Crystal smiled in return. "Fair enough. Let me explain the theory first and then we will try to see how it could be useful in your circumstances."

"Fair enough." Lydia allowed herself a smile. She relaxed. Despite her caution, she was beginning to feel trust toward Crystal.

"It is a simple concept. Everything that has ever happened to us is stored and accessible as memory. Hypnosis allows us to access memories that normally are unavailable."

"How is that possible?"

"Let me give you an example. Have you ever tried to remember someone's name, and no matter how hard you tried you couldn't? But later, when you weren't thinking about it, you suddenly could remember?" Lydia nodded her head. "That's because everybody has a subconscious mind that works in the background. When you were trying to remember the name with your conscious mind, your subconscious mind which sees all and records all, knew you wanted the information and went and accessed it for you. Your subconscious mind is subtle, and it has to wait until the conscious mind is idle before it can serve you."

"What do you mean serve me?"

"Our subconscious mind is constantly working to help us fulfill our goals and wishes. When we daydream, the subconscious mind can send us information. That is because our daydream mind is different from our thinking mind. The thinking mind is noisy and drowns out the daydream mind. All we do with hypnosis is make it easier to access the daydream mind. Both daydreaming and hypnosis are light trances. Our mind goes into that state just before we go to sleep. We usually experience it as we lie in bed half awake and half asleep. It is a normal function of our brain. All hypnosis does is allow us to control and harness the daydream mind. Do you ever daydream Lydia?"

Lydia was struggling to find a way to resist Crystal's logic. "Yes, but what does that have to do with it?"

"Like I said, daydreaming is a normal function of the mind and everybody does it. Hypnosis is no different except a professional like me guides it. This gives us access to all of your memories and can solve many personal mysteries." Crystal sat and waited for Lydia's reply.

"When you put it that way it sounds logical and safe. So, if I let you hypnotize me, how could that help?"

Crystal looked at her watch. "I tell you what. Why don't I tell you what I already know from your file and see if you can tell me what it is you want hypnosis, if it's warranted, to do for you?"

"Fair enough." Lydia laughed.

Crystal laughed back. "Fair enough."

Lydia listened as Crystal summarized Mary's notes. How well Mary documented their sessions impressed her. *I can't help but like her. Maybe she is an answer to my prayers. Maybe I should give God more credit. He sent her to me, right? If God had sent me to her then he had to have sent me to Mary. I wish now I hadn't been so closed-minded. Mary hadn't.* Lydia didn't realize that she had tuned out Crystal and was reliving one of her sessions with Mary. "Lydia? Earth to Lydia; did you hear my question?"

Lydia slightly shivered and refocused on Crystal. "Sorry, I must have been daydreaming." She blushed, realizing how easily her own mind had betrayed her and proven Crystal's point.

Crystal smiled. "It's a normal function of the mind. Bored with me rehashing old territory, your mind entertained itself. I do it all the time. What I was asking was, are you now convinced that your unusual conversations as a child were not the result of spiritual manipulation?"

Lydia nodded. Frowning, she tried once more to allow her mind to take in a new idea. "My mind won't accept the possibility of reincarnation."

"Let me tell you how I deal with paradoxes. It is easy if you can remember one key phrase."

"What's that?"

"I remind myself that I don't have to make a decision as I gather more information, but that I do have to let all the information have its 'day in the court of my reasoning mind.'"

Lydia smiled. "I like that."

"Now let me tell you how I came to consider reincarnation as a believable explanation of established facts." Lydia nodded for her to go on. "My whole purpose for going into psychology goes back to the death of my brother when I was seventeen. What began as a way to help myself understand the grieving process became a lifelong obsession to know what happens after death. I was one of the first people to start documenting what people experienced while they were clinically dead."

"People who almost died and then came back to life?"

Crystal leaned forward. "Some were people who were clinically brain and heart dead for two or three minutes. I have talked with hundreds of people in the last twelve years who claim that awareness did not end at death. I have hundreds of documented cases of people being able to view the efforts of the doctors and nurses trying to revive them. They were even able to remember the instructions of the doctors and the comments of the nurses. Others talk of going toward a bright light until pulled back into the body."

Lydia leaned back and took a deep breath. "So what. What does that have to do with reincarnation?"

Crystal grinned and said. "I have interviewed two different people who were pronounced legally dead who, after coming back to life, claimed to be someone other than who had died."

Lydia reached for an old comfortable line of reasoning. "Being dead for awhile made them vulnerable to a demon possessing them."

Crystal countered back, "You say demon, I say ghost, you say tamato, I say tomato. Don't be so quick to insist that everything be stated in a special semantic way. If one soul abandons a body at death and another soul can take over and take advantage of the body's miraculous recovery, then couldn't one soul have more than one body over a series of lifetimes?" Lydia spluttered trying to find a retort. Crystal continued, "If some people can remember what happened after they were clinically dead—and there are many documented incidents by many observers—might it also be possible, *just possible*, for some people to access memories from before birth?"

Lydia's eyes widened. "I need to think about this."

Crystal looked at her watch. "Our time is almost up. I told my student aid to reserve this time, every week for the next two months, just in case. Think about what all I have talked about and come back and tell me what it is you want to know. Here, let me walk you out of my jungle."

The Seven Paths

The next morning after breakfast, Master and Chester were sitting on the porch watching it rain. "I have never seen so much rain in my life," exclaimed Chester. "It has rained almost every day for three months. When will it end?"

"It should stop raining in about a month. The rainy season lasts from June to September."

"At least while it's raining hard the mosquitoes don't come around. I can see why you have this mosquito netting over the beds and around this porch. The rain must create a million places for them to breed."

They both watched the rain. Chester was lost in thought. After almost a half hour of quietly sitting, Chester broke the silence. "I have so much information, but it hasn't jelled yet."

"What do you mean jelled? I'm not familiar with that phrase." The Master didn't look at Chester but continued to watch the pools in the garden as they filled up and overflowed.

"Your English is so good I forget it is not your first language. Back where I come from, we eat a food called Jell-O. It's made by putting sugar, flavoring and gelatin in boiling hot water. When it cools it turns into a colored transparent pudding. When I was a kid my mom made it as a dessert. She would put it in the freezer to make it cool faster. I hated having to wait. She would always tell me it hadn't jelled yet. That is what all this information in my head is like. It's all mixed up, and I can't see how it all goes together."

"This is to be expected. Without a Master to guide me, I would have never seen the big picture to use a phrase you Americans like."

"The War of the Angels, all these religions, the seven paths to sainthood, evolution, creation, reincarnation, resurrection, Buddha, Christ, God—it's all so confusing. I remember you told me the religions all fit together, but I don't see it."

"I'll try to explain it so you can put it together. I once had the same problem. I grew up in a Vedic household and my father taught me to be devout in surrender to God."

"Vedic?"

"Many masters of The Understanding have been Vedics. It is the closest religion today to the original Understanding that was lost after God confused mankind's language."

Chester nodded. "What Genesis records as the Tower of Babel incident? I remember you told me about that not long after I got here."

"Yes. Vedism is the oldest spiritual path in India that has sacred texts called the Vedas. It's the origin of what is now called Hinduism."

"Wait, what do you mean *now called*?"

"The word 'Hinduism' is an English word coined by Europeans at the beginning of British rule in India around 1830. This is why the religion we call Hinduism is so hard to define. All the beliefs and myths that make up India's culture are all grouped under the broad phrase of Hinduism. Vedism is the proper term for the ancient religion that has its roots in India's distant past. The Vedic religion isn't like any other present-day religion nor is it exclusive or confined to India. It is universal and doesn't trace back to a single prophet or seer. Vedism teaches that truth is always complementary, not contradictory. This path never feared the advancement of science either. In fact, I was taught the Vedas contain the origin of religion, ethics, morality, and the sciences. Back at the dawn of time there were no temples, mosques or churches.

Everyone worshipped the same God and God was only addressed according to His Nature, Attributes and Characteristics. There is archeological evidence that many countries have Vedic roots dating back 4, 000 years or more. My Master told me that my upbringing prepared me well for receiving what he called *The Mahartha.* This is a Sanskrit word which in English means: 'fullness of understanding' or 'fullness of meaning.' That is why I use the English phrase, The Understanding. The original word was lost to the masters as the languages evolved, but its approximate meaning was to 'know fully' or 'to understand completely.'"

"Yeah, but every religion claims to be the one true religion. What about the seven paths I saw in the vision? Is that the same as seven different religions?"

"The word religion is also a confusing term. The origin of the word 'religion' is from the Latin word *religare*, which means 'to restrain' or 'to hold back'. This is the opposite of the meaning of path, which represents 'going forward' or 'to progress along.' The word religion has more in common with the word 'culture' than it does 'path.' Religion is designed to control large groups of people. Take for example the religion called Christianity. There are 3,000 plus different Christian sects that all believe something different. Some are similar to others, but as a whole they don't make a religion. What Christianity is today is simply a culture that has it roots in the teaching of Christ. The same idea of a common culture also applies to Taoism, Hinduism, Buddhism, Judaism, science or any other religion you can think of."

You aren't suggesting science is a religion, are you?"

"Science is the essence of trying to understand everything. So in a way, science has more in common with the original religion than even modern-day religions do. Let me put it this way, science and the world's religions are pieces to a puzzle that need one another to form a complete picture. What I am about to tell you is how these puzzle pieces all fit together."

"Now you're talking. I want to see you pull this off." Chester still hadn't lost his cynicism. Chester's next words were lost in a clap of thunder. Instead of repeating them he shook his head and said, "Never mind. It's not important. Go ahead."

The Master slightly bowed and smiled. "It all begins with the Seven Wisdoms and the seven paths to God. Even though the religions of today are a collection of truths and errors, seven religions have as part of their culture a true path hidden among the myths, rituals, and confusion of differing beliefs. Each path is composed of at least two wisdoms, sometimes more. In fact, there are three special religions that I call blended religions or double religions." The Master held up his hand to stop Chester from interrupting. "Hear me out, and you can ask questions in a minute. Each of the seven paths are in what are now known as Taoism, Hinduism, Buddhism, Judaism, Christianity, Sufism and science." Chester still wanted to challenge the Master on science as a religion or path but held off. "Three religions are actually two paths joined together. They are Zen, Sikhism and Sabbath Christianity or Messianic Judaism."

Chester couldn't stay quiet any longer. "Science is *not* a religion. And how do the Wisdoms tie into these so-called religions?"

Ignoring Chester's outburst the Master continued. "Each religion or culture has within it two or more Wisdoms. All of them have the Wisdom of Holiness and one other. The exception is science."

"Wait, I think I see where you are going. When I first got here you told me that science had discovered five Wisdoms. Let me see, they are Eternity, Infinity, Awareness, Oneness, and Balance. I remember you said that no religion had as many wisdoms in it as science did. I didn't realize at the time that you were calling science a religion."

The Master pointed out. "Science has many divisions in it much like religions have sects or branches and scientists have a culture all their own. Agreed?"

"I see your point. Go on. I'll try to be quiet." Chester grinned because he knew the Master didn't believe him.

The Master laughed and shook his finger at his student. "If you cause any more trouble, this lesson will end and you can go help Sanjiv do his chores."

Chester saluted and sat up straight, but his grin didn't waver.

"Where was I? Oh yes, it all begins with the Seven Wisdoms. Except for science, all the 'religions,' the Master made quote marks in the air when he said the word 'religions,' have holiness in common. This wisdom is essential to any path that leads to God because without virtue or a moral code, the path only leads to suffering, misery and false values."

Chester raised a finger and his eyebrows. The Master nodded for him to go ahead and speak. "Well, in that case, science has the Wisdom of Holiness in it because science is based on integrity, honesty and ethical behavior in its search for ultimate truth."

"Hmmm. I never thought of it that way. This means that science only lacks the Wisdom of Faith."

"Of course, science takes nothing on faith. Only that which can be proven and verified is considered truth." Chester bobbed his head with a proud look. Then he licked his finger and mimed adding a point to an imaginary scoreboard.

"I said back at the beginning we had much to learn from each other. I guess I owe you another gold coin. But if you don't take that smug look off your face, you won't get it. Humility is the foundation of holiness, and your foundation could use some work." The Master's gaze was penetrating and serious. "Don't take this information lightly. What you are learning is more precious than all the gold in the world. The gold in the coins is a physical reminder of the true wealth these Wisdoms represent."

Chester dropped his grin. "I apologize. I am grateful to learn all this, and I didn't mean to belittle it at all."

"But now we have found out that the seven paths all have in common the Wisdom of Holiness in one way or another. Now I will tell you what wisdom accompanies holiness in the other six religions."

Chester nodded and did his best to look interested and engaged in what the Master was teaching.

"Taoism contains the Wisdom of Balance. The Ying and Yang icon of Taoism speaks for itself. Hinduism has the Wisdom of Infinity. Have you ever wondered why a picture of a god often has six or more arms? That represents the infinite diversity of God's creation. God is Omnipresent. This means God is in everything and in every being. Over the millennia this has been corrupted into making everything a god. God is infinite and unlimited, and this Wisdom is reflected throughout the culture of Hinduism. Buddhism contains the Wisdom of Awareness. Buddha became fully enlightened when he became connected with the Absolute Awareness which is the cornerstone of the Absolute Realm."

Chester nodded his head and furrowed his brow. "You know, this sort of makes sense. I guess you're going to talk about Judaism next, but I can't even begin to imagine what Wisdom it contains."

"It contains the Wisdom of Eternity."

"Eternity? You must have told me a dozen times that eternity and now are the same. You told me the past is an illusion and so is the future. How does that translate to Judaism?"

"*The Now* is the ever-present canvas that reality is projected on. What we call reality is actually an ever-changing pattern. I have to admit, it is a very complex pattern; but it is just a pattern that is constantly moving and evolving. In the created realm, there is no such thing as absolute stillness."

Chester added, "I believe Einstein said, 'nothing happens until something moves.' So you agree with the smartest guy that ever lived."

"What we call the past is a memory of the pattern that was once in *The Now.* What we call the future is a possible pattern that might someday appear in *The Now.*"

Chester frowned. "I'll buy that. What the heck does Judaism have to do with Eternity?"

"Judaism is God's special project. God created a society of people who were descendants of Abraham and called them his people. God used the Hebrew people to perform several duties. Part of their purpose was to record and preserve history and prophecy. The Old Testament is mostly a book of history, but one third of it is prophecy. Not all the prophecies have been fulfilled yet."

"I get it. The history represents the past and the prophecies represent the future and both are recorded so they are always available in *The Now*. Hmmm…"

"Many of the prophecies are about the Messiah. Some were about Christ's first coming but others are about Christ's second coming. Christianity holds the Wisdom of Faith."

"How so?"

"Faith that Christ died for the sins of mankind. Faith that Christ will return. The whole religion is all about faith and believing God and the Messiah."

"So that leaves Oneness since you said all of them have Holiness. The only religion left is Sufism."

"Correct, Sufism traces its origins to Abraham through his son Ishmael. Even though it is considered a mystical sect of Islam, it is far older than Islam. The actual connection between the two is the fact they are both associated with Arabic culture. Sufism is totally dedicated to becoming one with God just as Abraham was. It teaches that everything is subordinate to seeking Oneness with the Supreme Eternal God."

"I'll admit that all makes sense. Now what was this about blended religions?"

Before the Master could answer, Sanjiv knocked on the door. After opening it, he carried in two bowls piled high with salad. Both men were silent as they ate. When they finished, they set their bowls aside and watched the rain. The Master commented, "Rain is letting up. Once the sun comes out, it will get hotter. Let's go inside where the fans are."

Chester got up with the Master. He grabbed the two bowls and forks and followed him into the interior of the house. After depositing them in the kitchen, he made his way to the cool interior. The design of the house allowed for plenty of air to circulate. The fans were left off unless the sun was shining. This was to prevent them from unnecessarily draining the batteries. Chester had gotten used to living with the realities of a solar-powered house and had come to admire the simplicity and the efficiency of the Master's lifestyle. Chester joined the Master in the sitting room and waited for him to continue his explanation of the blended religions.

"Before lunch showed up, I was going to explain what a blended or double religion is. The best example is Zen. After Buddha died, Buddhism spread from India to China. When the Chinese taught Buddhism to the converts in Japan, they used Taoist words, thoughts, expressions, and ways of communicating to teach the essence of Buddha's teachings. This resulted in the blended religion we know of as Zen. Zen has both the Wisdom of Balance and the Wisdom of Awareness because it has roots in two paths. Another blended religion is Sikhism. Some say that Sikhism is a blend of Islam and Hinduism. But Sikhism is not a mixture of Islam and Hinduism in the way Zen is a blend of Taoism and Buddhism. It may seem so to an outside observer at the most casual level of observation, but that is a wrong impression. Sikhism is a revealed religion in its own right. The Guru Nanak is the teacher that originated Sikhism. He grew up in an area that had a blended culture. Where he lived there were many Muslims and Hindus. Yoga is considered a sect of Hinduism and is a mystic path that teaches how to join the individual soul to the infinite divine soul. Sufism is chiefly found in the Muslim culture. As a result some Sufi masters accepted his teachings as did some Yoga masters. That is why the history of Sikhism has several Sufi and Yogic saints that are also considered Sikh saints. The more accurate way to describe Sikhism is to say that it is a double path religion that is compatible with Sufism and Yoga. In either case, because of its origins, it has both the Wisdoms of infinity and oneness within it. A study of the Sikh scriptures would bear this out."

Chester shook his head. "You've given me a whole lot of information, but I still don't see how all of this fits together."

"Sabbath Christianity is almost self-explanatory. It is Christians who also keep the Sabbath and the Holy Days. Messianic Jews are the Jewish equivalent. They are Jews that keep the Sabbath and the Holy Days and believe Jesus is the Messiah. The biggest difference between the two groups is the Messianic Jews call Jesus *Yeshua*. In either case, they accepted Christ as the prophesied Messiah and they dropped animal sacrifice and other minutia of the Old Covenant. But they keep the Ten Commandments including the Sabbath. They also keep the Holy Days. So it's less of a blended religion and more of a religion that never split up. Historically, Christianity abandoned everything Jewish. This resulted in two separate cultures with a common ancestry. But like the other blended religions, this one also has two wisdoms as well as holiness, in this case, eternity and faith."

Chester got up and stretched. "I need a break. Can we finish this later tonight?"

The Master also got up. "Sure, I need to help Sanjiv check the solar panel before dark anyway. Sometimes a hard rain like that causes some damage. Talk to you later."

Crystal and Lydia Meet Again

Lydia was running a little late for her next visit with Dr. Gibson. Her student aid was waiting for her and escorted her back into what she called the research room. Crystal was already there. The bright smell of mint filled the air. Crystal was holding a teacup. "I'm sorry I'm late."

"Don't worry it's only a couple of minutes. Would you like some warm mint tea? It's caffeine-free."

Deciding whether to accept her offer gave Lydia a chance to slow down. "Sure, that sounds nice."

Crystal looked up at her aid and nodded. Lydia didn't see her go. Lydia found her seat. Crystal waited for her aid to deliver the hot tea and leave. "Try it, you will find it relaxing. It's a blend of peppermint and spearmint."

Lydia sipped and smiled. "I can feel it all the way down."

"Yes, mint tea is also good for calming an upset stomach. Speaking of calm, you seem calm. Have you had a chance to think about what it is you want to accomplish with your visits here?"

"I guess I want the nightmares to stop."

Crystal prompted, "Do you remember what my line of research is?"

Lydia thought for a minute. "You are a research psychologist?"

Crystal amended. "In the area of near death-experiences, my primary tool is hypnosis for aiding memory recall."

Lydia hesitated then resolved herself. "Do you think my nightmares are memories? I have never been on a train. How could I remember being in a train wreck?"

Crystal tried another approach. "I was thinking of helping you remember what you told your mother when you were a little child. It is possible that what you told her back then is related to your nightmares. The technique is called Age Regression Therapy and is a useful tool in resolving issues. It will help you remember. A reason you can feel comfortable about this is that you have a unique opportunity for credibility. Since you haven't read your mother's journal except the first page, we will have dual proof if your memories coincide with her account of what you said as a child."

Lydia seized that word. "Proof of what?"

Crystal laughed. "Lydia, that is what we want to know. But we will have proof of whatever it is if your memories and the journal match."

"What if my memories don't match the journal?"

"I believe that would lend credibility to your opinion about the journal. That they were stories you made up. This could all still be related to how your father treated you before he left. We don't know. But I'm positive I can help you find out."

Lydia jutted out her chin. "I want to know the truth." She dropped her chin. "But I'm still afraid of being hypnotized."

Crystal shifted in her chair. "Let me give you some more background on hypnotism and see if that helps, okay?" Lydia nodded. Crystal continued. "There are three main levels the mind can reach while hypnotized. The first level is a level that almost anybody can reach. It is a trance so light, that many people don't realize they are hypnotized. While at this level the patient is open to suggestion. Now remember, you can't be made to do anything while hypnotized that you wouldn't normally do. Even at the deepest level of hypnosis your value system stays in place. In fact, no one can be hypnotized against his or her will. The next level of hypnosis is a medium trance."

Lydia jerked her head. "I don't want to become a medium. The Bible condemns it."

Crystal seemed caught off guard. "No not medium as in a séance, but medium as in low, medium, high. At this level you will know you are in my office, but you also will experience enhanced memory. I will guide you with questions, if you can even reach this level. I don't need to take anyone into the deepest level of a trance to do credible research. I have met a few patients that naturally and easily reached that level, but it isn't something I try to achieve because it isn't necessary. Just think of it as me talking to you while you do some daydreaming. Unless we go into the deepest level, you will remember everything that happens during the session. You will be your own best judge whether the experience is dangerous or not. I think we can find out why you are having these nightmares with just a few sessions. Are you willing to try?"

"I guess."

"I need more of a commitment than that. Either you do or you don't."

Lydia paused. "I'm willing for one session to see what happens."

Crystal kept her cool professional manner. "All right, before we start I want to go over what it is we want to accomplish this session."

Lydia nodded. She wasn't eager to get started and any delay was welcome.

"All we want to accomplish this session is two things. One, let's see if you can even be hypnotized. Second, if you can, let's see if we can access useful memories of when you were a young child. After that, you and I will discuss what you want to accomplish from that point on. Fair enough?"

Lydia laughed, "Fair enough."

Crystal took Lydia's hand, "Let's have a moment of silence so we can pray for safety."

Lydia felt comfortable praying. *Please God, protect me from wicked spirits. In Jesus name, I pray.* Lydia ended her internal prayer with an audible, "Amen."

Crystal echoed back, "Amen." Crystal reached over and clicked on the tape recorder. Only the hum of the tape recorder broke the silence. Crystal's voice sweetly filled the room and coached Lydia to relax. "Lean back and start with your toes and go upwards to your feet. Clench your muscles just before relaxing them. Do this progressively up your body. Now your thighs, your rear and belly and now your hands and arms. Roll your neck around and squench up your face. That's right. Now concentrate on your breathing and don't move a muscle. Now imagine that all the parts of your body are pieces of limp string. Imagine your thighs are strings just lying there. Your back and arms are strings." Crystal gave Lydia time to make the visualizations. "Imagine you are lying in your bed in your bedroom. Imagine the closet door is open. Now in your mind, get up walk to the closet and open it. Instead of your clothes being inside, you see a spiral staircase made of stone. Walk down the spiral staircase slowly. Every five steps you see a soft candle on a ledge giving out light. You are comfortable walking down the stairs. As I count backwards from 10 you will continue to go lower and lower down the stairs. Crystal's voice became progressively softer and slower as she counted backwards. "10, 9, 8, 7, 6, 5, 4, 3, 2, 1. You have reached the bottom. The door at the bottom of the stairs opens out onto a quiet gentle lake with a soft sandy beach romantically lit by the full moon. The clouds move slowly overhead. A warm and gentle breeze makes you feel secure and safe. You see a boat with a bed in it. You lie in the bed and the boat drifts in the water." Lydia was motionless and her breathing was gentle. "Let your boat drift to any place you want. I will count to five. When I get to five, your boat will put you in an important time in your life. [Slowly] 1, 2, 3, 4, and 5. Where are you?"

Lydia continued to sit still. Crystal could see her smile. "I'm in a restaurant. I'm celebrating when I graduated from college."

"Who all is there?"

"My mother, my aunt and my two best friends."

"Where are you?"

"At the Red Lobster near the Parks Mall."

"Now Lydia, when I count to five, I want you to go further back in time to another important time in your life. 1, 2, 3, 4, and 5. Now where are you?"

"I'm getting baptized."

"How old are you?"

"I'm seventeen, and I'm at the Crossroads Bible Church." Lydia was silent as she experienced again the time she gave her life to Christ and was baptized as a symbol that her former life was dead and buried in a watery grave.

Crystal gave Lydia time to enjoy the moment. "Tell me what is happening now."

"I'm drying off with a towel. All of my friends are congratulating me and giving me hugs."

"Now Lydia, when I count to five, you will wake up and remember everything that happened." Crystal spoke softly and slowly, "1, 2, 3, 4, and 5. You can open your eyes. Lydia's eyes fluttered open. She looked around and stretched. "Now tell me what that was like."

Lydia smiled as she remembered. "It was like I was there taking part in and watching at the same time."

"Did it feel uncomfortable or dangerous?" Lydia shook her head. "Good. For someone resistant to hypnosis, you did a lot better than I expected. I'm going to give you a recording of my voice with instructions to help you practice relaxing. If you listen to it every day between now and the time we see each other again, it will help our sessions go by faster and more productively. Are you willing to take this assignment home?" Lydia paused, still cautious. "Now don't listen to this while driving. If you want to make sure it is safe, listen to it sitting up and alert. If afterwards you trust the messages and suggestions, then lie down, relax, and listen to it again. At one place in the tape, I will give you a special phrase known only to you and me. The purpose is to make hypnosis easier and faster the next time we meet."

Lydia nodded before holding her hands palm up. "Are we finished?"

Crystal looked at her watch. "I would rather quit a little early sometimes as opposed to running overtime. Why don't you use your practice tape and come back to see me next week, and you can tell me how you want to continue?"

Anticipating what Crystal would say next she responded to Crystal in unison, "Fair enough."

Reincarnation and the Resurrection

Chester rubbed his eyes. He looked out of the small window in the library and saw that it was almost dark. He had decided to go back to the Master's library to do some research. With the Master's explanation about the seven paths and the blended religions, some of what he read made more sense than when he read it the first time. For every question that his research had answered, another had blossomed in its place. He was able to find harmony between the different religions if he ignored the semantics and concentrated on the core message. One particular question lodged in his brain like a prickly burr. His inability to figure what the core question really was frustrated him. This changed when he read a particular passage in the Bhagavad-Gita. Using a trick learned in college, he read it out loud. Sometimes hearing it as well as reading it helped him understand. He was reading Barbara Stoler Miller's translation. One particular passage struck a nerve. He read it out loud again. "*As a man discards worn-out clothes to put on new and different ones, so the embodied self discards its worn-out bodies to take on other new ones.*" He put down the paperback and went looking for the Master. He found him in the kitchen helping Sanjiv prepare dinner.

"Chester, here take this and put it on the table. It's time to eat."

Chester carried the bowl of steamed vegetables to the table. Sanjiv followed with large glasses of chilled apple juice, and the Master carried the forks and plates. As they sat down, Chester started to ask his question. The Master and Sanjiv had their heads bowed. He bowed his head and silently thanked the maker as he had been taught to do. When he raised his head, Sanjiv was passing him the bowl. The vegetables smelled good. He didn't miss meat as much as he used to. He was never told not to eat meats; they just didn't have any around. The Master liked to eat in silence. Chester was eager to ask his question, but he knew it was best to wait. It was his night to clean up in the kitchen. Normally, he didn't mind but tonight he was ready to challenge the Master. He believed he had found the fatal flaw in the different religions all teaching truth from a different perspective. As he cleaned the dishes in the kitchen, he rehearsed his question and tried to anticipate what the Master would say. His background in debate made this a natural way to deal with problems and puzzles. When he finished, he found the Master sitting on the porch. The rain had stopped and the insects were beginning their nightly symphony. Sanjiv must have sensed that a discussion was about to take place. He was sitting in the corner where he liked to listen to Chester and the Master have their discussions. He was so quiet that many times they forgot he was there. When Chester sat down on one of the pillows, the Master handed him a stick of sugar bamboo. It was the closest to dessert they ever had. It was like using a sweet toothbrush after dinner. Instead of chewing on the end, he asked the question that wouldn't leave him alone. "You have said there are seven paths or religions and that each contribute to the total understanding of God."

The Master nodded in the darkness and chewed his bamboo.

"I think I have found a flaw in all of that."

The Master didn't reply but continued his chewing.

"I was rereading the Bhagavad-Gita and realized for the first time that it teaches reincarnation. Buddhism teaches it, too. Judaism and

Christianity teach a resurrection. It occurred to me not to long ago that they aren't the same. One involves being born again and the other being raised from the dead."

The Master spat out some chewed bamboo fibers and answered him. "You are right. They aren't the same."

"How can they both be right? I'm sure Christians don't believe in reincarnation. I've seen nothing in the sacred texts of Taoism, Hinduism or Buddhism that says anything about a resurrection. I guess they don't believe in it. So this is a paradox. Which is right? Wait. Don't tell me. You're going to tell me they both are. So let's skip that part."

"If you know the answer before you ask, why do you ask the question?"

"Just because I know the answer doesn't mean I know why that is the answer. Find a way to convince me they are both right. It seems your whole theory depends on it."

"You remind me of myself. I once had a similar conversation with my Master. I grew up accepting the endless cycle of birth and death and could not understand a resurrection to judgment as taught by Christ. In fact, I couldn't see a need for Christ to come and die. If karma always delivered the blessings or cursing of one's actions, either in this life or the next then why is a judgment needed? In some ways you are better prepared for the answer than I was. You have never believed in either so believing in both will be easier once you know why. Even after my Master explained it to me, I had a hard time accepting a resurrection or a judgment."

"What changed your mind?"

"A parable. Once I heard the parable, all the pieces fell in place. Perhaps I should tell you the parable first."

"It's up to you."

The Master leaned forward and lit a candle. Chester had figured out long ago the Master did this so Chester could watch his face as he taught. He had done this many times before; and if it was dark, he had always lit a candle. He could hear Sanjiv moving closer. Sanjiv's interest stirred his own. "Once upon a time, there was a King that had no Kingdom. He lived alone for there was no one in the world but himself. He decided that a King should have a castle. So he made a giant castle of gold and silver and precious gems. It was glorious and a beauty to behold. In the castle were many rooms. Each room was different yet lovely in its own way. This King was skilled at building and creating, and he passed his time building his castle. When he was finished, he lived in his castle and went from room to room enjoying the pleasures and delights that each one offered. Still the King was not satisfied. He made himself servants to care for the castle. He gave them names that represented the work they did. There was peace and goodness everywhere. The King made a throne, sat on it, directed the affairs of his castle, and his servants were happy."

Chester was wondering if this story had any point to it but kept his peace. As he listened, he chewed the sugarcane and enjoyed its sweet flavor. The Master continued his story. "The King and his servants wore no clothes for the castle was perfect in every way. They lived and worked in the castle without cares or worries. Since it was never dark, the King and his servants never slept and never grew tired. But still the King felt something was missing. After pondering the emptiness in his heart, he decided he wanted children to share in his happiness. So the King made children out of his heart and gave them noble names that were fitting for princes and princesses. Soon the castle was filled with children laughing and playing. The many rooms were a source of delight and fascination for his children. One day his children came to him and said they wanted to see what lay outside the castle. The King loved his children dearly so he granted their wish. Right outside the castle he built a large garden. He planted trees and flowers of every color and variety in his garden. He crafted ponds and waterfalls and built paths and benches. His skill at making things of beauty knew no bounds. He even made birds and animals to live in his garden. Everything he made was perfect and pleasing to the eye. He built a wall around his garden to protect it. He gathered his children and told them that outside the castle they would have to wear garments. He gave each one a white robe and told them they must keep their robes clean. He had his servants also wear robes and watch over his children whenever they went out and played in the garden. When they wanted to come back inside the castle again, they would hang their robes at the castle entrance. One day his children asked him what was beyond the walls of the garden, and he told them it was a world full of loneliness and sadness. When he told them that was the reason he had made a castle and a garden, they were satisfied for awhile and stopped asking about the outer world. But, eventually, some of his children came to their father and told him they wanted to leave. When he asked them why, they said they wanted to go out into the world and build themselves castles and gardens. The King realized that since he had made his children from his heart they would be like him and would wish to build and create just as he had done. Before he let them go, he told them they had to come back with clean robes or they couldn't get back into the garden. He told them he loved them very much, but he couldn't allow anything unclean in his garden or his castle. He called his most faithful servant, gave him a garment, and told him to go with his children and help them keep clean so they could come back to him whenever they wanted. He gave him a new name and called him 'Guardian.'"

Sanjiv clung to every word of his Master and his excitement made him break his normal silence. "Master, were they good children? Did they stay clean?"

The Master smiled and nodded his head. "Yes, they went out and played in the world. Sometimes they would come back and tell their father of all they had done and the places they saw. Every year more and more children asked their father for permission to go out and play in the world. Soon all of his children had left him but one. His first-born never left his side. But because so many wanted to play in the world, he had to send more and more servants to help them stay clean and safe. All the servants answered to the Guardian and did as he commanded. But the children wandered so far away for so long that their robes became worn and damaged enough that they had to make new ones. They would have to find a place to shelter themselves until they had new robes. Afterwards, they would don new robes and start another adventure in the world. As time passed, fewer and fewer of the King's children would come back and visit their father. They had wandered so far away that it took many, many years to make it back to the garden and the castle."

Chester began to see where the story might be going. The air acted as if it were listening. The thunder started to rumble when the Master pointed out there was trouble in paradise. Chester and Sanjiv looked at each other when it started raining. Chester still wasn't used to the eerie coincidences that surrounded the Master. "The King wanted his children back. He sent out a message for the Guardian to return. He told the Guardian to go back and tell all of his children that he was declaring a grand festival and to invite all of his children. To make sure they would come, he told the Guardian to tell them that at the festival's conclusion the King would give all of his children their inheritance. To give them all time to make the journey back, he scheduled the festival for the 100th year anniversary of the building of the garden, which was ten years away."

Chester commented, "Some of them must have been far away."

"When the time for the festival came, none of his children showed up. Concerned, he ordered his most trusted adviser to go into the world and find his children. The adviser came back with bad news. He had found the children asleep in a cave. Some of them were lying in dirt, mud, or ashes. Even those away from the dirt and mud still had stains on their robes. All the children had soiled their robes as taught by their trusted guardian. All of them were unaware that a festival had been awaiting them. The Guardian had lied to them and told them their father never wanted to see them again. He slyly told them that dirty robes would be the perfect revenge for their father rejecting them forever. The King became outraged and demanded to know what had happened. His adviser told him a tale of treachery and betrayal. The

Guardian had decided that it wasn't fair that someday the King's children would inherit their father's kingdom and he would get nothing. He had also convinced all the other servants that he knew a way for them to get the kingdom instead of the children. So they tricked the children by giving them wrong directions leading away from the festival so they would become lost. The plan was to get the children's robes so dirty that they would never be able to return to the garden."

"How did the King handle this betrayal?"

"The King sent his firstborn son out to give his children a message. He knew he could trust his son to deliver the message and come back. He told his firstborn exactly what to tell them and to come back and tell him what happened. So his firstborn went out and found his brothers and sisters with the dirty robes. He told them what they had to do to get their robes as clean as possible. He also explained that he would be back in two years to take them to their father for a special inspection. He also warned the evil servants that if they continued to deceive the King's children they would end up in prison forever."

Sanjiv squirmed on his pillow. "What happened to the children?"

"Yeah, what happened if they didn't get perfectly clean?" Chester was getting into the parable.

"Those that tried to get clean would be given a second chance. Some didn't believe their brother and didn't heed his warning. They continued to play in the dirt and mud, and they didn't care how dirty they got."

"Does story have a happy ending?" Sanjiv pleaded.

"After the two years was up, the King commanded the adviser to take as much of his army as needed and to bring the Guardian and the evil servants back to face his wrath. The adviser and his army delivered all the evil servants bound, gagged, and tied together. The adviser threw them before the King and asked what should await them. The King ordered his adviser to dig a deep pit and to cast the evil servants in it. Then to cover it with heavy iron doors so they could never get out."

Sanjiv asked breathlessly, "What about the children?"

"Just as promised, the firstborn of the father came and gathered all of his brothers and sisters outside the gates of the garden for the King's inspection. Those who had tried to get their garments clean were given new ones and allowed back into the garden to receive their inheritance. Those who hadn't tried to get their garments clean were denied access to the garden."

Chester spat out the rest of the sugarcane. "I think I understand."

The Master smiled and asked. "What is it you think you understand?"

"The garden represents the Paradise of God. The world represents all of us as his children playing away from God. The robes represent the bodies needed to leave the Realm of God to go among the Created Realms. A worn out robe represents death and a new robe represents rebirth. Had Lucifer not rebelled and deceived the world, God's children would have had plenty of time to make their way back to God." Chester snapped his fingers. "So reincarnation was the original plan all along to let the children play in the world and still make their way back to God."

Sanjiv spoke up. "But Master, why did some of the children stay dirty and not try to get clean?" He grabbed his feet and leaned toward the Master.

The Master explained, "Satan did a good job of deceiving them. That is why they would not listen to their older brother. The older brother represents Christ who had to help his brothers and sisters since they had been betrayed and led astray. The inspection in the parable is symbolic of the resurrection when the dead will be judged whether they are worthy to return to the paradise of God or not."

"So you're saying that if Lucifer had never rebelled then there would have been no need for a resurrection to judgment?" Chester asked.

"Correct my student. Before the rebellion, the original plan of God was reincarnation. The natural cycle of birth and death would have resulted in all the children of God sooner or later making it back to their Father. Each life cycle (birth and death) would give more experience, more stored wisdom in the soul for access in their future lives to make better choices. After enough lifetimes, the law of karma would naturally bring them all the blessing of peace, truthfulness, and holiness. This would draw them closer to the source of these over the lifetimes until they would find the Garden of God. The War of the Angels changed all of that. This resulted in our planet's surface being frozen and covered in darkness. Just as God had to repair the world, the original plan of God needed repairing also. Only Christ who had never sinned could repair the damage done by Satan. God knew Satan would influence the world to sink deeper into evil every lifetime unless it was somehow reversed in the future. That is why Christ had to come and resist the temptation of Satan in the desert and qualify to replace Satan as ruler over our world."

Chester stuck to his position. "Why did Christ have to die such a horrible death?"

"The law of karma requires a price to be paid. Christ took on the bad karma of all of his brothers and sisters. This is why in Revelation it says, '…*These are they who have come out of the great tribulation; they have washed their robes and made them white in the blood of the Lamb.*[1]' Does that solve your paradox, Chester?"

"It's logical. But why do we have so many spiritual viewpoints?"

The Master sighed. "Several enlightened masters have come into our realm to help their brothers and sisters learn how to walk the path of righteousness. Those that show no interest in a life of righteousness will be denied access to the Garden of God and put in a place with others who hate righteousness. Those that walk a path of holiness will be guaranteed a place in the Garden. But I have a couple of questions for you. Have you ever heard that Christ is prophesied to return and reign on earth for a thousand years?" Chester nodded. "What about the belief that only those who accept Jesus' message could enter the King-

1. Revelation 7:15

dom of God?" Once again Chester nodded. "Well, if that is true, then what about people who never heard the message?"

Chester frowned. "I never thought about it before but it sounds like a major flaw in the resurrection plan, especially for all the people who lived and died before Christ was even born. That's really unfair. If they never heard Christ's message they are doomed to hell?"

The Master shook his head. "Come on, think. The resurrection to judgment isn't until the thousand year reign of Christ is over. You've read the book of Revelation. Satan is bound for a thousand years, and Christ sets up a utopian society that lasts one thousand years." Chester just sat there and looked dumb.

Sanjiv exclaimed, "I know. I know. Everybody that has ever lived will be reincarnated at least once during the thousand year reign of Christ."

Chester smacked his head. "Of course, that way no one will be able to say they didn't have chance."

The Master explained further. Think of reincarnation as the original plan of God and the resurrection as part of the amended plan of God. The Master continued his explanation. "The seven day week represents God repairing the damage caused to the original plan of God by the War of the Angels. The seven day week is symbolic of both a physical and a spiritual restoration. First was the physical repair necessary to allow life to flourish on the earth. The seven day week also represents the seven thousand year plan of God to restore the Earth to spiritual health. The first 6,000 years is almost over. The last 1,000 years begins at the return of Christ."

"Like I said before, I knew you were going to say both were right. Oh, so *that* is where 'to God a day is like a thousand years and a thousand years is like a day' comes in."

The Master chuckled. "Now do you see how reincarnation and the resurrection work together? It's not about one being right and one being wrong. It's about seeing the big picture."

"I guess I can buy your explanation for now, but I will look into this further. I'll start by rereading the book of Revelation."

The Master reached for a piece of sugarcane. As he started chewing, he nodded his head as if to say, *Of course, I would expect nothing less of you.*

Paul Flies to Dallas

Paul was excited to finally be in the Dallas area. The project he had accepted would probably last at least three months. If Tina turned out to be the real thing, he would figure out a way to stay in the area. He was so caught up in thoughts about Tina that he almost missed the rental car bus. He had to flag it down just as it was pulling away from the curb. Since the plane had landed a bit early, he would have plenty of time to get his rent car, find the corporate apartment he'd be using while in the area, and grab a shower before meeting Tina at the restaurant. She had promised him that it was easy to find because it was right across the highway from Six Flags Over Texas. When he emerged from the apartment where he would be staying for the next few months, he was sporting a light blue polo shirt, stonewashed jeans, and a pair of new Nike's. The casual dress didn't blunt the effect he had on several women as he passed by them. Smiling at them with his boyish grin, he had kept walking. One woman at a time was all he could handle, and Tina was shaping up like someone who could get his mind off all the others. He was hoping he would have plenty of opportunities to see her while he was here since they had developed a cozy friendship over the phone. He was tired of phone dating. They had talked almost every week but both of their jobs were demanding. He was determined to find a way to balance his work life and his personal life this time. The problem would be getting away from this new project, especially at the first. When he started a new project, his workday often stretched into night as he tried to get a feel for a company's current players and norms. The corporate immune system would sabotage the project every time if he suggested changes without knowing the lay of the land and forming good relationships with key players. This would be the first time he would be working on two kinds of relationships at once.

*   *   *   *

Paul didn't have any trouble finding Mariano's Mexican Restaurant since it had a huge sign that was easy to see from the highway. Apparently he had gotten there before Tina. Since it was a nice day, he decided to wait outside on a bench. He grinned as he saw the surprise on her face when she rolled passed the front door. She pulled into the parking lot on the west side of the building. She almost didn't stop the car before jumping out to greet him. Her purse caught on the car door in her haste causing her to jerk backwards and almost fall down. His grin changed to concern as he rushed over to rescue her. Tina shook her head laughing and said, "Hi, I'm *Grace!*"

"Glad to meet you *Grace*. I'm *Early*," Paul joked as he hugged her.

"You sure are. I thought I'd get here way before you did. I'm so glad to see you. You look wonderful. How was your flight?"

"Flight was good, but I'm starving. The pretzels I got on the plane didn't last long. Remember, you promised me the world's best guacamole when I came to Texas and it's pay up time." They headed into the restaurant laughing and leaning against each other.

It was a little too early for the dinner crowd so they were seated immediately. The waitress came right over with chips, hot sauce and a couple of menus. She was attractive and tried to flirt, but Paul kept his eyes and conversation directly focused on Tina. He'd learned from prior mishaps never to flirt with a waitress no matter how tempting she might be. Tina acted as if the waitress was invisible. "How's Chester. Did he get back from that job overseas?"

"No he hasn't. I'll have to tell you about that after I order some guacamole to go with this salsa and chips."

"Let's hurry. It's an avocado emergency!" Tina announced.

After taking their guacamole and drink order, the waitress gave up on getting Paul to respond to her and left. Paul leaned over and said, "I expected Chester to be back from India by now. I only got that one letter."

"You didn't tell me he was going to *live* in India."

Paul laughed. "We had better things to talk about." After squeezing her hand, Paul acted interested in his menu.

Tina picked up a chip and threw it at him. "That's not fair. You have to tell me why he's still in India."

Grinning, Paul looked over his menu. "What are you having?" Tina picked up the entire bowl of chips and acted like she was going to throw them at him. "Okay, okay. I'll tell you. I didn't know this was going to be a full contact meal."

Tina scrunched her nose and wiggled it at him. "It doesn't have to be if you'd behave."

Paul chuckled and leaned forward again. After looking around, he spoke in a conspiratorial whisper. "Chester is being paid to learn about religion."

Tina leaned in and whispered back. "No!!…How did he swing that?"

Paul was distracted when their drinks and guacamole arrived. Mumbling around a mouth full of chips and dip he said, "He finished his part of the Torah Codes project and somehow ended up in the jungle learning ancient secrets or something."

"Is he lost or what?"

After drinking some tea, Paul continued. "It's not that simple. Chester's a consultant like me. His letter said it was a profitable opportunity and that's about it."

"I don't get it. Why would somebody pay Chester of all people to learn about religion?"

"Chester is not just a programmer he's also a top-notch researcher. I'm sure it's a collaboration of some sort. Besides, he's a shrewd guy. He's making a bundle or he wouldn't still be there."

Before Tina could explore Chester's project further, their waitress showed up to take their food order. They decided to split an order of fajitas, and Paul asked about Lydia. "Tell me about your friend. Is her travel agency doing okay?"

"All Lydia does is work. She's depressed. She said she is seeing a psychologist. If Lydia is going to therapy it must be serious. Normally, she won't even see a regular doctor."

"What's bugging her? Is her business slow or something?"

"Remember, I told you that losing the debate really hit her hard? You'd think after all this time she would get over it, but she's getting worse not better. I'm worried."

Paul finished the guacamole and moaned with pleasure. "This stuff is great. I'm so full I don't know if I can eat any fajitas. I always do this when I eat at a Mexican restaurant. I get so full on chips that I don't have room for dinner."

As if on cue a hot sizzling plate was placed in front of them. They could hear it before they could see it. The smoke billowed up into the rafters. Tina rubbed her hands together. "Gosh that smells good. I don't know about you, but I'll find room somehow. I have eaten here before. These are worth it."

Both were silent as they prepared and ate their fajitas. They ate and ignored the uncomfortable silence that had joined their table. Paul finally pushed himself back from the table and groaned. "I just went from stuffed to overstuffed. These are awesome. Normally I quit when I'm full but these are so good they would tempt a saint. Trust me, I'm no saint." He punctuated his last remark with a wink.

Tina laughed nervously. "Neither am I, but I have to be a good girl tonight. I have to get up early and go to Houston."

Paul got the hint so he switched gears. "How is that going by the way?"

"I won't have to be in Houston a lot once I get trained. Since the company started in Houston, they won't need me down there as much as they will here. Looks like I'll only be down there about a week out of each month. How about you? What is your schedule going to be like?"

Paul cleared his throat. "For me it is usually ten to twelve hour days for the first week or two including weekends. Once I get the lay of the land, I usually can avoid weekend work; but I usually have no time for anything but work and sleep during the week." Tina wilted. "What is it? Did I say something wrong?"

"No. It's just that the weekends are the busiest times for the limousine service. I'm off on Mondays and Tuesdays so I can be there for the peak times."

"Cheer up. I'm sure we can see each other for lunch and stuff. Heck, if I have to I'll rent a limo from you and you can see me that way."

"How sweet." She reached over and held his hand.

After paying the bill, Paul walked Tina to her car. She leaned against the door and pointed to the south. "There is a mall with a movie theater about a mile or so that way. Want to see if we can find something to watch?"

Paul looked at his watch before replying. "I'd like to but I have be a good boy tonight, too. I need to go back to my apartment, unpack, and get caught up on some e-mail. Besides, you said you have to get an early start, too. Maybe we can catch a movie when you get back from Houston?"

Tina sighed. "You're right. It was good to see you."

Paul smiled and pulled her to him and gave her a gentle lingering kiss. When they pulled apart he winked and said. "There's more where that came from. Just give me a few weeks to get my foot in the door, and we can spend a lot more time together, I promise."

"I would love that." Tina was all smiles as she got in her car. Paul waited until she had driven off before getting in his own car.

The Temptation

Chester and Sanjiv were in the stables cleaning out the stalls of the donkeys. From the porch the Master called out to Chester. "Chester, come here. It is time."

Chester poked his head out of the stable and said, "Time for what?"

The Master motioned for Chester to come over. "You have more to learn."

"What's left to learn? I can meditate as well as you. I've studied all the major religions."

"It's one thing to know the path. It's another to walk the path. That is what I will teach you now. See this path that goes from the porch to the contemplation garden?"

"Yes."

"Walk with me as I explain." The slight crunch of crushed oyster shells marked a rhythm with the Master's words. "I want you to start walking this path every day. But don't just walk it. I want you to learn how to be mindful of the moment. It's called *walking meditation*."

"What's the point?"

"To be mindful of the moment is to be aware of your surroundings and yourself without the distractions of the past or the future. When you walk this path, remember it represents Eternal Holiness. Until you have walked all the way to the pond and back, do not leave the path for any reason. This will represent walking the path of holiness."

"I thought holiness was being close to God like during the Sabbath. How does walking down this path help me do that?"

"Holiness is also knowing right from wrong and choosing the right. By choosing not to leave the path for any reason represents walking with God for only the righteous walk with God. In Buddhism, the eightfold path represents holiness or righteousness. Yoga calls it the five restraints. In Judaism and Christianity it is the Ten Commandments. In either case, you must walk to the end and back without straying from the path. Before you begin always say 'I walk the path of holiness, and I shall not depart from it.' This is how you make it a holy walk instead of a regular walk."

"It seems silly, but I'll do it. It should be easy to walk up and down this path every day."

"As you walk, keep your mind on the *Now*. As soon as you begin to remember the past or to anticipate the future, stop. Keep your mind as clear of thoughts as you can. Practicing mindfulness of the present is to practice the discipline of Eternal Holiness."

"Eternal Holiness?"

"Remember, Now and Eternity are the same. By making sure our mind is in the present free from judgment and desire is to walk with God. Do not think this is easy. To walk in perfect holiness, even though it is just for the time it takes to do this exercise, is difficult and challenging."

Chester and the Master rounded the corner and saw the pond and the garden up ahead. "Remember, on the way back do not think of the past or the future. Do not let your imagination wander or your thoughts be of hate, greed or violence. Keep them pure and righteous. Every time you have a thought that is not pure or is not of the present, stop. Do not move another step until your mind is back on the path of holiness."

It surprised Chester how often he had to stop. It seemed easy, but it was turning out to be more challenging than he expected.

* * * *

For several days, Chester added walking down the path to his routine. The rainy season was near its end, and the mornings were beginning to be rain free. It was easier to walk the path in the morning before the heat of the day was in full force. One day when Chester was returning from his walk, the Master was waiting on the porch. Chester shook his head. "I guess you're going to tell me you know what happened."

The Master just sat and waited.

Chester joined him. "I feel silly." The Master waited. "I was walking this morning, free from thoughts when I saw what looked like a pile of silver just to the right of the path. I completely forgot this was a holy walk instead of a regular walk and went over to get the silver."

The Master kept silent.

"I should have finished the walk and came back afterwards. Anyway, when I went over, it wasn't a pile of silver. It was a pile of donkey dung glittering with the morning dew. I felt stupid."

"Tell me the lesson in this."

Chester sat and tried to think. "I give up. I mean, I know I'm not supposed to leave the path but…" His voice trailed off.

The Master offered. "The lure of riches that causes one to leave the path of virtue is an illusion without value."

"Like donkey dung."

The Master got up. "Like donkey dung." The Master left Chester to ponder the lesson.

* * * *

Chester was walking the path. It had been over a week since the incident with the donkey dung. Just as he rounded the corner, he halted. Right in the middle of the path was a coiled up cobra. It raised its head and spread its hood. The taste of fear was in his mouth. He decided to walk around the cobra and continue the walk. He left the path for just a few steps. He looked back to make sure the cobra wasn't following. When he returned the snake was gone. When he got back to the porch the Master was waiting. "Now wait a minute. It was a cobra. Give me a break."

The Master was silent. Chester sat down and waited, but the Master didn't say anything. "I guess meeting a serpent wasn't a coincidence?"

The Master merely blinked.

"The serpent represents Satan making me leave the path of goodness, right?"

"The serpent didn't make you leave the path; you chose to leave the path." With that said the Master got up and left Chester on the porch.

Chester spoke to know one in particular. "This is harder than I thought."

* * * *

The next day the serpent was in the same place. "I'm not playing this game." This time he turned around and went back to the porch. The Master was waiting. Chester nearly shouted. "Now what? I didn't leave the path!"

The Master spoke softly. "Giving up is worse than leaving the path and returning later."

Chester didn't say anything. He just sighed and turned around and walked back down the path. He had to stop several times because he couldn't keep his mind on the present. *This whole God thing was not my idea. I'm a computer consultant not a holy man. That kind of thinking isn't helpful. I've never backed down from a challenge before. I can get through this.* Chester cleared his mind and continued walking. When he got to the bend in the path the cobra was waiting. *I can't go around and I can't go back. I don't think I'm supposed to let him bite me. Their bite is deadly.* Chester cleared his mind and waited. *I need help. That's it.* "God, I need your help. I want to walk the path of righteousness but the cobra is blocking me. I can't do this without you." As soon as the prayer had left his lips, the cobra lowered its head and crawled away. A surge of pride in figuring out the solution surged through him as he continued his walk. When Chester got to the pond he saw a beautiful double rainbow, the brightest he had ever seen. Its vibrant colors framed the contemplation pond. A few minutes later he heard the crunching of someone coming up the path. It was the Master.

He walked up and stood next to Chester. "You're just now starting to learn." When the rainbow faded, they both turned around and walked back to the porch.

* * * *

For the next few weeks Chester's daily holy walks went by without incident. There was one place where the path went near a large tree that was hundreds of years old. Its roots had caused the stone wall that marked the edge of the Master's property to crumble and fall. As he passed the tree he heard a female singing. He didn't understand the language but whoever it was had an incredible voice. He stopped to listen. *I didn't know anyone else was out here.* Chester continued his walk. When he came back from the pond he could hear singing again only louder. Determined not to leave the path, he continued the walk. When he got back to the porch, he turned around and went back down the path in a half run. When he got to the tree, the singing had stopped. *Oh well, at least I didn't leave the path.*

Every day when he walked past the tree, from either direction, he heard the singing. He had meant to ask the Master about it but decided he was spiritual enough to handle this one on his own. Every day after he had completed the path, going back yielded the same results—no singing. The singing started to weigh on his mind. It found its way into his meditations. Finally, one night as he lay in his cot he decided that leaving the path just once to find out who was singing couldn't be all that bad.

The next day as he went by the tree and the broken down wall, he didn't hear any singing. Chester felt relieved and disappointed at the same time. *Oh well, it's probably for the best.* But on the walk back he heard singing. Without hesitation he left the path and crawled over the rocks that had once been part of the wall. Just on the other side of the break in the wall was a faint path that was on a gentle incline. As he made his way down the singing got louder. As he got closer, he could hear the sound of a stream softly bubbling as it flowed by. *It must be the stream that feeds the contemplation pond.* The path ended next to a large tree with broad leaves. Peaking around the tree he saw who was singing. The most beautiful woman he had ever seen was taking a bath in the stream. She had flawless olive skin and long black shiny hair. The sunlight sparkled on the water and on her hair. Before she could discover him watching her, he hurried back up the path, his heart pounding. *Come on, you've seen naked women before.* His heart raced with fear and excitement. He hadn't felt this way since he had been stranded on the bus. He expected to see the Master waiting for him as he neared the porch but neither he nor Sanjiv were in sight. He quickly made his way to his room and shut the door. He lay on his cot and replayed the images of her beautiful naked body over and over in his mind.

The next day he hurried through breakfast. Neither Sanjiv nor the Master was to be found. Both must have eaten breakfast earlier. Chester felt relieved. He was sure the Master would see his nervousness. As he started his walk, his thoughts were on the gorgeous woman singing in the stream. Instead of stopping and clearing his mind until he was focused on the present, he hurried to get to the break in the wall. His heart skipped a beat as he heard the singing. He made his way down to the large tree and peeked around it. He tried to get his eyes around the tree without his head following. He caught his breath. She was getting out of the water. She was even more perfect than he remembered. If Venus had been Indian, this is how she would look. As she dried herself off, he forced himself to leave. He trembled and his heart raced as he made it back to the path. Surely the Master would be waiting when he got back this time. He forgot to make the trip to the pond before turning back. He dreaded the meeting with the Master when he got back and was surprised to find the porch empty. He started looking for the Master and found him in his library. He looked up from his reading and motioned for Chester to take a seat next to him.

"You have done a great job translating the *Yoga Sutras of Patanjali*."

Chester wasn't expecting praise. He hesitated. He looked into the eyes of the Master. Did he see concern? "Thanks, I guess. Your explanations helped me a lot."

"Were you looking for me? Can I help you, Chester."

Chester started to tell him about the girl but instead just shook his head. "I was just wondering where you were."

The Master's voice revealed no emotion. "Make the best of your time here. I sense you will be leaving soon. Stay as long as you want and take advantage of the peace and quiet for your meditations. Let me know if I can do anything to help." The Master got up and left Chester wondering why suddenly the Master seemed oblivious to what he was going through.

The next day during breakfast the Master and Sanjiv were discussing what Sanjiv needed to get when he made his monthly trip for supplies. When Chester left for his morning walk, they were both engrossed with the details of the list.

He almost ran to the gap in the wall. His excitement swelled when he heard the sweet melody of her singing. He had been afraid she wouldn't be there. He hid behind the tree and watched her bathe. As she got out of the water, she looked straight at Chester and pointed to a towel hanging on a bush not far from where he was standing. He heard her in his mind inviting him closer. Somehow he knew she wanted him to bring her the towel. She acted as if he belonged there. When he tried to give her the towel she raised her arms and waited. Once again he felt the brush of her mind with his. She wanted him to dry her off. As he rubbed the towel over her soft wet skin, she turned around so he could have access to all of her. She closed her eyes and sighed whenever his hands would caress her instead of the towel. Her skin was so soft and smooth. When she was dry, she pointed to where her dress was hanging on a tree limb. It was a soft cotton weave with a leopard print design. She showed him how to pull it over her head and onto her body. The fit was tight, and she encouraged him with her mind to smooth it over her body. Chester became lost in the sensations of his hands on her body, and the way the garment clung perfectly over her soft curves mesmerized him. She smiled and pointed to a blanket that was laid out nearby. As they knelt on the blanket, she picked up a brush and handed it to him. She spoke for the first time. "You please me." She sat down cross-legged and waited. Chester sat behind her the same way and started brushing her long black hair. When she was satisfied, she turned around and looked at Chester. "You have a strong spirit. Greatness is your destiny." She leaned forward and kissed him on the mouth. Chester felt both lost and excited as the heat rose within him. She motioned for him to get up. He helped her fold up the blanket. After he handed her the brush, she tucked the blanket under her arm, turned around, and walked away. *She never told me her name, but I know it is Candy. This must be why I came to India. She did say I was destined for greatness.*

Chester was grateful the Master was leaving him alone. He barely saw him except at meals. That night, his meditation session was a long desire-soaked session of remembering her kiss and her incredible beauty. When he drifted off to sleep, he dreamed of holding Candy in his arms.

Lydia's Third Visit

Lydia was on time this time. Crystal had a fragrant hot cup of mint tea waiting for her. As she settled in, Crystal broke the ice. "So, how is it going?"

Lydia held the cup to her nose, enjoying the relaxing smell of mint. "Everything was fine until the air-conditioner went out in my office building. For two days we sweated. I'm just glad it didn't happen last month when we had all those days over 100."

Crystal nodded. "I think the college keeps it too cold in the classrooms. Some of my students bring sweaters to school in the middle of the summer. What else is going on, have you had anymore dreams?"

Lydia nodded her head. "It wasn't a scary dream so I didn't bring the recording. But I distinctly remember it was about me and my family, but it wasn't my real family. It was the dark-skinned family I always dream about."

Crystal reached for a folder sitting on a table near her chair. She flipped through the pages until she found what she was looking for. "I have Xeroxed all the handwritten pages and have had them typed up so I can reference the important material faster. Don't let me forget to give you the originals when this is all said and done. I won't read it to you; but in your mom's journal, it says you talked about dark skin back then, too. Have you decided where you think we should go from here?"

Lydia drank the rest of the tea before answering. "That stuff is so good." She put down the cup and leaned back into the plush leather chair and blew out a soft sigh slowly. "I don't know. I was hoping you had some ideas."

Crystal laid the folder back down and folded her hands in her lap. "Are you interested in finding out exactly what you were talking about when you were a little girl?" Lydia slowly nodded. "Did you listen to the practice tape I gave you?"

"Well, almost every day. The last couple of times I felt refreshed, and it seemed to be over almost before it had begun."

"That's a good sign. Remember how clear your memories were of the time you became baptized and when you graduated?" Lydia nodded again. "We can access earlier memories just as easily. Now, before we move forward I want to warn you. It is possible we will face memories that are unpleasant as well as pleasant ones. If I see you experiencing distress, I can tell your subconscious to detach from the painful parts by using one of those code phrases on your practice tape. You will switch from experiencing the memory to watching the events as they unfold. Do you understand?"

"I think so."

"Okay, let's get started." Crystal reached over and clicked the recorder on. "Close your eyes and count backwards from 30 to 1 slowly in your mind. With each number relax a different part of your body." When Lydia's body showed no signs of tension, Crystal prepared her to accept the prearranged phrase. "I'm going to count slowly to five. As I count I want you to imagine lying in your boat on the lake with a full moon overhead. 1, 2, 3, 4, and 5. Boat Relax Now." Lydia's didn't move. "As you drift gently in your boat, you feel yourself floating. I want you to go you back to the time when you were six years old, and you drew a picture of a mountain for your mommy." Lydia smiled but kept her eyes closed. "Tell me what you are doing."

"I'm at the kitchen table drawing with my new crayons."

"Who is with you?"

"Mommy is washing the dishes."

"Where is your father?"

Lydia dropped her voice to a whisper. "He is watching TV, and he doesn't want anyone to bother him."

"Tell me what is happening."

"I have just finished drawing a picture of a train. I'm showing it to mommy. She wants to know what I'm drawing." Lydia frowns and sighs.

"What is happening now?"

"She wants to know why the train isn't on the tracks."

Crystal got out the drawing she thought Lydia was talking about. On top of the page was a mountain. Underneath was a crudely drawn train, broken in half with two girls lying on the ground.

"Now, Lydia, I want you to sit up and open your eyes. I'm going show you a drawing and I want you to tell me if this is the one you are talking about."

Lydia sat up and opened her eyes. She looked over the picture. "This is mine, but it looks old. How did you get this?"

Crystal knew from experience that Lydia's reaction was normal. "Don't worry about that. Close your eyes and lean back." After Lydia was reclining in the chair again, she asked. "What did your mommy say when she saw your drawing?"

"She asked me if it was a train wreck. I told her it was a drawing of the train wreck where I died." Lydia frowned and whispered, "Oh no!"

Crystal leaned forward. "Tell me what is happening."

"It's my daddy. He heard me tell mommy about the train, and he's mad at me. He walked in as I was trying to explain to mommy that I really did die on a train. He is taking me to my room to whip me for lying."

"Lydia, when I count to five you will watch what happens but won't feel any pain or discomfort. 1, 2, 3, 4, and 5. Watch from the boat."

On the tape Crystal had suggested to Lydia that she could watch any memory from the boat and be safe from harm. She often had to do this for patients reliving a traumatic near-death experience. "Now tell me what is happening."

"Daddy whipped me hard for a longtime and locked me in my room. He told me I had the Devil in me and the Devil wasn't welcome in his house."

"Now what is happening?"

"I can hear Mommy and Daddy shouting in the other room."

"Lydia, I'm going to count to five. When I do, I want you to wake up and be here with me. 1, 2, 3, 4, and 5. Land the boat. "She used the wake-up command that she had prepared on Lydia's practice tape. The boat was a tool for moving Lydia around in her memories as well as getting her in and out of a trance state. Lydia blinked her eyes a couple of times and sat up. She stretched as if she had just awakened from a nap. "What do you remember?"

Lydia scratched her nose. "Everything I guess. It was like I was six years old again. I remember I was convinced I had died on a train."

"All of this is consistent with your mother's journal. I think it is quite possible that your mother's journal is in fact what she claims it is. If there hadn't already been thousands of other documented cases of young children remembering what appear to be previous lives, I wouldn't have mentioned it."

"Maybe I was just making it all up."

Crystal picked up a pen and made several entries in her notebook. Lydia craned her neck to see what she had written. When Crystal finished, she handed her note to Lydia. "I was just making a note of your resistance to the idea of having lived a life before this one. Actually, from a research perspective, your insistence that these memories are fantasies removes any doubt that you have manufactured these memories for my benefit."

Lydia handed Crystal's notes back to her. "I don't understand."

"I'm always doing research. I have found numerous works aimed at discrediting the validity of memories revisited via hypnosis. A common one is the subject makes up a fantasy or memory to please the researcher." Crystal reached over and turned off the recorder. She looked at her watch. Lydia had learned that was Crystal's body language for our time is up. "Do you think we have made any progress?"

Lydia nodded her head. "Kind of. I mean, I guess that means my mom wasn't crazy or something. I did talk about all of those things."

"How do you feel about your father? You had blocked from your memory all of those times he whipped you."

Lydia sat for a moment and pondered the floor as if the answers were down there. Not looking up she slowly conjectured. "I feel angry and glad he's gone. I feel guilty for being glad he's gone." Lydia looked up. "I don't know what I feel."

"That is actually quite normal. It could be the dreams you are having is your subconscious mind's way of trying to get you to deal with the suppressed emotions about your father. Your drawings and the stories you told about dying on a train were what triggered your father's rage."

"You think my dreams will go away now? I mean, now that I remember what happened at all."

"Perhaps the dreams will go away; perhaps they won't. For the next week, I want you to keep a journal of anything that seems important in this area. Feelings, thoughts, memories of your father. Anything that will help us figure out what your subconscious is trying to tell you."

"Mary used to talk about that. What is the deal with my subconscious wanting to send me messages?"

Crystal sighed and looked at her watch. "Let me give you the short version. If you want, we can talk more about it the next time. Have you ever heard of someone complaining that they always end up in the same kind of relationship over and over?"

Lydia smiled. "I have a friend who tells me she has only been in one relationship all of her life, just the names change."

"Tell me more about that."

"She always ends up in love with a guy who is too busy to give her any attention, you know, works all the time, stuff like that. In fact I think she is doing it again. She has fallen in love with guy who doesn't even live here in Texas."

Crystal laughed. "If you read any good books on relationships, you will find that the subconscious is constantly trying to set up situations so you can fix what is wrong. I call it the unfinished business syndrome. Perhaps your friend's father ignored her when she was growing up."

"Yeah, she told me her dad was a work-a-holic. I see what you mean. All the men in her life have been work-a-holics, too." Lydia shook her head and looked amazed.

"I can see the light bulbs going off or is that fireworks? It's funny how we can see patterns like that in others and are blind to it ourselves. Whatever *your* unfinished business is, I think we are on the right track." Crystal looked at her watch and stood up. She walked over to her file cabinets and opened one of the drawers. She flipped through the folders until she found the print-out she was looking for and, smiling, handed the single sheet to Lydia. "Here's something you might find enlightening as well as entertaining. And by the way, listen to the tape I gave you at least a couple of more times. I'll see you next week."

Chester's Trouble

"Where are you going?" The Master asked with a concerned look.

Chester smiled nervously, "My meditation walk."

The Master tried to smile but shook his head instead. "Do not leave the path placed before you or you may find yourself tested by powers you are not ready to face. You are not strong enough for the lion that wants to devour you."

Chester laughed and started to leave as if he was in a hurry. Turning as he went out the door onto the porch, he tried to reassure himself as well as the Master. "There aren't any lions around here."

As Chester turned to leave, the Master called after him, "Remember, without God you are nothing!"

The Master sighed, sat, and waited. He could see out the door to the clean-swept path that Chester had made a habit of dashing down every morning after his energy exercises. Sanjiv walked in carrying a glass of water, the ice chunks tinkling like a wind chime. The Master didn't even look up as he took the glass and started sipping. Sanjiv frowned and said, "Why Master sad?"

The Master acknowledged his dedicated friend and servant and smiled. "Not sad, just waiting. Chester will pass this trial or he won't, and I will have to wait for another student. I had a trial much like the one he will face today. He has learned much, but he is still attached to the pleasures of the flesh. But it is not the flesh I fear for Chester today. It is the dark spirits that wish to take my student from me." Sanjiv shook his head in wonder at what the Master spoke of. He decided to leave his Master alone but stayed close in case he was needed.

As the day wore on Sanjiv ministered to his Master by bringing him lunch and tea. He wasn't used to his Master being in this type of mood and hovered nearby hoping to catch his eye. The Master just sat and waited. The shadows were getting long and the sky was turning red when Chester finally came back from his walk. He had never been gone that long before, and he looked tired and scared. He saw the Master waiting for him and stopped just inside the door. When the Master said nothing, he looked around and saw the lunch that he had missed still sitting on the table in the corner. He glanced at the lunch then back at Master and decided to sit down in one of the chairs across the room. The Master said nothing. The silence felt thick and uncomfortable. Finally in desperation Chester blurted, "How was I supposed to know?"

The Master simply asked, "Will you be going back to be with the girl you have been seeing?"

Chester stammered, "You know?"

The Master pointed over to the corner. In the shadows was a painting covered by a white cloth leaning against the wall. Chester got up and uncovered it. He picked it up and brought it closer to the door so the light from the setting sun fell over it. It had been painted years ago. Portions of the paint had small cracks that only age inflicts. It was a picture of Chester, on his back, in lush green grass with a stunning young woman sitting on his chest. Her brown beautiful body was scantily clad and her black long hair almost covered Chester's face as she leaned over him. She held a mushroom, dripping with honey, up to his lips. Dancing around the couple were dark sinister shapes painted in hauntingly wispy strokes of black and red. Chester put the painting back where it had been but left it uncovered. Shaking his head in disbelief, he slumped back into the chair. "After all that has happened to me since I got here, you'd think I wouldn't be surprised anymore; but the painting scares me almost as much as she did today."

Master sat and waited.

Chester said, "Do you know what happened or do I have to tell you."

The Master said, "I know you faced a great trial today, but I don't know any details other than what I saw in a vision years ago. From that vision came this painting. The spiritual test you had today is faced by all that walk the true path. Buddha faced Mara; Christ faced Satan; I faced the demon of malice many years ago when my Master was training me."

Chester looked up and said, "I thought you said Mara and Satan were the same being?"

The Master just laughed, "Good old Chester, it sounds like you are back. Now tell me your story before you test my patience."

Chester sighed. "Oh man, I'm sorry. I'm so keyed up. I don't know where to start. I thought you would me angry with me. Then I saw the painting, and I thought you knew what happened." Chester leaned forward and pleaded with his eyes. "I almost failed the test. I almost blew it!"

The Master's face softened as he leaned back. "If you hadn't almost failed then it wouldn't have been a true test. The evil ones are real and very strong. Now tell me everything."

Chester was getting his color back as he sat on the edge of the chair. His shame and fear were almost gone, and he was eager to share his adventure. Running his left hand through his hair he said, "Can I get something to drink first?"

Master called toward the kitchen, "Sanjiv, two teas." With a look that said I've waited long enough, he gestured at Chester.

Chester looked up at Sanjiv as he hurried in with two glasses of tea. Chester sipped the liquid and waited for Sanjiv to leave before he began. "Every morning after exercising, I did that special walk you taught me, you know, where I try to be calm and mindful and in the present. One day, about a couple weeks ago as I was going down the path around the big tree on the edge of your property, I thought I heard something. It sounded like a woman singing. I know you told me not to leave the path, but I saw no harm in checking out who was singing. I thought we were alone out here, and I had to know who was out there. Just past that break in the stone wall that marks the north part of your property is a trail that goes downhill."

Master nodded, "The path to the stream that empties into the contemplation pond."

Chester nodded back, "Yeah, that one. I walked down the path until I was near the stream. There I saw this extraordinarily lovely woman taking a bath in the stream with no clothes on. She was singing and her voice was compelling and beautiful. The water was shallow enough that I could see all of her from her knees up when she stood up. She had enchanting eyes and a perfect body. I hid behind a tree and watched her. It was like I couldn't take my eyes off of her."

"Did she see you?"

"I don't think so, not the first time." Chester rubbed his hands together nervously. "So every morning I would go and watch her bathe. She was so beautiful, I couldn't help it." Chester looked up. The Master cocked his head and raised an eyebrow. "Okay, I know I could have helped it. But I guess I didn't want to."

Master smiled and nodded his head.

Chester continued, "Then one day she looked right at me. As she got out of the water she pointed at the towel she had left hanging on the tree near where I was hiding and watching. I could hear her in my mind invite me closer. Somehow I knew to grab the towel and take it to her."

Master leaned forward, "She used mind speech?"

Chester nodded and breathlessly added, "It was scary and exciting. It was like we had this mental connection, and I could hear her voice in my head." The Master seemed especially interested in this piece of information and leaned forward. Chester stopped and asked, "What?"

Master shook his head and said, "I will tell you later, please continue."

Chester rubbed his hands again, his eyes flashing eagerness and excitement as he told his tale. "She wanted me to dry her off. It was like she had been waiting for me. Sometimes I would caress her skin with my hands, and she would look at me and smile, encouraging me. Her skin was so soft and smooth, I found myself wanting her more than I had ever wanted a woman. When she was dry she showed me where her dress was. It was made of soft cotton with an exotic animal print on it. She guided me in pulling it over her head and onto her body. It was a tight fit and she encouraged me to smooth it over her so it was comfortable for her. I was spellbound at how it barely fit over her body, gently clinging to her soft curves. She looked even more beautiful with just a little clothing on than when she was nude."

Master shook his head and said, "She was a…" His voice trailed off, instead of finishing his thought. He motioned for Chester to continue.

Chester gulped most of his tea before continuing. "Then she finally spoke to me. She told me I pleased her and asked me to brush her hair. She must have laid out a blanket earlier because we sat on it as I brushed her hair. We both sat cross-legged, her back was to me as I brushed. I tried to talk to her, but she just quieted me. When I had finally finished, she turned around and sat facing me. She told me I had a strong spirit and that I was destined for greatness. Then she leaned forward and kissed me on the mouth and asked me to come back tomorrow. I felt bewildered and disappointed. After that I helped her fold the blanket. Then she disappeared into the woods, singing. It wasn't until she was out of sight that I realized she had never told me her name, but somehow I knew her name was Candy. She also knew mine because she used it in her mind speech."

"This was a couple of weeks ago, right?" The Master pursed his lips, waiting.

Chester hung his head and murmured, "Yeah."

"After that what happened?" The Master sat back deeper in the chair to listen.

Chester sat up and admitted, "From that moment on she was all I could think about. Even when I tried to meditate, all I did was fantasize about being with her. When I was with her, it was like I was in heaven and when I was away; it was like I was in hell. She started having me bathe in the stream with her. We would play and splash and laugh together. Afterwards we would dry each other off and dress each other. She kept promising me that in the future she would teach me this wonderful spiritual secret that would allow me to have all I wanted and more. Sometimes, we would talk about you. Candy told me you meant well but that you were teaching me a path of bondage. She said that it was nonsense for us to try to keep the Ten Commandments or to walk the eightfold path of Buddha. She said the true path released us from all rules and gave us unlimited power."

The Master interjected, "It was she who drew you into bondage. She was binding you to her so you would do anything for her. You became attached to pleasure. The bondage the pleasures of the flesh and the lust of the mind have on our souls is extremely difficult to break."

"I thought I was in love with her. One day I told her I loved her. When she heard that, she started kissing me. I have never felt a kiss so sweet and passionate. Just the tip of her tongue would ignite my whole body. I also loved feeling her soft warm body press against me. And when I was away from her, all I did was crave her." Chester shivered; the memory was too vivid. His eyes pleaded for the Master to understand. "She was everything I have ever wanted in a woman. Her face was like an angel, her body was flawless, her skin like silk. Nothing mattered to me anymore but pleasing her."

The Master said, "I noticed you became distant and you stopped challenging me when we had our discussions. It seemed you just wanted me to finish so you could go on your walks. It was about a week ago you started slipping off at night to meet her, right?"

Chester hung his head again. "It was at night when she wanted to make love. I knew I shouldn't, but I didn't care anymore about right or wrong. I just wanted to feel the pleasure she gave me. Afterwards, we would lie on the blanket and look at the stars. She told me soon it would be time for her to show me the true spiritual path and for us to go away together. Every night for the past week was like that, and every day was the same. Soon I was just pretending to be your student."

"But today was different, wasn't it?" The Master sighed. "Today I knew you would either come back, or I would never see you again."

Chester shook his head as he sat back in the chair. "I almost didn't come back."

"What happened today?" The Master leaned forward.

"Today when I went down the path to where we would bathe together, she wasn't in the water. She was sitting on the blanket waiting for me. She motioned for me to join her on the blanket. Her mind speech was strong, more than usual. As I sat down I leaned forward to kiss her, but she stopped me. She whispered in my mind that it was time for us to experience the ecstasy of the spirit. In a basket were some mushrooms and a jar of honey. She had me open the jar of honey and hold it. She held the basket of mushrooms in her lap. She took one of the big ones and dipped it in honey until it was covered and dripping. She took a big bite out of it and held it up to me to eat also. I thought it was an aphrodisiac, so I wasn't afraid. I was eager. The mushroom was bitter but the honey made it easier to chew and swallow. After we had eaten about six mushrooms, she told me to wait and relax."

The Master asked, "You had no idea what those mushrooms were for?"

Chester shook his head. "It wasn't long before I knew they weren't an aphrodisiac. I started getting high, and I could hear everything around me with remarkable clarity. I could tell she was feeling it too by the way she was grinning and looking around. I asked her what was happening and she told me to relax and enjoy it. She reassured me that soon I would understand everything. About that time the trees started looking brighter and more vivid. I looked around and saw bright sparkling points of light on anything I looked at. She started giggling and so did I. I couldn't help it; everything was incredibly funny. As I laughed and laughed, I noticed that everything had a second skin over it that moved and breathed."

The Master asked, "What do you mean *a skin*?"

Chester looked up trying to remember. "It was like a double image overlaid anything I looked at. But the second image had many different colors that moved and swirled. It resembled colored smoke that clung to everything. I looked around in awe. I knew I was starting to hallucinate. That's when I figured out the mushrooms were psychedelic. I figured that somehow she knew about me doing mushrooms when I was in college, and she was doing this to surprise me. That must have been why I wasn't scared or worried that she was trying to harm me. I didn't resist when she pushed on my chest so I would lie on my back. By this time I was really enjoying the high and the bright vibrating colors that formed patterns and shapes. That is when she got on my chest like in the painting. Only we were on a blanket, not on grass."

"I never get all the details perfect when it's a vision of the future, but I got close enough." The Master crossed his legs and waited.

Chester looked back at his master and continued, "As I lay on my back, I noticed the colors were moving and swirling more. Instead of just looking like a kaleidoscope overlaying the trees and bushes, the colors started making face-like patterns. At first I liked the shapes and patterns. The colors started to drift and shift like smoke. Nothing felt wrong at first, but I did sense a change. Even though it was a bright sunny day, it started getting dark and gloomy where we were. As the mushrooms affected me more and more, the patterns started turning into the faces of demons and devils."

Master leaned forward, "How did you know they were demons?"

Chester kind of shrugged. "I could see silhouettes of faces that had an evil and scary look. No matter where I looked the colors and patterns would turn into leering frightening faces. Many formed faces like gargoyles or monsters. I felt and heard a sound I hadn't noticed before. It was a deep growling that surrounded me. It sounded like huge boulders were grinding against each other. That was when she leaned over me and put her hands on my wrists. Her face looked demonic. I realized she was possessed. I could see her, and I could see the demon that was using her to get to me. I went from enjoying the experienced to being terrified in a split second. I was horrified to the point that I became petrified. I literally couldn't move a muscle."

The Master's eyes widened as he listened. "Did she say or do anything weird?"

"No, but she kept saying that it didn't hurt, just to relax and let my spirit guide help me." Chester's face looked strained as he licked his lips. "That is when I felt the pressure on my mind."

The Master studied Chester. "A demon was trying to control you; and you could tell, right?"

Chester nodded hard. "I'm sure of it. I tried to fight him; but the more I fought, the deeper he went into my mind. I panicked when I realized he wasn't alone. The grinding, growling noise got louder; but I also started hearing other demons cackling around us like the laugh you hear witches make in the movies. It got dark and cold even though it was hot and bright outside. I could see the spirit world around me almost as clearly as the real world. I could faintly see about a dozen demons surrounding me. But one demon was using Candy to take me over. I tried to get up, but I was too weak to even get her off my chest. I started shaking my head back and forth but nothing helped. It felt like I was being raped in my mind. I shouted at the demon that I was a being of power. In my ears it reverberated louder and louder until I realized it wasn't me saying it. It was the demon."

The Master couldn't stand the suspense. He got up and started pacing. As he paced, he shot Chester some questions. "What did you do next? How did you fight back? What did the girl do?"

Chester looked up with alarm. He hadn't realized how much the Master cared for him. "Master, it was your words that saved me."

The Master stopped and pivoted around. Looking at Chester he raised his eyebrows. *"My words?"*

"Remember, just as I left you reminded me that without God I was nothing." Chester licked his lips before continuing. "As I was being attacked by the demons, I also remembered your warning of me not being strong enough for the lion that wanted to devour me. That grinding, growling noise reminded me of a lion's rumble. Just as I was almost overwhelmed by the demon, I quit relying on my own power and started praying."

The Master focused on Chester's next words. In a near whisper he simply said, "Go on."

"As soon as I called out to God everything froze in place. The demon quit making more progress into my mind, but he wasn't backing out either. It was like someone pressed a pause button and God was waiting for the next words of my prayer. I looked past Candy onto the sky straining with my entire being to connect to God with my prayer."

The Master sat down but stayed sitting on the edge of his chair. "Try to remember the exact words of the prayer."

Chester looked up and rubbed his chin before looking back at the Master. "I think I have it. I remember saying, 'God, please God, I need you. I know now I haven't been doing right. I know all of this is my fault. I know now that I should have stayed on the path. I know I should have resisted temptation. I ask for your forgiveness God. I know now that without you I am nothing. I realize how much I need you. If it is your will that these demons take me over I accept it as my punishment. I completely turn myself over to you, God, to do as you will. Not my will but your will be done.' Right then I completely relaxed and was ready for whatever happened next."

The Master was smiling, sharing the moment. "Then what happened?"

"The scene changed quickly. Candy screamed real loud, 'NO,' and got off me. The darkness was replaced by light, and I felt supremely grateful. All the moving colorful patterns that reminded me of smoke shifted suddenly as if disturbed by rapid movement. It was like a puff of wind moved the smoky colors. I could hear Candy screaming that she hated me as she got up and left me alone on the blanket. It was like she was chased off by something. After she left; I couldn't get up I was so weak. Everything got brighter and brighter and I heard a beautiful sound like a keening of joy. I went from terror to ecstasy. I felt so much joy I was overwhelmed. Every cell in my body felt like it was alive for the first time, and every single one of them was a tiny pocket of joy. I felt like I had been born again. I believed at that moment that I had passed an important milestone in my life. I felt myself changing into something spiritual instead of physical. As I moved my head, I could see portals everywhere."

The Master frowned. "Portals?"

Chester replied, "I don't know how else to describe it really. The colors and patterns formed a honeycomb of entrances into other dimensions. This world got fainter and fainter until I had passed over into another reality altogether. It seemed more real to me at the time than this world does now. The new place I was in was a blank, gray featureless plain that extended in all directions. The sky was also a soft gray with no features. Somehow I knew that this place was mine to do whatever I wanted. My thoughts manifested themselves instantly. I was overjoyed to have such marvelous creative powers, and I started creating gardens filled with flowers, butterflies and sweet slow moving animals that were gentle and friendly."

The Master looked shocked. "I have never heard of an experience like that from any of our past Masters. Please go on." The Master leaned forward with a glint of interest in his eyes that Chester had never seen before.

"Let's see. I tired of creating gardens and trees, so I decided to make something different. In the middle of a garden I had created earlier, I added a golden pool filled with a clear crystalline dark blue liquid. Then in the middle of the pool, I made a special tree fashioned out of a sparkling red crystal. I gave it a special quality that was unique to all that I had created. When any creature got near it, the tree would resonate with a bell sound like a crystal glass. Not just any sound. It matched the mood of the animal near it. I was so filled with joy at the result of my creation that I just stood and sang a song of gratitude and happiness in harmony with the heavenly chiming of my red crystal tree." Chester stopped and took a deep breath.

The Master leaned back in his chair with a look of wonder. "How long were you there in this reality you created?"

Chester scratched his ear, "That's the funny part. It seemed like I was there a couple of weeks. After I finished my song everything started fading, and I passed through a portal again. After the honeycomb of portals faded, I was back on the blanket and the sun was going down. I felt exhausted but grateful. I came back here and, well, you know the rest."

Sanjiv walked in carrying a dinner of cheese, bread and vegetable soup. "Perfect timing. I'm hungry."

Instead of more conversation, all three sat around the table and began eating. The Master didn't ask any questions, and Chester felt too embarrassed to say anything. After the meal was over, he helped Sanjiv clear off the table. When he got back from the kitchen, he asked the Master, "If you knew what was going on, why didn't you stop me?"

The Master had moved back to his favorite chair. Chester went to his usual place and waited. The Master looked at Chester for a moment before responding with a question of his own. "Do you think I could have had any influence over you after you started seeing her?"

Chester thought a minute and finally shook his head. "No, I guess not."

"At least you came back here after every visit with her. Had I tried to intervene you may have left and never come back. I didn't want to risk running you off. Who knows where she would have taken you."

"What do you mean?"

"You know nobody lives around here for miles. Had you been thinking just a little you would have realized something strange was going on. Where did she come from and where did she go every day?"

"I guess I should have thought of that. I guess I wasn't thinking at all was I?"

"It has always been a Master's job to prepare his student for the trials and tests he will face, but not to face them for him. If I had intervened, you would have had the same temptation somewhere else, probably with disastrous results. It was best I left you alone."

Chester thought about that for a minute. "I feel so stupid."

"Actually you did okay considering who you were up against." Chester looked puzzled. The Master picked up a book sitting on the table between them. "This book has a list of all the Hindu gods and goddesses. All the Sanskrit names are also listed in English. See if this helps to clear it up for you."

Chester took the book but wasn't sure what to look for. "There are so many. What am I looking for?"

"Look under the Cs and let me know if anything jumps out at you."

Flipping back to near the first of the book. "Oh, I see a goddess called Candika with a footnote saying it is sometimes spelled Chandika." Chester looked up. "She is the slayer for she is the goddess of lust and desire. So I passed this test?"

"No, you failed the test but survived the trouble that you brought on yourself for failing the test. God forgives us our mistakes, but we still experience the consequences. You failed the test when you left the path to see who was singing. You failed it again when you allowed your lust to be fulfilled. This also means that until you successfully resist the temptation of lust you will face it again and again."

Chester raised his eyebrows. "Why me?"

The Master laughed. "Remember, in the *Yoga Sutras of Patanjali* it specifically warns the advanced yogi to beware of the deities of temptations. Because of your spiritual advances you have become a threat to the powers of darkness."

"Why do you say I'm now a threat?"

"All that you have learned here is for a reason. My Master told me of a prophecy that states that when the entire world can hear, The Understanding will not be withheld. I believe it is you who are to share this to the world. I believe you're the prophesied messenger of the ancient Understanding. There are many dark forces that will strive to keep it from coming out. I wish I could tell you that your path will be easy."

"I don't want to be the messenger."

"Your fate was sealed when you were born. Why do you think your last name is Messenger?"

"Well, if I'm a messenger, I'm a *reluctant messenger*."

"Reluctant or not, you did turn your life over to God today. I'm sure God took you seriously. Your life is not yours any more, it belongs to God."

Chester got up. "If you need me, I'll be in my room. I have a lot to think about."

The Master added, "And a lot to pray about."

Lydia and Tina

Tina was coming over. They hadn't seen each other since their trip to Six Flags. Lydia was in the kitchen when the doorbell rang. She quickly put some rolls in the oven before answering the door. "There you are. You're on time."

Tina waltzed in holding a paper sack. "Don't look. Let me put this in the refrigerator. It's a surprise."

Lydia put her hands on her hips. "What are you up to?" Lydia couldn't hear Tina's answer in the kitchen. "What did you say?"

Tina came out of the kitchen with a silly grin on her face. "Don't tell me you don't remember?"

Lydia shrugged. "What?"

"You'll find out soon enough. That smells good in there. What are you cooking?"

"I made a roast. As soon as the rolls are done, we can eat. Tell me how things are with you as I set the table."

"I'll help."

Tina set out plates and bowls while Lydia made a salad in the kitchen. "Well, do you like your new job?"

"I love it. Working at Hertz was okay, but I like having more responsibility. Did I tell you I got to meet some of the Dallas Cowboys?" As Lydia brought out the dinner from the kitchen, Tina told her all about meeting Michael Irwin. By the time Lydia had delivered the rolls to the table, Tina had run out of steam.

"Let's eat."

"Okay, let me get the surprise out of the refrigerator." Tina almost ran into the kitchen.

"Why are you so excited?"

As an answer, Tina grandly presented two bottles of Dr. Pepper to Lydia. "Ta, da! Remember, I told you I was going to get some original recipe. I want you to try it before you eat anything. Don't put a bite in your mouth until I get back with the glasses of ice." Lydia could hear the ice clinking in the kitchen. "Where is your bottle opener? These aren't the twist off kind."

"Look on the refrigerator."

Tina reappeared with two glasses and a bottle opener. "It's magnetic. How cute."

"I never lose it that way."

Tina made a big show out of opening both bottles and pouring the dark fizzing liquid over the ice slowly. "Wait until you taste this. You'll never want to go back to mass market Dr. Pepper again."

Lydia sipped it slowly, like it was a fine wine instead of a soda. Nodding her head she smiled. "I see what you mean. There is no after taste."

"I know, isn't it great?" Tina beamed with pride.

"Can we eat now? I'm starving." Tina and Lydia both bowed their heads for a few seconds and silently gave thanks before beginning the meal. "Here, have a roll while it's still warm. Want some butter?"

Tina and Lydia both piled their plates high. It was a tradition of theirs. Once a month they would get together and eat and talk. It was a way to celebrate their friendship. They never talked about anything serious during dinner. Tina finally had enough. "I don't know which was better, the roast or the mashed potatoes."

Lydia just grinned as she cleared the table. "You had *two* ears of corn."

Tina got two more bottles of Dr. Pepper and refilled the glasses with ice. Lydia joined Tina in the living room. "Gosh, if I'm not careful I'll fall asleep."

"Are you still working weekends?"

"Yes. I wouldn't mind, but I never get to see Paul. He has weekends off and I don't."

"How's that going?"

"He's been here almost a month, but I *never* see him. We talk on the phone and he's met me for lunch, once. I don't know. I thought him being in Dallas would be different. He might as well still be in Atlanta." Lydia made listening noises and let Tina vent. "At least when he was in Atlanta I could understand. But now, it's like…" Tina didn't finish her sentence. Instead she just stared into space.

"It's like what?"

"He says I complain too much. I wouldn't complain if I didn't care. It isn't fair." Lydia started to say something but stopped herself. "What?"

Lydia tried to wave it away. "Never mind."

"No what. Come on tell me."

"It's just that this isn't the first time you know."

Tina scowled up. "What does that mean?"

"You always complained about Richard never being around. That's why you dumped him. And remember Marcus, the work-a-holic?"

Tina crossed her arms. "This is different."

"Why is it different?"

"I don't know, but it is."

"See, this is why I didn't want to say anything. But I recently learned something about myself. Maybe it will help you, too."

"What? That I always pick the same kind of guy? I don't want to."

"Here, let me show you something my shrink gave me. It explains it better than I can." Lydia got up and went down the hall. When she came back she had a single piece of paper. "Here, read this."

Tina took the page and read the simple message.

Autobiography in Five Short Chapters

I.

I walk down the street.
There is a deep hole in the sidewalk.
I fall in.
I am lost...I am helpless;
it isn't my fault.
It takes forever to find a way out.

II.

I walk down the same street.
There is a deep hole in the sidewalk.
I pretend I don't see it.
I fall in again.
I can't believe I am in the same place;
but it isn't my fault.
It still takes a long time to get out.

III.

I walk down the same street.
There is a deep hole in the sidewalk.
I see it is there.
I still fall in...it's a habit.
My eyes are open.

I know where I am.
It is my fault.
I get out immediately.

IV.

I walk down the same street.
There is a deep hole in the sidewalk.
I walk around it.

V.

I walk down another street.

Portia Nelson
There's a Hole in My Sidewalk

Tina looked up. "Ouch!"

"Crystal says that our subconscious draws us to making the same painful choices over and over again unless we recognize the pattern and consciously change it. Remember you always complained about your father never being at home because he worked all the time. You tried so hard to get his attention, but you never really could."

"Yeah, but."..

"But what?" Lydia raised an eyebrow. "Every man I've known you to be attracted to has been a work-a-holic and/or emotionally unavailable."

"I don't choose them. They choose me," Tina defended.

"Really…?" Lydia teased. "How do you respond to the available, supportive, dependable men?"

Tina started laughing. "They're bor..r..ring."

"Got ya." Lydia giggled. "I guess we're both still on Chapter II."

Rolling sideways off the couch onto the floor laughing, Tina threw a pillow at her friend.

The Parable of the King's Diamonds

Chester was sipping his coffee as the Master walked in to join him for the morning meal. The Master pulled up a chair and sat down at the bamboo breakfast table. A large bowl of fruit was in the center. The peels of an orange lay scattered before Chester. The Master started peeling a banana. "How are your studies and contemplations?"

Chester put down his coffee and shook his head. "I've been going over in my head what you were telling me about the soul. Those books you gave me to read haven't helped me much either. I read what they said, but I don't understand. To me, it doesn't make any sense."

After swallowing his bite of banana, the Master pointed at Chester's head. "What is troubling your head?"

Chester scratched his head in reply. "You say and the books say that everyone has a soul, but Buddha said that even the soul is an illusion. You explained that all souls are identical and thus not separate. At the core of who we really are is the same spirit. My soul is a part of God and every other soul is a part of God. God is God and there is no other. Yet if we are all the same, then why are we all different?"

The Master mumbled around his banana, "Karma."

Chester frowned. "If karma is what makes us different, then what do you call that which is the same in all of us?"

The Master started peeling a grape. "Truth."

Chester was growing frustrated, but he knew better than to lose his cool with the Master. He tried a different tack. "Okay, if I recite what you asked me to memorize, will you please explain it to me?"

The Master smiled. His pleasure showed on his face. His student was learning self-control even when frustrated. The man that used to shout and argue had come a long way. The Master cocked his head in a half nod toward Chester and peeled another grape.

Chester closed his eyes and starting reciting in his deeper voice, "There is self and there is truth. Where self is, truth is not. Where truth is, self is not. Self is the fleeting error that creates the endless cycle of births and deaths; it is individual separateness and egotism which begets envy and hatred. Self is the yearning for pleasure and the lust after vanity. Truth is the correct comprehension of things. It is the permanent and everlasting, the real in all existence, the bliss of righteousness, and the purity that is Eternal Brahma. The existence of self is an illusion, and there is no wrong in this world, no vise, no evil, except what flows from the assertion of self. The attainment of truth is possible only when self is recognized as an illusion. Righteousness can be practiced only when we have freed our mind from the passions of egotism. Perfect peace can dwell only where all vanity has disappeared. Blessed is he who has understood the Dharma. Blessed is he who does no harm to his fellow-beings. Blessed is he who overcomes wrong and is free from passion. To the highest bliss has he attained who has conquered all selfishness and vanity. He has become the Buddha, the Perfect One, the Blessed One, the Holy One."

Chester opened his eyes to see his master smiling. "Very good. I will now explain this as my master explained it to me. He called it The Parable of the King's Diamonds."

Chester poured himself some more coffee from the urn on the table. As he stirred in sweetened cream, he commented, "Well, a diamond is forever."

The Master settled back in his chair. "Once there was a King who owned the most perfect diamonds in the world. Each diamond was priceless. Each was the size of a man's fist and would sparkle with a rainbow of shimmering hues from just the glow of a candle. Each of the King's diamonds was identical yet precious and sought after for they were life. If the King gave a diamond to one of his subjects, he or she was free to travel anywhere without fear. The diamonds were magical and could never be lost or stolen. When his subjects finished their travels, they were to bring their diamond back to the King and tell him of their travels and what they had learned. The King gave two brothers each a diamond and gave them leave of his palace to travel as far and as wide as their hearts desired. One brother went to the north and one went to the south. The brother who went to the north cared for his diamond every day and made sure it was washed in pure water every night before bed. He protected the diamond and didn't let even a speck of dust linger on the King's precious gift for more than a moment. He traveled far and wide and shared the story of the King's gift and brought the light of truth to all he met. His brother went south and was proud of his gift of the diamond yet cared for it not. He traveled far and wide and let the dust of his travels coat the diamond. His sweat dried on the diamond and mixed with the dust to form a haze that blocked the beauty of the gift. He was a violent man and the blood of those he killed stained the diamond. He stole from others and had to hide in caves. Mud from the wet dark caves covered the diamond until it was a black rock of dried mud and blood. He grew afraid. Even though he could not lose the diamond, he hid it from others for he was ashamed of its appearance. One day the word went out throughout the Kingdom that the King was recalling all of the diamonds back to the palace for an accounting. Both brothers obeyed their King and returned as instructed. The first brother who went north gave the diamond to the King and told him of his travels. The King blessed him for the wise and special care he took of the King's gift and gave him a position of authority and power over many more diamonds. The brother who went south reluctantly handed the King the diamond that was caked with dried blood and the filth of his travels. The King was angry and threw the evil brother into a deep dungeon. He was not allowed out until he could deliver the diamond back to the King in its pristine form. The evil brother only had his tears to wash the diamond with; and he suffered for many, many years. Finally he was able to bring the diamond back to the King in its original form. The King forgave his servant but never trusted him again with another of his diamonds."

When the Master was finished, Chester just shook his head. "Was that supposed to make it easier to understand the soul? I'm more confused than ever."

The Master smiled and leaned forward. "We all have a soul that is like a diamond from the King. God is the King and we are the diamonds that can never be harmed or lost. Yet our deeds are carried with the diamond. As long as we do evil, our diamond is covered in its filth. Until we can clean our diamond completely, we are not allowed back in the King's palace. Good karma is like washing the diamond with pure water and bad karma is like the blood and mud. Bad karma causes suffering and good karma causes blessing. Even though we are all the same inside, our deeds are what make us different. Some have very dirty diamonds and some have very clean diamonds. Buddha learned how to clean his diamond completely by removing the lust, envy and hatred that covered his diamond. The truth that we are all part of God can be blocked by the illusion of separateness called the ego. All souls are identical but not all have the same baggage. Christ was one with the Father only because he was not deceived into thinking that he was separate from God. He was righteous and perfect and never lost union with the Father. We are all one. This is why Christ said that he who is generous and kind to another in his name is being generous to Christ."

Chester stroked his chin. "Is this another one of those stories that the more you think about it the more it makes sense?"

The Master pushed back from the table and cocked his head in a half nod toward him, then left Chester to further contemplate the Parable of the King's Diamonds.

Lydia Has Another Dream

Lydia sat up in her with her eyes wide open and felt relief. Relieved it was just a dream and not something real. She turned to her right and picked up her tape recorder. She pushed 'record' and held one corner of it up close to her mouth. "I just had the dream again, but I remember more now." The slender strap of her gown fell to her elbow as she propped herself up. "This time I remember getting on the train with my mother, but she wasn't white. She was a beautiful dark-skinned woman with almond eyes and dark black hair. Her name was Panini and she called me Kamna. We both said goodbye to my papa. He was at the train station and wasn't pleased with her but didn't say anything. It had all been said before it seems. Momma and I rode the train until there was a horrible crash and that is where I woke up. But I didn't wake up right away like I usually do. I remember what happened right after I died because I watched them take my dark-skinned bloody body away in a stretcher. Then I woke up." Lydia blew the hair out of her eyes and said to the empty room. "Coffee!"

* * * *

Lydia made sure she was on time for her weekly appointment with Crystal. It wasn't until after she had settled into the soft lounger that she allowed herself to relax. She blew out a noisy sigh. "Finally!"

"You seem more anxious or eager today or something. What is it?"

"I don't know, well, yes I do. I had another dream. This time I remembered it perfectly, in fact I still do. I don't need to listen to the tape recorder or anything."

"Why do you think this particular dream is so vivid and memorable?"

Lydia paused. "I feel weird even saying this but I dreamed I died, and I was able to see what happened after I died." Crystal smiled in response. "What's so funny?"

"If I had a dollar for every time I heard that I could buy this college."

"Oh yeah, I forgot, you talk to people who remember dying all the time."

"Not all of them remember unless I help them."

"I want to find out why I'm having this dream."

Crystal stated with calm authority, "If we find out why you are having this dream, I think you will have your answers. Are you willing to let your subconscious help you again like last week?"

"I am, but what are we going to do this time?"

Crystal paused for a moment. "I have to be honest with you. I am going to attempt something that I have never done before but other people have. Earlier this week, I had a long phone conversation with a colleague of mine that lives in California. He has done many, what he calls, past life regressions. He told me it is very similar to what we did last week, only instead of asking you to go back in time to when you were a little girl, I will ask you to go back in time even further. If we are successful, you may be able to remember what happened even though it is before you were born."

"But I don't believe in that."

"He said it doesn't matter. He has regressed many patients. He told me that the subject's ability to reach a deep enough trance is the key, not the subject's belief system. When I told him about our previous sessions, he told me you should be an excellent subject. Are you comfortable with this?"

"Yes. Before I came here I asked God to protect me like I did the last few times. I trust God to make sure nothing bad happens to me."

"Do you want to pray now?"

"No, that's okay."

"So does that mean you are ready? It should be a learning experience for both of us."

For an answer Lydia wiggled into the soft chair and leaned her head back just a little as she closed her eyes. Crystal reached over and clicked the recorder on. "Close your eyes and count backwards from 30 to 1 slowly in your mind. With each number relax a different part of your body." When Lydia's body showed no signs of tension, Crystal prepared her for the prearranged phrase. "I'm going to count slowly to five. When I get there, I want you to visualize lying in your boat on the lake with a full moon overhead. 1, 2, 3, 4, and 5. Boat Relax Now." Lydia's didn't move. "As you drift gently in your boat you feel as if you are floating. I want you to go you back to an important time after you were born and tell me what you see." Lydia smiled but kept her eyes closed. "What is happening?"

"I got a puppy for my birthday."

"How old are you?"

"I'm five."

"I'm going to count to five, and I want you to go back a few more years. 1, 2, 3, 4, and 5. What is happening?"

"I'm lying down looking up at mommy."

"What is she doing?"

"She is changing my diaper."

"I'm going to count to five, and I want you to go back even farther. 1, 2, 3, 4, and 5. What is happening?" Crystal learned later this wasn't exactly the best way to regress someone, but it didn't matter since it worked."

"I'm eating. This is very strange."

"What is strange?"

"I feel like I'm still Lydia, but it's like I'm looking through someone else's eyes."

"I believe this is normal; tell me what you are experiencing."

"I'm with some people and somehow I know they are my family. There is my mother, my father, and my brother. We are at a restaurant. The food is spicy but good."

"Can you see yourself?"

"I can see my hands as I eat. I have dark skin and my nails aren't done."

"What is your name, and what are the names of your family?"

"I'm Kamna, my mother's name is Panini, my father's name is Darshan, and my brother's name is Etash. Our last name is Radhakrishnan."

"What are you and your family talking about?"

"We are planning a trip we will take together."

"What kind of trip?"

"We will travel by rail to visit my mother's family in Ariyalur."

"On the count of five, I want you to move forward in time to where another important event happens concerning the trip on the train, 1, 2, 3, 4, and 5. What are you doing now?"

"I am reading my mail. I have been offered a job as a hostess on a luxury cruise ship that will go from India to the United States."

"How old are you?"

"I will be twenty next month."

Crystal ventured deeper. "Does your father know you've been offered the job?"

"Papa wants me to go back to school, and I want to go to America. I have to tell him tonight."

"On the count of five, I want your boat to take you to the conversation with your father about the job offer."

Lydia's breathing increased almost immediately. Her eyes moved back and forth quicker under her eyelids. Crystal wanted her to keep talking. "Tell me what is happening."

"My father has forbidden me to accept the job. He refuses to listen to what I want." There was a long pause before Lydia said anymore. "I have insulted him deeply. Before he left, he told me he no longer had a daughter."

"What did you say to insult him so?"

"I told him he was the worst father in the world, and it was time I did what I wanted not what he wanted."

"On the count of five, move forward to the next significant event before the train ride. 1, 2, 3, 4, and 5. Where are you now?"

I'm at my new apartment with my mother. My mother and I have decided to go ahead and take the trip to her people just before I take my new job."

"Won't your brother be on the train with you?"

"My father has forbidden him from ever speaking to me again. I moved out of the house three weeks ago. My mother is all I have left."

"Why didn't he forbid her from going?"

"My mother has her ways. She told him she still has a daughter and will never forsake me."

"At the count of five, I want you to go forward to the next important encounter with your mother concerning the train. 1, 2, 3, 4, and 5. What is happening?"

Lydia was quiet for a moment as if collecting information. "I'm on a train."

"You are on the train?"

"We are going to see my grandparents."

"Who are *we*?"

"My mother and me. It is a long train ride. Something is wrong. Oh my God!"

"When I count to five, you will watch what happens but won't feel any pain or discomfort. 1, 2, 3, 4, and 5. Watch from the boat. Tell me what is happening."

"The train has fallen. Water is coming in. None of us can get out. I can't breathe, and I'm drowning." Lydia became very quiet.

"What do you see?"

"There are people with a boat." Lydia paused. "They are trying to rescue us. I can see my body and my mother's body on the bank of a river. I can see the train. The bridge has collapsed. All of the train is in the water. I think a lot of people have died. This is strange."

"What is strange?"

"I know I am dead, but I feel at peace."

Crystal waited about a minute before bringing Lydia out of her trance. At the count of five, I want you to come back to the present. You will remember everything. 1, 2, 3, 4 and 5."

Lydia blinked her eyes open and stretched. "Um. I don't know what to say."

Crystal pursed her lips in thought before responding. "Let me ask you something. Did those feel like memories?"

"What do you mean?"

"Does the experience of what happened in India feel like memories or something else? I guess what I mean is, did it feel like the memories of when you were a little girl?"

"Yes and no."

"That doesn't help. Please explain what you mean by 'yes and no.'"

Lydia sighed. "I don't know how to put it in words. It felt the same in one way. But the whole time I was remembering arguing with my father in India, part of me felt like I was watching someone else. I didn't feel that way when I was watching my memories as a child."

"Could it be you identified with your memories as little Lydia but couldn't identify with the other memories?"

"That's probably it." Lydia brushed back her hair with her hand. "I mean, I couldn't have been someone who lived in India, right?" Instead of responding, Crystal picked up a pen and her notes and started writing something down. "What are you writing?"

When Crystal was finished she put down her notes and looked at Lydia. "I wrote down that you couldn't accept the experience today as proof that you have lived before. I also wrote myself a reminder to see if any of the details you revealed could be verified."

"So where does that leave us?"

"I don't know. Mostly that will depend on you. On the one hand, what you experienced today could very well be memories of a previous life. In my opinion, that theory fits the facts. But, my opinion isn't important because you didn't come to me to find out about whether or not you have lived before. You came here because you wanted help with your nightmares. As a scientist, I am willing to keep an open mind. Perhaps all you did today was remember some very vivid and lifelike dreams. Who knows what the mind is capable of? Today we gathered data. One of my college professors told me something that I will always remember. She said that *facts are facts and interpretation is interpretation. Don't get the two confused.* The facts are that today, under hypnosis, you described in detail experiences that appeared to have occurred in India. It is too soon to know what that means."

Lydia stood up. "Okay, I guess that means I will see you next week."

As a reply, Crystal stood up and said, "See you next week."

AND GOD SAID...

Chester sat quietly meditating by the contemplation pond as the Sabbath began. In this part of India twilight turned quickly into darkness. It was a warm night and the frogs were competing with the insects on who could make the most noise. It wasn't the noise that distracted him; it was a question that was trying to form in his mind. As he contemplated the events of the past months, he knew that soon he would have to leave. He felt he had learned much yet he also felt he had so much left to learn. He began reciting in his mind the Seven Wisdoms: Eternity, Infinity, Awareness, Oneness, Balance, Faith and Holiness. The Master taught him to begin each Sabbath by contemplating the seven wisdoms. It was oneness that nudged his mind closer and closer to a question. In concert with his contemplation the frogs croaked in unison, "One God." Yet why did the thought of One God seem contradictory to him? He mentally reviewed the lessons of the Master. His mind focused on one of his first lessons. He realized the Master had left an important concept unexplained when he taught him the true meaning of Genesis 1. If there is just one God, why does it say *God said let us make man in our image, after our likeness*. Who are *us*? The question, now fully formed, prevented any further progress in his meditations. With a sigh he unfolded from his meditation position and made his way down the path to the Master's home.

* * * *

The Master looked up from his reading as Chester cleared his throat. He could tell by the look on his face that he wanted to talk. Motioning to the chair next to his, he waited. "It's funny I hadn't thought of this before; but if there is only one God, why does Genesis quote God as saying, 'let us make man in our image?' Who is this 'us' speaking?"

The Master looked proud. "You ask well. I was wondering if you would ever ask this important question. It shows progress on your part to ask. Once again we will need a Bible and the concordance. You know where they are."

Chester smiled. As the time came nearer and nearer to his departure, these sessions with the Master had become less frequent. It seemed the Master was content to leave him to his meditation practice. Little did he realize that soon he would miss the luxury of having nothing better to do than meditate all day. After lifting the books from their spots on the shelves, he placed them on the table next to the chairs that they would be sitting in. The Master didn't reach for the books. Instead, he began in his teaching voice. "The Buddhist teach that an omniscient Buddha comes around every 25,000 years or so. They say that Siddhartha Buddha was the fifth such Buddha. The ancient religion now called Hinduism has a history that goes back at least 50,000 years. Yet what Genesis describes in verse two happened only about 6,000 years ago."

Chester frowned. "Yes. That is one of the first truths you taught me. The rebellion of Lucifer is why God came down to repair the Earth. That explains why we can have a fossil record that goes back 3.6 billion years and why the Genesis account of creation is also true at the same time. How does that explain God in the plural?"

The Master replied, "The answer to your question is also why they killed Jesus."

To Chester this did not make any sense. As usual, the Master began by speaking in riddles. Instead of losing his cool and starting an argument like he used to, he sat patiently and waited for the Master to continue. Soon the Master filled the silence with a suggestion. "Turn to John chapter 10 and read to me verses 30 to 36."

Chester turned to the passage and read it out loud. "*John 10:*
30 I and my Father are one.
31 Then the Jews took up stones again to stone him.
32 Jesus answered them, Many good works have I shewed you from my Father; for which of those works do ye stone me?
33 The Jews answered him, saying, For a good work we stone thee not; but for blasphemy; and because that thou, being a man, makest thyself God.
34 Jesus answered them, Is it not written in your law, I said, Ye are gods?
35 If he called them gods, unto whom the word of God came, and the scripture cannot be broken;
36 Say ye of him, whom the Father hath sanctified, and sent into the world, Thou blasphemest; because I said, I am the Son of God?"

Looking up he said. "I know that Jesus is the son of God. I know from John 1 that he was the creator God before he came down to Earth in the flesh. That still doesn't explain God saying *let us*, does it?"

The Master pointed at the Bible he was holding. "Jesus was quoting a scripture from the Old Testament. Now turn to Psalm 82:6 and read it to me."

Chester flipped back to Psalms and read. "Psalms 82:6 *I have said, Ye are gods; and all of you are children of the most High.*"

The Master continued his instruction. "Use the concordance and tell me what Hebrew word was translated as gods in the verse you just read."

Chester knew the drill by now and quickly found the proper reference. "It says it is from the Hebrew word *Elohiym* and that it is the plural of *Elowahh*, meaning God. Hmmmm."

"There is another scripture that may help. Read what Joshua 22:22 says."

Chester flipped to it and read. "Joshua 22:22 *The LORD God of gods, the LORD God of gods, he knoweth, and Israel he shall know; if it be in rebellion, or if in transgression against the LORD, (save us not this day,)*" He looked up at the Master. "The God of gods?"

The Master nodded. "Look up what the Hebrew words are for 'LORD', 'God' and 'gods.'"

Chester looked eager as he made the necessary references. "LORD is from *Yehovah* which means 'self-existent.' God is from *El* which means 'God' and gods is from *Elohiym* which means 'more than one god.'"

The Master explained. "The God of Israel has a name which means 'self-existent one' and the Old Testament records that he is the God of gods. Now turn to Genesis and find the scripture that reads *God said let us* and tell me what is the Hebrew word that they translated as God."

It took a moment for Chester to find the scripture. It was in Genesis 1:26 and it read, *And God said, Let us make man in our image, after our likeness*. After finding the original Hebrew in the concordance, Chester frowned and looked up. "It says God in English but the Hebrew word is *Elohiym*, which is a plural noun."

The Master laughed. "If your translators had done their job right, it would have read. *And the gods said, let us make man in our image, after our likeness*" The Master let his words hang in the air as Chester struggled to understand.

Finally Chester just shook his head and held out his hands palm up. "I give up."

The Master laughed. "Do you think that God the Father, who has always existed, who is omnipresent and pervades all of reality looks like a man? You've memorized the definition of Brahman. What is it?"

Chester quickly quoted. "Brahman is the transcendent absolute being that pervades and supports all reality. That which is Absolute, fills all space, is complete in itself, to which there is no second, and is continuously present in everything, from the creator down to the lowest of matter." He rattled the definition off quickly and with an obvious sense of pride.

The Master shook his head. "You have memorized well, but they are just words if you do not have comprehension of their true meaning. How can the Eternal Transcendent God that pervades all matter look like you or me?"

Chester frowned and looked dumbly at the Master. "I guess I never thought of it like that."

"Do you remember the story of Enoch?"

Instead of answering right away, Chester flipped to the chapter in Genesis that spoke of Enoch. He read out loud verse 24 of chapter 5. "*And Enoch walked with God: and he was not; for God took him.*" He then turned to Hebrews and read, "Hebrews 11:5 *By faith Enoch was taken away so that he did not see death, and was not found, because God had taken him; for before he was taken he had this testimony, that he pleased God.*"

The Master said, "I'll give you one more hint. Read to me Romans 8. To make it easier for you, read it in the New International Version. I have a copy over where you found the King James. After Chester got the other Bible the Master said, "Read Romans 8:14 through 17."

Chester complied. "Romans 8:14-17, *because those who are led by the Spirit of God are sons of God. For you did not receive a spirit that makes you a slave again to fear, but you received the Spirit of sonship. And by him we cry, 'Abba, Father' the Spirit himself testifies with our spirit that we are God's children. Now if we are children, then we are heirs—heirs of God and co-heirs with Christ, if indeed we share in his sufferings in order that we may also share in his glory.*" Chester commented. "I remember these scriptures. You explained they showed that it is our true destiny to become God just as Christ is God. But this verse speaks of our yet unrealized God potential."

The Master was patient. "Chester, how long has man as we know it been on the planet?"

"Well, it's estimated that Cro-Magnon man was about 50,000 maybe 40,000 years ago. Let's see, Neanderthal arrived about 100,000 maybe 150,000 years ago. Some say possibly even longer ago than that. But, the first proto-man was at least 2 million years ago." The Master prodded further. "And why did Lucifer rebel?"

"Because he discovered that God was creating God beings that would forever be more glorious than even he was."

"How do you think Lucifer came to this discovery?"

Chester suddenly slapped his forehead with the palm of his hand. "Of course, when men started achieving their God Consciousness, it became obvious to Lucifer why God had created a universe that could evolve beings such as man. I remember you telling me about the legends of ancient Hindu Yogis who had become so pure in thought and deed that they became gods."

The Master leaned forward, his eyes shining as he watched his student understand. "The Bible records Enoch becoming eternal, right? What religion do you think Enoch was practicing 5,000 years ago? Judaism? Christianity? No, of course not. Enoch practiced what we would call Vedism today. Remember the Dance of Shiva?"

Chester exclaimed. "Right. Just because Enoch was translated into immortal life after God repaired the Earth doesn't mean others hadn't done it before the Earth was repaired. That must have been how Lucifer learned of God's true purpose for man."

The Master sat back with a look of triumph on his face. "Now tell me my stubborn student. Who said *let us make man in our image, after our likeness*? Who? Hmmm?"

Chester laughed so hard he could hardly answer. It seemed so obvious now. "The men and women who had become god-beings in the centuries leading up to the rebellion of Lucifer were the gods repairing the Earth so the rest of mankind could continue its journey. So we could have our opportunity to become gods, also." Chester leaned back and shook his head at his own denseness.

The Master and Chester both sat in silence, grinning and enjoying the moment.

Lydia and Crystal's Last Meeting

Lydia was being quiet. She had been that way since she had come in for her appointment. Crystal had waited several minutes hoping Lydia would say something. "It looks like I need to get us started. Are you okay?"

Lydia nodded then shook her head. Crystal nodded then shook her head then raised her eyebrows. Lydia laughed before breaking her silence. "I'm sorry. I just came by to say goodbye. I don't want you to hypnotize me or anything."

Crystal smiled. "That's good, I think. Does that mean you're not having any more nightmares?"

Lydia nodded then looked at her hands before trying to explain. "I appreciate everything you have done and all, it's just that…" Instead of continuing Lydia shrugged. "I mean what's the point. I'm not depressed anymore. I'm not having nightmares. I'm all better."

"I see." Crystal slowly nodded with a big smile. "You think I will be mad or you will hurt my feelings if you stop coming."

"You're right. I don't want to be a guinea pig. I just want to get on with my life."

"That's great. Whatever we did here helped. Right? That was what this was all about."

Lydia nodded her head and looked relieved. "So are we finished?"

Crystal nodded and held up her hand. "Just a few items before you go. Let me get you your baby book and drawings. I won't need them anymore. Besides I have copies. I do have one question before you leave. Do you want to know what I found out last week about India?"

Lydia frowned. "India? What do you mean 'found out'?"

Crystal sat up and placed her hands on her lap. "Being part of a university has its advantages. I was able to do some research into India and came up with some interesting historical facts that fit the details we uncovered in our last session."

Lydia narrowed her eyes. "What do you mean *details*?"

As a reply, Crystal picked up a folder sitting on a table next to her and handed it to Lydia. "You might find this interesting."

Lydia looked inside. In it was a single typewritten page with a few short paragraphs.

> **Radhakrishnan:** Surname Common in southern India
> **Kamna:** Female Indian name meaning *Wish*
> **Panini:** Female Indian name meaning *Skillful*
> **Darshan:** Male Indian name meaning *Paying Respect*
> **Etash:** Male Indian name meaning *Luminous*
>
> **Ariyalur:** City in Southern India. It gets its name from the legend that ages ago, Lord Vishnu, also known as Ari, once lived there; thus the name "Ariyalur".
>
> **November 25, 1956:** Ariyalur witnessed a railway accident, which is the saddest of that type in the state. The mishap was in the monsoon season of 1956 when Maruthai River was overflowing. While Rockford Express plying from Chennai to Trichy was on the bridge over Maruthai River, the bridge collapsed and the train went under water. More than 144 passengers died and many were rescued in critical condition. The incident shook the whole country. Lal Bahadur Shastri, the railway minister of India at the time resigned because of the tragedy.

Lydia looked up from the sheet. "What does this mean?"

Crystal held up her hands in disbelief. "Isn't it obvious? Every detail you described in last week's session has checked out. The last name you gave for the family is common to the region you described. Every name you mentioned for you and your family is a common name for that culture. The town you and your mother were traveling to, not only exists, but history records that in 1956 a terrible train wreck happened just like you described. All this happened just six years before your birth. Don't you see? Those details couldn't have been just a dream. Nobody has historically accurate nightmares unless they had access to the information somehow. You didn't know any of this before today." Crystal's voice rose in excitement. "This is incredible."

Lydia sat stunned shaking her head. "I don't know what to say."

Crystal laughed. "You don't have to say anything. But I thought it was only fair you had this information. Besides, if I were you, I would want to go to India and see if this checked out."

Lydia shook her head and handed the paper back to Crystal. "I don't know, maybe I don't want to know. But..." Lydia let the word hang in the air.

Crystal echoed her. "But? But what?"

Lydia let out a nervous laugh. "Funny coincidence happened in church last Sunday. Our minister's sermon was about how everything happens for a reason. Now you tell me that my dreams are in the history books. I am a travel agent. It would be easy for me to travel to India and see if what I dreamed about happened or not. Not that I don't believe you, but..." Lydia let out a big sigh. "I wasn't expecting this. I need time to think. This is too much for me right now."

Crystal got up. "I understand. Let me get you your belongings." She took the folder that had the details about India and placed it on top of Lydia's baby book. "Take these. They are yours. Maybe now you can read your mother's journal, and it won't be so frightening to you."

Lydia gave Crystal a big hug. "Thank you for all your help."

"Will I see you again?"

"I don't know. Let's just see what happens, okay?"
Crystal laughed. "Fair enough."

The Final Challenge

Chester waited for the Master to join him in the study. He took a deep breath. He hadn't challenged the Master in a while but one particular question burned in his mind like an unanswered rebuttal. The Master was so silent that Chester didn't notice him until he placed a glass of chilled fruit juice next to him. Startled, Chester looked up and said "Thank you."

The Master sat down with a pleased look. "It has been too long since we talked. But I wanted to leave you alone as you finished your notes. I will miss you when you leave here." He sipped the fruit juice from the glass he was holding.

Chester held up a thick pile of papers as an answer. "I'm almost finished. But I have one question that won't leave me alone. You tell me that this secret knowledge has been passed down from master to student for almost four thousand years. How is it possible to keep a secret that long?"

"You have a mind that misses nothing yet overlooks the obvious. The Seven Wisdoms are scattered throughout the world's religions. I told you that long ago."

"I'm not talking about the Seven Wisdoms, I'm talking about the fact that Satan is responsible for the mess we are in. I'm talking about the knowledge that Satan wanted to stop the reincarnations so no soul on this planet could achieve full God Awareness. Certainly this information had to have been leaked before. If so, why doesn't history record a hint of it?"

"There were a group of Christians who had beliefs similar to what we are talking about. You may have heard of the Gnostics."

Chester frowned. "Weren't they killed off?"

The Master nodded. "Supposedly all of their writings were destroyed, but it turns out not all of them were. They believed in reincarnation and of the culpability of Satan. They were persecuted and wiped out about three hundred years after Christ. Some of their sacred writings were discovered buried at Nag Hammadi, Egypt, in 1945. Just before the sect was wiped out they buried their sacred texts. The Gospel of Thomas was found among the scrolls unearthed at Nag Hammadi. In some of their sacred texts, you will find an alternate version of creation. In it they claim that our world was created by an evil God who caused many souls to become trapped here. Jesus, according to their scripture, came to show us how to escape the clutches of the evil one by giving us special knowledge of ourselves. One of his sayings recorded in the Gospel of Thomas expresses that belief. In it Christ is quoted as revealing that '*when you know yourselves, then you will be known, and you will understand that you are children of the living Father. But if you do not know yourselves, then you live in poverty, and you are the poverty.*'"

"But Satan didn't create this world, God did."

"When Satan was still holy he found the blue and green jewel we call Earth, thus manifesting it from the infinite probabilities. Your quantum science teaches that unless something is observed, it is not real. God created the infinite possibilities, but we are the creators who manifest reality from day-to-day. When Lucifer discovered our planet he in a sense created it. After God gave him Lordship, he was and still is the god of this world. Paul wrote of this very fact in a letter to the Corinthians[1]. Obviously the way the Gnostics put it is a little different from how you would explain it, but essentially it is the same story told from the perspective of a culture almost 2,000 years old."

"Are you saying that Christ was one of the Masters or that he learned it from a Master?"

"Christ traveled the world from the time he was 12 to when he was almost 30. Obviously he picked up the information from somewhere. It is recorded that he traveled into India and Tibet." Instead of continuing the Master shrugged.

"Recorded where?"

"I thought the subject was whether this information I have been teaching is recorded in history?"

"We can explore Jesus traveling to India later. Was during the time of Christ the only time the information has leaked out? Christ wasn't a secret at all so he can't be one of your secret masters. Christ doesn't count on this one. Has there ever been a time in recorded history when the secrets you have told me have leaked out instead of being kept secret?"

The Master face grew grim. "Are all Americans so ignorant of history that isn't directly about them?"

"I had World History in college, and it didn't mention anything that even remotely resembles your ancient secret. Your past Masters kept the secret too well it seems. That is why your story lacks credibility."

"History is written from the perspective of the winners not the losers. There was a Master who allowed the information to leak out before it was time. His teaching took hold and swept through whole communities. Thousands were killed because of it. History records them as heretics, and they were hunted down and killed because of what they believed."

---

1. 2 Corinthians 4:4 The god of this age has blinded the minds of unbelievers, so that they cannot see the light of the gospel of the glory of Christ, who is the image of God. NIV

Chester frowned. "You're not talking about the Gnostics again, are you?"

The Master shook his head. "Haven't you heard of the Inquisition?"

Chester jerked his head in disgust. "Of course, it is the most heinous part of Christian history. In someways, what the Inquisition did was worse than what Hitler did. The Inquisition committed their crimes under the name of Jesus."

The Master seemed reluctant to continue. He sighed and hung his head. "History records that the office of the Inquisition was formed in 1233 A.D. and the first town-wide massacre under its authority occurred in 1234 A.D. The whole town was wiped out including women, children, old people, everybody!"

Chester was visibly shaken by the date. "I didn't know that."

"Aren't you just a bit interested in what was considered so terrible that a whole town was murdered?" Not waiting for Chester's response the Master stood up and almost shouted. "I was there. I was the student that leaked the information! The Inquisition was my fault." The only clue that the Master was struggling to maintain his composure was his fists clenched at his sides. "Read about the Cathars and what they believed. There is a book in my library called *The Great Heresy*." The Master had tears in his eyes and he trembled. "I didn't listen to the warnings that it wasn't time to reveal the secrets. I did it anyway and the horrible consequences that resulted weigh on my soul."

Chester was stunned; he had never seen the Master act like this.

Sanjiv ran into the room and confronted Chester. "What you do to Master?"

"I didn't do anything."

Sanjiv wasn't there to argue. He had gone after the Master. Chester started to follow but thought better of it. He went into the Master's library to read about the Cathars. He found a book titled *The Great Heresy: The History and Beliefs of the Cathars,* by Arthur Guirdham. The hairs on his neck slowly rose as he read of a Christian sect that existed for awhile as the Dark Ages raged across Europe. They believed in reincarnation, and they believed that Satan or the Devil had created the world and was at war with God. Except for eating fish, they were vegetarians. Their teachings spread into northern Italy and southern France. When he read about the formation of the Inquisition in 1233 A.D. for the express purpose of eradicating the planet of these people and their beliefs, he couldn't hold back the tears any longer.

He put the book down and went to look for the Master. By accident he had discovered the Master's dark secret from one of his past lives, and he felt that somehow he shared in the Master's guilt. He hoped he would find the Master at the contemplation glade. It was dark but the path was white, and he was used to its curves and slopes. Before he could see him, he heard him.

"Here I am."

Chester saw the outline of Sanjiv and the Master sitting near the water. He joined them and felt the silence of secrets straining to be released.

The Master must have regained his composure because his voice was strong and even. "Years ago I was able to pierce the veil of forgetfulness, and I remembered every one of my past lives going all the way back to when I was with God in perfect Oneness. One of those lives was of a young man who thought he knew better than his Master. In a monastery in northern Italy, I was the Master's favorite of about a dozen monks under his tutelage. We were dedicated to a life of companionship with God through Christ. This lifetime was near the end of the first millennium. One of my most vivid memories was arguing that the beginning of the new millennium would be ushered in by the return of Christ. I was so sure because the Abby Master had been sharing with me mystic secrets about how to totally surrender to God. He had chosen me to receive ancient secrets passed from master to master for over 3,000 years. After about fifteen years of training, he had instructed me in how to share the secrets with another before I died. He was almost 70 years old when he died. Back then that was an extremely long time."

"How old were you when he died?" Sanjiv asked.

Chester was surprised at how clear Sanjiv's English was. He had forgotten he was listening to the Master's story as well.

"I was nearly 40, and I felt old. The 1,000th year since the death of Christ was only twelve years away, and I believed so strongly in His imminent return that I decided it was time to share the secrets to help usher in the new millennium. I preached what I had learned to towns and villages over parts of France and Italy for fifteen years. I was wrong about the new millennium. I quit sharing what I had learned in embarrassment of being wrong that Christ would return. I lived to be almost 60, and I did teach and instruct a new master before I died but the information was out and it was slowly spreading. I died not knowing the tragic results of my disobedience. It took about a hundred years before the Church noticed that a form of Gnosticism had returned. Of course by that time, it wasn't exactly what I had taught; but it was enough to cause a revolution in thought and lifestyle."

"You can't blame yourself for the Inquisition. It was over 200 years later." Chester shifted, the grass was damp and so were his pants. "Can we go back into the house?"

The Master answered by getting up. As they all three made their way back in the starlight, the Master chuckled. "Want to hear a perfect example of karma in action?" Rather than wait for a reply he continued, "I was one of the first people ever tortured and killed by the Inquisition for believing in Catharism. Of course, that was in my next life. I didn't know at the time that actions from a previous lifetime were shaping my fate in that lifetime. But I remember that I was proud to die for my beliefs. It wasn't until this lifetime that I had the strength to see the karmic expression of one lifetime to another. I know now to keep all this secret."

Chester had forgotten all about the original challenge.

The Master parted the mosquito netting for Sanjiv and Chester. Chester felt the Master was still holding something back as he waited for the Master to continue. He followed him and Sanjiv back to the study where the conversation had started in the first place. "No, the karmic irony has just begun." Chester narrowed his eyes. The Master was using his serious voice. "History repeats itself. I was wrong by about 1,000 years. For a mistake I made five lifetimes ago, I will fulfill my destiny in a different way. I was originally supposed to share these secrets with the world just before the return of Christ. Instead it became my destiny teach the one who will reveal it to the world. You are the one."

Chester's flesh crawled. "Look, every time this information gets out a lot of people die. I think keeping it a secret is much better."

The Master smiled. "That is how I know it is time. Because of the world we live in, there is a way you can safely release the information."

Chester cocked his head. "What are you up to?"

"All you have to do is find a way to expose to others what you have experienced here. Those that are ready for the message will hear it, and the rest will be entertained by an interesting story."

"First, I don't think anyone will believe me, anyway. And secondly, it's not a story. This has really happened!"

The Master got up and left Chester with a nugget to focus on. "Don't make them uncomfortable with the truth. Entertain them with it. Think of it like this. A lie is an invented story told to conceal the truth. Fiction is an invented story told to reveal truth. Don't use my name, change a detail here and there, and call it a novel." The Master's eyes sparkled with laughter at Chester's look of disbelief.

Chester glanced over at Sanjiv who just shrugged as he turned to follow after his master.

APPENDIX

For up to date information concerning scientific and historical evidence supportive of the War of the Angels, visit The Reluctant Messenger website at:

Http://reluctant-messenger.com/rebellion.htm

About the Authors

Stephen W. Boston, creator and author of ***www.reluctant-messenger.com***, holds a Ph.D. in Comparative Religion and a M.A. in Biblical Studies. He was a computer and network engineer with a major utility company before devoting his energies to researching, teaching, and writing about religion and spirituality. He teaches The World's Great Religions at a state university.

Evelyn McKnight Boston holds a Ph.D. in Theocentric Business and Ethics, M.Ed. in Behavioral and Career Counseling, and B.A. in Sociology/Psychology. Her efforts in the human development field have focused on assisting corporations, individuals, and families resolve productivity and safety issues in the workplace, community, and home. She is a Certified Employee Assistance Professional, Licensed Chemical Dependency Counselor, executive coach, crisis interventionist, and national human resource trainer. Her current professional affiliation is with an international energy services corporation.

0-595-26821-8

48125698R00195

Made in the USA
San Bernardino, CA
17 April 2017